BLINK

www.**transworldbooks**.co.uk

www.transworldireland.ie

BLINK

Niamh O'Connor

TRANSWORLD IRELAND

TRANSWORLD IRELAND
an imprint of The Random House Group Limited
20 Vauxhall Bridge Road, London SW1V 2SA
www.transworldbooks.co.uk

First published in 2013 by Transworld Ireland,
a division of Transworld Publishers

A CIP catalogue record for this book
is available from the British Library.

ISBN 9781848271401

Addresses for Random House Group Ltd companies outside the UK
can be found at: www.randomhouse.co.uk
The Random House Group Ltd Reg. No. 954009

The Random House Group Limited supports the Forest Stewardship Council®
(FSC®), the leading international forest-certification organisation. Our books
carrying the FSC label are printed on FSC®-certified paper. FSC is the only
forest-certification scheme supported by the leading environmental organisations,
including Greenpeace. Our paper procurement policy can be found at
www.randomhouse.co.uk/environment

Typeset in 11.5/15pt Sabon by Falcon Oast Graphic Art Ltd.
Printed and bound in Great Britain by
Clays Ltd, Bungay, Suffolk

2 4 6 8 10 9 7 5 3 1

BLINK

1

18 January 2013 – 6.30 p.m.

Lucy Starling claps a GHD down a length of two-tone hair
– dark at the roots, peroxide blond at the tips – tilting her
head with the tug. Her fingers scissor a strand, and she
examines the split ends with a frown. Steam billows from
the straightener, making a crackly noise. If it so much as
drizzles tonight, her hair will go Afro.

Checking her make-up in the mirrors of her French dressing table, she jerks her face to different angles, lips pursed.
Her fake eyelashes are even and glob-free. Her liquid eyeliner has a retro kink at the corners – Amy Winehouse style.

Rolling her pearly pink lip gloss, she makes a *'pa-pa'*
sound and then sweeps her blusher brush over her cheek-
bones to give them a heavy dust of bronze. She needs to look
perfect. Knowing Red Scorpion intimately from chatting
online is one thing, but meeting face to face is different. She
is going to record everything on her phone and upload it
once they are done. It is so going to go viral . . .

Slugging back a mouthful of her can of vodka-laced Coke,
she waves the hairspray over the mini-beehive perched
behind the hair band set towards the front of her scalp and
zaps. The fumes choke up the air and she leans away from
the fug, fanning with one hand while walking the fingers of

the other through the contents of her handbag on the floor: iPhone, check; keys, check; condoms, check.

'Woah, head rush,' Lucy says to herself, straightening up. A piercing in the middle of her tongue flashes when she talks and gives her a slight lisp.

She always preloads before heading out, but tonight she needs more Dutch courage than usual. She spewed her dinner so as to fit into her skinny jeans, and the alcohol has gone straight to her head. She blinks away the colour spots in front of her eyes.

Springing up, Lucy picks a light-headed path through the clothes strewn on the floor, searching for her jeans. She spots the glimmering sequinned Gucci black hot-pants she nicked from TK Maxx and roots them out, holding them at arm's length, trying to decide: with or without 500 denier tights? On the one hand, it is January, and freezing outside. On the other – why waste all that Christian Dior shimmering skin by covering it up? She puts her blinged-up acrylic toenails into the shorts, zips and pulls on her shiny black knee-height boots to complete the rock-chick look. Bending sideways, she gives herself one last check in the mirror. She looks hot. She knows it's shallow wanting to look good, given everything going on, but this is the moment she's been waiting for, planning. She wants everything just so.

Lucy starts. Her gigantic blue eyes slide from her own reflection to the space where her father is standing, framed by the bedroom doorway.

'Even if it wasn't a school night and you were allowed out, you know right well you would not be allowed to dress like that,' he says. His Welsh accent is thick as ever.

Lucy slumps back on to the bed. 'Are you ever, like, going to knock first, Nigel?' She sighs every last cubic inch of air out of her lungs.

He walks over and examines her more closely. 'Since when did you start wearing make-up?'

Lucy sits up quickly. She arches her back, shoulders drooping to give off the practised mall-vibe of intense boredom, rangy arms dangling between her gangly legs. The correct answer is 'a year ago', but her parents don't know that, because she normally puts it on *after* she leaves the house. Tonight, she has other things on her mind. After tonight it's not going to matter any more anyway . . .

Her father steps back and points at the door. 'Can you go and talk to your mother this instant? She's between appointments. The next one is in ten minutes.' A pause. 'Now.'

'For once, I'm the one who doesn't have time to fit into her window, and whatever happened to being entitled to privacy? Jeez.'

Moving to a dressing-table drawer, she pulls her diary out and zips it into her bag quickly. She checks over her shoulder to see if he is still watching. He is.

Nigel has the look of someone counting to ten. After a prolonged pause, he says softly, 'Do you know you've actually got an American twang from all the episodes of *Hannah Montana* you used to love? We should sit down some time with popcorn and Coke and stick on one of the box sets like old times.'

'Seriously, can you just fucking go now?'

'Do not curse in this house, young lady.'

'Dick, balls, cunt, douchebag . . .'

He waits, lips pursed, and then pleads, 'At least tell me you cleared it with your mother earlier?'

Lucy looks him up and down. He is wearing the kind of saddo jumper most men would only be seen dead in at Christmas, and the kind of glasses you get for free on a medical card. His thinning fair hair is shoulder length to compensate for the bald patch, which she reckons is also the reason for his sideburns.

Lucy folds a stick of gum on to her tongue slowly, 'Hel-lo? She was, like, working.'

'She's never too busy to take your call, you know that, sweetie.'

'I am so not phoning someone who's on the other side of that wall. It's just creepy. And can you stop calling me that, I'm not, like, four any more.'

'You're only fourteen! And even when you're forty, you're always going to be my baby.'

He sits down on her bed. 'Don't be too hard on Mum. She needs to look professional in front of the patients. It's a surgery, you know that. I'm the first to accept that things are more hectic than usual. But you'll always come first for us. Always.'

Lucy withers him with a look, chewing hard. 'I'm going. End of.'

Nigel sighs hard through his nostrils and crosses his arms. He's at the end of his tether, where she wants him. 'Who with?'

'Melissa.'

'I thought you two didn't get on.'

'We made up.'

'I want her mum's number.'

'Whatever.' Lucy catches a glimpse of her reflection and flicks her hair. She realizes he is waiting. 'It's in the book. They're the only Brockles in it.'

'We were supposed to be going to choir tonight.'

'Yeah, right.'

'You've got a beautiful voice.'

'Can you just go? Seriously.'

'Have you even done your homework yet?'

Lucy shrugs and mutters, 'Whatever.'

In the old days, at this point he'd have been giving her an earful about living under his roof . . . by his rules . . . it being his duty to protect her until she was capable of looking after herself. But that was before she did something to show them she could think for herself. Since then, he will only push it so far, just in case . . .

'Well, where is it you want to go tonight anyway?' he asks.

'I don't *want* to go anywhere, Nigel. I *am* going to the Phoenix Park to a gig.'

'I'll drop you.'

'No, I'm getting the bus.'

'You're joking, it's bucketing outside!'

Her eyebrows go up a notch at the mention of rain, but she studies her nails, stealing a glance at him once his back is turned. Nigel stands, knits his fingers behind his head, points his elbows at the ceiling and stares up. After a few seconds, he asks, 'So who's playing then?'

Lucy stretches the gum to snapping point. 'Nicki Minaj.' She pauses. 'Ever heard of her? She's only, like, the biggest star on the planet.'

'Nope. Is she good? What kind of songs does she sing?'

She rolls her eyes.

'Why don't you show me, on that YouTube thingy? You know I'm useless on the computer. Go on. Otherwise I'm going to be waiting at the Phoenix Park to collect you. I mean it.'

'Fine.' Lucy leans over to her desk and grabs her pink laptop, flicking it open and typing Nicki's name in the search engine. She clicks on 'Beez In The Trap'.

The smouldering rap star appears on the screen behind barbed wire, twirling the ends of her long green hair and dropping to her hunkers in her short skin-tight pink leotard, opening and closing her legs.

Instinctively, Lucy joins in and starts to walk her shoulders to the beat as Nicki moans, *'Maan!'*, flaring a nostril.

Nigel looks horrified that his daughter thinks 'bitches' can't tell her 'shit' and 'motherfuckers can't tell her nothing'.

Lucy turns the volume up and pumps the air with her hands.

The laptop starts beeping. She starts, realizing Red Scorpion is trying to Skype her. His name flashes on the bubble, and a ticker-tape line of chatroom text appears on the bottom of the screen. It reads: 'Don't be late, Honeytrap' – her chatroom name.

'What's that?' Nigel points a finger at the screen with a frown. 'Who's—?'

Lucy slaps the computer shut and cuts him off. 'Nothing, no one, and give me some space or I'm so phoning ChildLine. I'm serious.'

He stands, his face pleading. 'Open it up again and I'll show you David Bowie. Now that's real music.'

'Not now, Nigel, OK? I seriously need to get ready.'

He bends over and starts picking up her clothes, folding them against his chest and placing them on the unmade bed. He doesn't want to go yet. Lucy stands up suddenly and reaches behind her back to unhook her bra clasp, bending an arm and reaching into her sleeve to pull it off. She tosses it on the floor, the padded red-lace number that makes her look like a B-cup. She does not stop staring straight at him, despite his obvious mortification.

'I've got a beez problem in the attic myself,' he says, avoiding eye contact.

He hands her a pair of jeans from the bundle and turns for

the door quickly. 'You better get these on before you go. You'll catch your death.'

Lucy opens and shuts her hand. 'Good. Bye.' She moves to the window to check out the rain as Nigel leaves the room. It is belting down. She will look like shite later if she goes out in that, and the whole world will remember her that way. That would be so, like, tragic.

Her gaze slides down the street to where her mum's car is parked, further away than usual to accommodate the number of patients in the surgery.

Flicking the door shut with the sole of her boot, she moves to her wardrobe and kneels down to get to the tampon box in the bottom. She keeps one eye on the door as she transfers the contents to her bag. She knows Nigel is still out there; she can hear him breathing.

'Are you absolutely sure you want to get the bus?' he calls.

Lucy eyes the door. From the pitch of his voice, she'd have bet any money he is peering through the keyhole.

'Positive, Daddy,' she says sweetly, miming sticking her fingers down her throat.

'Nobody ever let me go on a bus at your age,' he grumbles on the far side of the door.

She mouths 'Loser' silently, and makes an 'L' with her index finger and thumb which she jabs in his direction.

At the sound of his footsteps moving off, she goes to the door and looks through the keyhole. He's gone. She presses her ear against the door to work out where he is, hears his steps getting fainter, and reckons he's in the kitchen. Rumbling her leather jacket free from the clothes mountain, she fumbles in one of the pockets for the spare key for her mum's car.

Lucy is not afraid of anyone or anything, but even she does not dare to keep an actual murderer waiting.

Ten Days Later: Monday

2

DI Gavin Sexton sees the yoga mat as he enters the office. His anger management counsellor is crouched down, rolling it up. Her arched back bows and kinks. She's late thirties, and barefoot in a pair of bell-bottom jeans, worn with an Adidas tracksuit top. No bra line cuts across any one of the seventeen vertebrae that run from the base of her neck to the top of her pelvic bone, he notes. Strands of escaped long brown hair, twisted in a bun at the base of her skull and skewered in with a ballpoint, give her a frazzled look despite her efforts to relax. The tinkles from a wind chime at the front door were drowned out by the sound of traffic on the South Circular when he arrived. A low hum travels through the rotting wood held together with layers of emulsion in the bay window.

'Not even a couch?' Sexton asks.

'It wouldn't fit,' she answers with a pronounced Australian accent, scooping up an armful of books to free up a chair. The top one on her pile reads *Daily Zen*. It's the first time they've met, but she barely glances at him as she leans the yoga mat in a corner.

'I'm Dr Victoria Baker. You're Gavin?'

He nods. He presumes she is reminding him of her title to create a professional distance, perhaps because her practice is based in her home.

A small boy, maybe six years old, pushes past Sexton's legs. 'Mum, what time are we going swimming?'

She kneels down and cups his face. 'In an hour, sweetheart, when you hear the clock bong. Come and get me. Read your book until then so I can finish up working, OK?'

The child runs off, giving Sexton a dead leg as he passes that makes him wince. The shrink doesn't notice, she is clearing space on her desk – it is festooned with finger-printed paintings and blobs of paint on pieces of paper folded in half to make butterfly wings.

'Sorry about this,' she says, closing the door. 'I don't usually work on Mondays, but your sergeant said your appointment couldn't wait.'

'He's been on my back for the last few months. Gave me an ultimatum at the weekend, thinks I'm a ticking time bomb,' Sexton jokes as he sizes up the chair in front of her desk warily. It's going to be a squeeze. He's put on several stone over the last year, and he eases himself down, holding his breath.

'No qualifications on the walls either,' he says, looking around. There was no secretary on the way in. 'That's a first.'

She takes a seat behind the desk. 'You've been to many psychiatrists?'

'No,' Sexton says, adjusting himself. 'When my wife was alive, she thought we needed counselling.'

'But you didn't?'

'I would have found confiding in a friend about our problems excruciating.'

She makes a note of something in an A4 pad. 'You don't believe people should talk about their feelings?'

'People can do whatever they want, but it's too hippy dippy for me.'

She looks confused.

'Like badminton, for instance,' Sexton explains.

'And what's the problem with badminton?'

'It's not natural . . . all that wrist action, leaping about like gazelles, it looks more like it was invented for porn stars, not sport enthusiasts.'

He frowns when she doesn't laugh. 'Oh, come on, play nice. I'm joking. I have absolutely nothing against people who want to swing.' He waits, then blurts, 'That was a joke too, by the way . . . woah, tough audience!'

Dr Baker tucks her escaped hair behind her ears. 'Have you always used humour to deflect from your problems?'

'Oh, now, I've got issues with my sexuality. I'm probably a closet homo, is that it?' Sexton says. He points to her notepad. 'That was another joke.'

'I know,' she says. 'It wasn't funny.'

'Could we start again?' he asks. 'I could maybe knock next time and you could look me in the eye and shake my hand as I introduce myself?'

'Why? I know who you are.'

'You know my name, there's a difference.'

'You're going to great lengths to avoid the actual reason you're here. Are you in denial about what you did?'

'Can we lose the jargon, for Christ's sake?'

'You're here because you need help,' she reminds him.

'I'm here because I want to keep my job; the same reason you are.'

The kid bursts through the door again, crying. 'Mommy, I fell off the chair and banged my knee.'

'I'm sorry,' she tells Sexton, standing, lifting the child up and taking him out of the room, whispering soothing assurances in his ear.

Sexton stands and turns her notepad around, sees the words 'Tea, milk, sugar'. A shopping list. He sighs and sits back down.

When she comes back, he notices she's put on trainers.

'All I ask, before we start, is that you don't put a report together based on generalizations that have nothing to do with what happened that night,' he explains. 'You have a view of me, just as I have of you, based on the couple of minutes we've been in each other's company. It doesn't mean either is right.'

'I'm a professional, Detective.'

'So am I,' he clips.

'You attacked a man in a holding cell.'

'You have a child running in and out of the consultation room,' Sexton retorts.

Her eyes narrow. 'What was the name of the man you almost killed?' Dr Baker asks coldly.

'You think me saying his name might change the fact that he was a scrote? It won't. I can see from your face that's not a word you're familiar with, suggesting to me you're more comfortable on a yoga mat than mixing it with the kind of people you're trained to help. Scrote is short for scrotum sack. I know you want me to play the game and show remorse, but, to be honest, he pushed my buttons. Saying his name won't change that.'

She reaches for a sheet of paper, near a phone, and scans it. 'I see that you're a juvenile liaison officer. In my experience, JLOs tend to be officers with a lot of patience, and not people with short fuses. Do you enjoy working with young people?'

Sexton looks at his fingers spread out on his legs. He can tell her the truth, or he can lie. Based on how things have gone so far, there's only one option. 'It's fantastic. My interest in social work is probably the single reason I trained to become a crime fighter.'

'I take it that's an attempt at sarcasm. You don't think JLOs are necessary?'

'Glorified babysitters? Of course. My colleagues call me J-Lo. That's how much respect I've got.'

'I would have thought that it was life-and-death stuff at the moment, given what I'm reading in the newspapers.'

'I preferred it when boredom was part of the job description of being a yoof.' He makes bunny ears with his fingers around the last word.

'Why are you doing it at all, if you'd rather be involved in some other area of policing?'

He sighs. 'Since the incident, I've been sidelined. Yes, they needed more JLOs to cope with all the suicides in the secondary schools. I got the gig. Yes, it has added to my sense of frustration, but no, I'm not impotent in bed. Yet.'

'The incident?'

'The reason I'm here.'

'The reason you still haven't spoken about. The name you won't say.'

'Philly Franklin, and he had it coming. There, are you happy now?'

She makes a note.

'Don't write that down, for Christ's sake. Can't we just have a basic human conversation without it ending up in your notebook?'

She stops writing and looks at him. 'Do you understand why you're here, Detective, and the nature of our relationship?'

'Yes, you get paid by the hour to see me, and you don't kiss your clients.'

She looks appalled.

He puts his hands up. 'All I'm saying is that if I were sitting in your seat, I could make all kinds of assumptions, not necessarily correct. Based on first impressions, you'd be a single mom trying to juggle work and childcare and not quite pulling it off. Your son's right hook combined with a borderline Attention Deficit Disorder suggests to me the absence of a father figure, which is going to add to your own feelings of guilt about your mothering skills.' He scans her blank expression. 'How am I doing? I know what you're thinking, and yes, you'd be right, I got the box set of *In Treatment* for Christmas.'

She waits.

Sexton opens the top button of his shirt and runs his finger around the inside. 'Is it just me or is it hot in here?'

She indicates the water dispenser and he leans sideways and glugs a cup out. 'There are techniques you can learn to cope when someone pushes your buttons,' she tells him.

Sexton cracks the cup after draining it. 'Oh please, cut me some slack. If someone hurt that boy of yours, you wouldn't stop to take deep breaths before deciding what to do next. You'd do what was required. That's the real world, not what it says in your books.'

Her expression changes. He knows this look from numerous interviews and countless interrogations over the years. The shutters have gone down.

'What happened to your wife?'

'My wife is dead. Look, what's this really about? Why am I here?'

She blinks. 'You mentioned her when you first came in. I thought you might like to talk about her.'

He turns and looks out the window. The door opens a chink.

'Why's the man shouting, Mummy?'

Dr Baker hurries out of the room, and it is a good ten minutes before she returns. Sexton can smell coffee off her breath. She doesn't go back to her desk; she stays by the door, holding her kid's hand.

'Look, I'm going to recommend you see a male psychiatrist.'

'Why?'

'Because you make me uncomfortable.'

'What are you talking about?' Sexton asks. 'This is ridiculous. Can you sit down and just get it over with? Are you going to say I'm a misogynist now as well as sexually frustrated? Because the consequences of just one of those phrases affect the rest of my career, and I don't mean in terms of promotion.'

She lifts her son.

Sexton stands, his fists balled. He is absolutely furious. Catching a glimpse of the expression on the child's face, he takes a deep breath and pulls a fiver from his pocket.

'Here, kid,' he says, trying to hand it over, but Dr Baker turns the child away and keeps him out of Sexton's reach.

His 'Perfect Day' ringtone starts to trill. He picked it to remind himself there's no such thing and that as soon as you start taking anything for granted, the shit hits the fan.

He rubs his forehead as he presses the phone to his ear and listens as DS Aishling McConigle, the station's family liaison officer, fills him in. Another day, another teen suicide. This one's a fourteen-year-old girl. She was found this morning, died the previous night. McConigle's about to do the death knock to inform the family, bring them to the morgue to ID their kid. She needs Sexton to tag along because the family have two other teenage kids, who may or may not need babysitting – she's not taking any chances. The eldest one is fifteen, the younger thirteen. They're both old enough to be left home alone, but in the circumstances she wants him there, just in case. McConigle's sorry. Foxy mentioned Sexton is otherwise engaged, but this can't wait. She needs to get there before the press.

He nods. 'I'm on the way.'

As Sexton leaves, Dr Baker hurries to her desk and picks up the phone.

3

On the TV, a young female reporter in a waxed shooting jacket is standing in front of Garda HQ in the Phoenix Park, delivering some breaking news:

'This latest death brings to twenty the number of youths under the age of fifteen who have taken their own lives in Dublin in the last four months. The most recent incident was just ten days ago. Leading experts have warned parents to be vigilant, as the copycat effect is now veering dangerously close to cult proportions.

'The girl, who has not been formally identified, is understood to have attended one of the schools affected in the cluster. Her name is not being released until family have been informed . . .'

Nigel aims the remote at the box and zaps, switching the TV off. He stands and lifts the tray on which his lunch is perched on his lap – ham, two potatoes, a sprig of broccoli and carrots – arranged like a still life. He carries the tray into the kitchen, scraping the untouched contents of the plate meticulously into the bin once his instep has summoned the lid to spring up. He puts the crockery and cutlery into the dishwasher and walks to the hallway, reaching for the phone. He dials a number he knows off by heart on the house phone and listens to Lucy's voice play back on her answering machine.

'I'm, like, not available right now, but if you leave your name and number, I'll suck your cock.' Lucy laughs. 'Just kidding,' she continues. 'I'll get straight back to you . . . if you send me credit.' More hysterics. 'Just kidding. Go ahead . . . dweeb!'

The phone beeps for him to speak. Nigel hesitates and hangs up. Tears roll down his face. He pulls the phone book out of a drawer in the hall table, flicks through the pages until he gets to the 'B's and then licks a finger to turn them one by one, trying to locate the surname Brockle.

As he runs his finger down the list, the ink smudges in a blurry trail. His finger stops at the only Brockle in the book: Martin and Marie. He dials the number. The call connects after three rings.

'Ah, hello, it's Nigel Starling.'

He waits for a response but, after a prolonged pause, clarifies, 'Lucy's dad. It's just that I was watching the news and I hoped we could . . .'

He pauses to listen intently to what's being said on the other end of the phone.

'I'm so very sorry to hear that.' He holds the phone away from his ear and pulls a face in response to the angry blast. When he listens again, it's only for long enough to establish that there's no longer anybody on the other end.

Hanging up, he redials the number, but it rings out. Nigel goes to the cloak stand in the hall and puts on his scarf and coat. He uses his big toes to push the backs off his slippers – his shoes are waiting neatly by the door. He studies the sets of keys hanging on the wall and runs his finger along them to try to find the spare for his wife's car, then realizes something that makes him start.

Suddenly, he bolts for the bathroom under the stairs,

drops to his knees and vomits. His wife, Nancy, runs in, kneels down beside him and rubs his back. 'What is it, love? What's happened?'

4

Grimacing, Lucy draws her hands off the steering wheel and covers her face as her mother's car careers out of control, hits the ditch and judders to a halt. Watching from her perch on a metal gate at the entrance to a paddock known locally as the Cider Field, Melissa Brockle tips a pair of bug-eyed shades down an inch and stares disbelievingly at Lucy over the rim.

Lucy peers back through her fingers as Melissa heads towards her. Even in her uniform, Melissa looks like she's just stepped off the set of Glee. *Her shiny ponytail has been meticulously curled in a tendril that bounces from side to side in time with each step. She pulls open the passenger door and climbs in.*

'You are such a loser,' Melissa says. 'You look like a complete tart, and you've been drinking. Your eyes are all over the place.'

'How come you didn't change out of your uniform, like we agreed?' Lucy demands. 'What if someone saw you?'

'He-llo? What do you think this is for?' Melissa asks, indicating the shades and ponytail wig. 'If I'd changed, my old dears would have copped something was up. BTW, You so scraped the bumper. It's going to need panel beating, which costs an absolute fortune. In other words, you're dead.'

'That is, like, the least of our problems,' Lucy says. 'I was

reading this old article online about how Red Scorpion is supposed to have, like, raped a woman as well as killed people, but they couldn't charge him because she was too scared to give evidence.'

'OMG,' Melissa says. 'I so told you this was a bad idea.'

She reaches for the handle. Lucy leans across her and pulls the door shut.

'We have no choice,' Lucy reminds her. 'We have to do it. Before any other kid dies.'

Melissa takes a deep breath. 'I'm scared.'

'You're scared? All you have to do is make sure Red Scorpion isn't a psycho who wants to slit my throat, or assault me, and ring the cops if he tries.'

'You still haven't told me how I'm supposed to manage it without being seen,' Melissa says.

'You can get out of that seat, for starters,' Lucy answers. 'He said to be sure to come alone, remember?'

'What do you want me to do? Like, lie on the floor in the back? I've, like, suffered from car sickness since I was two. Even if you put some kind of blanket or coat over me, if I puke, he'll smell it. Even if I take Motilium for motion sickness, it's not going to stop me cacking my pants.'

'Yeah, it will,' Lucy says, checking the rear-view. 'Motilium freezes the stomach.' She leans to the passenger footwell and rummages in her handbag. 'Want some?'

'Only you,' Melissa answers. She pauses. 'Don't you think it's weird he set up the meeting in Amy's Wood?'

'He's a freak – that's why we want to meet him, remember?' Lucy says, annoyed.

Melissa plays with her ponytail, curling it around a finger, all set to suck her thumb, which hovers near her mouth. Lucy knows if Melissa was on her own, it would have gone in by now.

'*So where is it I'm supposed to hide in this revised version of events?*'

'*There's only one place in this car you can go without being seen,*' Lucy replies, swivelling around and looking out of the back windscreen.

Melissa stares to see if Lucy is serious. Lucy presses a button and the boot creaks open.

Melissa takes her shades off. '*You're joking, right?*'

No answer.

'*And how the fuck am I supposed to open the boot from the inside to make sure you're not being boned by some guy with a boning knife, Einstein?*'

Lucy points to the button. '*I'll release it just before I get out, and you can hold it down from inside to make it look closed. That way, if anything happens to me, you can jump out and save me.*'

Melissa's jaw drops. She starts to shake her head, but Lucy grips her arm and squeezes. '*Don't even think about it. This is for Amy. You owe her, remember?*'

'*You just make sure you tell the others what I did, OK?*' Melissa says.

'*You bet,*' Lucy says.

'*Anyway, it's not like we're even going to get in with all the parent patrols to keep kids out.*'

'*They're, like, totally an urban myth,*' Lucy answers.

'*How do you know that?*' Melissa asks.

'*'Cos if they existed, Amy would have been the last one to die.*'

Melissa puts the flat of her palm up to Lucy and opens the door with the other. '*I cannot deal.*'

In the rear-view mirror, Lucy watches her stomp around to the back of the car and climb in.

5

The only thing worse than the nightmare view unfolding in the windscreen, where a jack-knifing lorry is hurtling towards the car at breakneck speed, are the sounds playing out in sync: a foghorn blaring, brakes screeching, metal chirping and groaning and glass shattering into a million tinkling splinters and shards. When everything stops moving and skidding with a thunder-clap smash, a soaring tongue of flame bursts from the place the car bonnet is supposed to be, and then everything goes black.

The crash that caused all Chief Superintendent Jo Birmingham's sight problems occurred over twenty years earlier, but flashbacks still come regularly and without warning. Like now.

'Describe what you can see?' her ophthalmologist prompts.

Dr James Griffen's voice is high-pitched and nasal.

Jo unclenches her fists. 'You wear glasses, right?' she asks, her face inches from his.

She heard his glasses clinking on the tonometer during the eye exam.

'Yes,' he says.

'Imagine them smeared in Vaseline,' Jo says.

Her husband, CS Dan Mason, takes her hand. Her gratitude isn't tinged with resentment for the first time in years. They're rock solid again after all the problems caused by his affair with his secretary, Jeanie. Jo just wishes it wasn't a side effect of her now needing him more than ever.

'That's how everything is now for anything more than a foot beyond my face,' Jo continues. 'Within that radius I can see perfectly; outside, it's like there's a haze or a cloud in front of things. If something is two inches in front of me, I can see fine, but any sort of range beyond that and I can't make out the outlines.'

'But that's normal,' Griffen reacted. 'It's only a month since you had deep lamellar transplants. I can still see multiple light reflections.'

'I still can't see my sons' faces,' Jo says, exasperated.

Dan's hand moves to her back. She knows he understands how badly she wants to see them, and she leans closer to him. Their eighteen-year-old, Rory, lost a friend of a friend to suicide in the spate that's gripped the city's secondary schools, and Jo feels useless trying to gauge how he feels without sight. Plus, she is missing major milestones in the development of their three-year-old, Harry. Motherhood has never come naturally to Jo. But she is as fiercely protective of her sons as anyone.

She grips Dan's hand.

'There's been no improvement. I may as well not have had the surgery.'

'Your progress is perfectly normal,' Dr Griffen says. 'It can take a year for your vision to stop being blurry, and two for it to return to its best. You knew this before the surgery. You just have to be patient. You're lucky. Think of all the people still waiting.'

'We know, and we appreciate everything you've done,' Dan says. His Manchester accent makes him sound like one of the Gallagher brothers. 'It's just that Jo's had almost a year of being virtually blind, and everything about our lives has had to adapt. She'd pinned all her hope on the operation changing that.' He squeezes her fingers. 'Losing your independence has been the hardest thing for you, hasn't it, love?'

Jo nods. Dan pulls her close and kisses the top of her head. She swallows. 'What happens if in six months' time this is still all I can see?'

There is a ruffle of papers. This is her third follow-up consultation since the op a month ago. Griffen banging a stack of paper off the desk always signals the beginning of the end of the meeting. Any second now he will mention another waiting patient. He's changed his aftershave since the last visit. Maybe he has a date.

'In that case we'll talk about performing the operation again,' he answers.

Jo draws a breath. The rising knot of worry that her sight will never fully come back sits like a permanent lump wedged in her throat. The fear of having to go back on the waiting list and endure the emotional roller coaster all over again is overwhelming. It's doing her head in.

'I can prescribe Valium, or anti-depressants, if that's what you feel you need,' Dr Griffen says.

'No,' Jo states. 'I just need to know if this is how it's going to be, so I can get on with it, or whether I can still hope.'

'You know that phrase about a watched kettle?' Dr Griffen says. 'You need to busy yourself doing something else. I think, all things considered, the best thing for you would be to go back to work.'

'Work? Don't you understand? I can't bloody well do anything!'

'Look,' he replies sternly. 'There are no guarantees. I really feel you need to occupy yourself now, even if it's in a reduced capacity. That way, should you be faced with a worse scenario, you'll have laid the groundwork for your changed circumstances, have taken the first steps to adapting. Just because you can't see doesn't mean you can't do . . .'

'I can't go back to work without my eyesight. They won't let me.'

She bites the inside of her cheek so she won't shout that the only reason she was so good at her job was her ability to see the world through the eyes of a killer. She'd caused that crash all those years ago, and kept it quiet, because of her father's death.

Dr Griffen clicks a pen. 'Then you may have grounds for a discrimination action against your employer. Prove to them that you have a contribution to make regardless of whether you're able-bodied or not. I think you need to start making the mental adjustment needed, just in case. Nothing heavy duty. There must have been something you put off when you were chasing your tail that you can turn your attention to now, some job you didn't have time to get to before this happened?'

There is one case that's been on Jo's mind. She promised Sexton she'd look into the circumstances surrounding his wife Maura's death. She just hasn't been able to, because of her disability.

'Now, I'm afraid I've got another patient waiting.'

Jo cannot believe he thinks she should be back at work. 'I can't even cook. I can't clean!'

Dan guffaws. She pulls back her hand. 'Sorry, love, but as a seasoned domestic slattern, even you have to admit that's pretty funny.'

Jo clicks her tongue. 'How can I work?' she asks.

'Adapt,' Dr Griffen says brightly. 'Instead of looking,

listen. You can still interview, deduce, delegate, I presume. Now, if you'll excuse me . . .'

'This is unbelievable,' Jo says, standing.

'Actually,' Dan answers, 'I think you going back to work part-time is probably a very good idea.'

He studies a text on his phone. 'Are we done? I'm going to have to make a call,' he says.

'What is it?' Jo asks.

'Another teen, and this one lived in our district,' he says.

Jo puts a hand across her forehead. 'What am I going to tell Rory?'

6

The middle-aged woman answers the door with a smile on her face that freezes when she realizes the people standing there are not the ones she was expecting. Her gaze flicks past Sexton and McConigle standing side by side to the squad car parked on the street right outside her home. She glances over a shoulder to the stairs, and turns back to face them slowly. The telly is on in the sitting room. Sexton knows she knows.

'Maggie Eccles?' McConigle asks gently, stepping inside the door.

A slow nod.

McConigle takes her arm maternally and puts another around her back to catch her if her legs go from under her.

The woman has already started the breathy pant marking the onset of hyperventilation.

'I'm Detective Sergeant Aishling McConigle from Store Street station,' she says as they walk. 'This is Detective Inspector Gavin Sexton. Is your husband, Frank, here? We need to talk to both of you. I'm afraid we have some very bad news.'

Sexton follows, but stays in the doorway to the sitting room, where McConigle invites Maggie to sit on the couch.

'Frank's out looking for Anna,' Maggie says, trembling. 'She didn't come home last night. I haven't sent the kids to school. Please tell me it's not my baby. Please.'

'I need you to ring your husband, Mrs Eccles,' McConigle says firmly. 'I need you to tell him to come home now.'

'Please tell me my baby is alive,' Maggie says. The tears still haven't had a chance to come, but her body is going into shock. She knows . . .

Sexton keeps his hands in his pockets and stays in the doorway, with one eye on the stairs. There's one of those black-and-white family photo portraits superimposed on canvas of Maggie and her husband and children – a boy and two girls. They're all blow-dried and barefoot in the shot, big fake smiles for the professional photographer. The boy has long hair and an AC/DC T-shirt. Sexton wonders which of the two girls is Anna. They look very close in years. One is thin as a wisp, the other has a roll of puppy fat on her jowls. He hears footsteps on the landing and looks up.

'Sexton,' McConigle summons.

He turns back.

'The phone,' she instructs.

He takes the cordless landline off a hall table and carries it in.

Maggie's hand is trembling too much to dial the number. She tells it to McConigle, who dials for her. There are two kids coming down the stairs when Sexton resumes his position. He recognizes the boy from the portrait. Sexton moves to the bottom of the stairs to block him. The kid looks at him in surprise and takes one of his iPod earphones out. The girl behind him – the heavier one from the shot – has her head tilted and is looking at the sitting-room door trying to work out the sounds her mother's making. The slight one must be the victim, Sexton realizes, glancing at Anna's face in the portrait.

'Please tell me,' a voice wails from the sitting room.

'Is that Frank Eccles?' Sexton hears McConigle ask. 'This is Detective Sergeant Aishling McConigle.'

'Guys, it would be better if you went upstairs, OK?' Sexton tells the teens through the bars in the banisters.

'What's going on?' the boy asks.

'Oh my God, it's Anna, isn't it?' the girl says, sinking down on a stair.

'She's not that stupid,' the boy says, bolting down the last of the stairs and trying to push past Sexton, who stops him by putting his hands on his shoulders. 'We need to wait until your dad gets home, OK?' he says.

'Is it my sister?' the boy demands.

The girl is talking aloud, but to herself. 'It's that video she got on her phone a few days ago, telling her how to do it.'

The boy turns. 'She laughed at it,' he says.

'It put the idea in her head, though,' the girl tells him.

'What video?' Sexton asks.

From the sitting room, a guttural cry. The boy pushes Sexton, who repeats himself robotically: 'We need to wait until your dad gets here.'

'You didn't even know her,' the teenage girl bawls. 'How come you get to know before us? You didn't even love her. What about us?'

7

Dan helps Jo through the front door and flicks on the light in the hall. Harry is asleep in his arms, and he heads for the stairs to put him down for the night. Jo's carrying a brown paper bag containing the stack of Chinese takeaways they picked up on the way home, and she puts a hand against the wall to guide herself towards the kitchen. Rory arrives in behind them and slings his coat on the floor, grabbing the top carton from the top of Jo's bag. He's doing his mock exams and they offered to treat him to the dinner of his choice after picking him up.

'Oi, pick that up, your mother could fall over it,' Dan shouts after him.

Rory snorts and lopes back out from the kitchen, wiping his mouth on the back of his hand. He peels the lid from his container of food and grabs a fork. Getting a plate doesn't occur to him; neither does giving it a blast in the microwave. He's all attitude as he carries his food into the TV room, turning the set up loud. The chants of a football match fill the house.

Jo is jangling out more cutlery from the drawer, setting two places and filling a big jug of water, without losing track of one ice cube in the kitchen.

'Turn that down,' Dan warns, arriving back downstairs and talking through the open sitting-room door to Rory.

'You'll wake your brother.' He turns to Jo to tell her incredulously, 'The coat's still on the bloody floor out there.'

'Go easy on him,' Jo tells Dan quietly as he puts plates and glasses at the settings and scoops her egg-fried rice on to the plate. Rory hasn't said a word about the latest suicide. One of the girls who died a couple of months back had been going out with one of his mates. Rory hasn't been himself since, though she suspects she is the one more freaked out.

Dan stands and lifts his plate. 'I know, I know, but how long do we have to pussyfoot around him? He's holding this house hostage. Mind if I eat in front of the match, love?'

Jo tells him to go ahead. She leaves the plate of food a minute later and goes to the sitting-room door to ask them if everything is OK. Satisfied that both her husband and son are still there, she heads upstairs to Rory's bedroom. He's repeating his Leaving Cert year to try and get the points for law, and most of his time is spent in his room these days. Jo is the first to admit that this has more to do with the PlayStation, laptop and TV rather than his schoolbooks, but she's not going to put him under any more pressure than he's already under with the exams.

She paces to the chair at his desk and bings his computer on. So far she has resisted snooping, despite a Parent/Teacher briefing in his school about the suicides which encouraged it. The experts had explained to worried parents the signs that had to be watched out for.

Jo presses 'CTRL' + 'H' to call up the computer's history.

She leans in close to read the text. Rory is an adult, but if he has something serious on his mind, as his mother she needs to know. The experts advised that parents talk to their kids about stuff, but every time Jo tries he fobs her off, saying 'Awkward,' or 'Icky,' or 'Seriously?' If she sits too close to him, to try to see his face, it gives the game away and he tells her she's invading his personal space.

The hairs on the back of her neck go up when she sees Amy Reddan's name appear in his recently viewed sites. Amy is the girl Rory knew. She had been going out with his friend Darren, even though she was a few years younger than him. Jo clicks a YouTube link and Amy appears, sitting on the edge of her bed, singing and playing guitar.

Jo frowns.

'Do you want me to put your food under the grill?' Dan calls up the stairs.

'You have it. I've lost my appetite,' she calls back.

Jo turns back to the computer. Amy's face is half hidden under her big side-swept fringe, her expression absolutely tortured. She looks studious in a pair of big-framed geeky glasses. Her T-shirt has a picture of a soldier kneeling with a bayonet in hand amidst a devastated scene that resembles a nuclear wasteland. The word 'Why?' is printed underneath. She's quirky as well as deep, Jo decides. Her short sleeves are rolled up and she has a tattoo on her arm of a bar of music with staggered minims and crotchets.

There is no denying the pain Amy is in. It's not some adolescent fit of pique, or someone who thinks suicide is romantic. Nobody can fake the expressions of agony that are crossing Amy's face on the screen. The angst makes Leonard Cohen sound like Beyoncé in comparison, she's so utterly lost in the pain of the performance she's giving. Jo spots the number of hits has soared to over 30,000. The tagline on the video reads: 'Welcome To My Life', the name of the song.

There are numerous comments underneath the video:

Forever a Superstar!! RIP Amy xxx
Hope you r happy now ☺ such an inspiration
Rip beautiful! <3
The amount of views !! you are amazing Amy And so brave
<3 xx
Well done Amy u a brill singer :* And an inspiration Love
you lots babe :'(R.I.P. :'(: '(xxxxx
RIP UR soo pretty ur one of the prettiest angels up there <3 XX
Not a day goes by that I don't think of you <3 I know your
smiling up there :*:* xx

On and on they go in the same vein. Jo scrolls down,
realizing the page is a virtual suicide shrine. The outpourings
suggest the kids don't think of death as the end, that Amy's
still listening somewhere, that they can still communicate:

RIP Amy, been listening to this non stop today can't believe
it's been a month . . .
Words can't describe how much it hurts knowing your gone.
Knowing your happy and no doubt partying like bad up
there makes it just that bit easier.. Love you baby girl :* xox
Till we meet again the sooner the better mega respect to such
a brave girl x

The kids go on to say how much they admire her, how
happy they are she is happy, and how they wished they had
the courage to opt out of their crappy existence. The
comments make Jo's blood freeze.

She listens to the track again and, given the fact that Amy
took her own life, the words of the song take on much more
sinister overtones. Jo realizes that Amy's not just heart-
broken, she's already decided what she's going to do, and
she's telling everyone so nobody has any doubt.

Leaning in closer, Jo scans the screen for the date the YouTube clip was uploaded. She spots 15 November and opens another window to Google Amy's name with the words 'sudden death'. Jo wants to remind herself when Amy died. An RIP website returns the death announcement for the same day – 15 November:

The death has occurred of Amy Reddan.
Suddenly. Reposing at her home from 12 noon until 10 p.m. tomorrow. House private at all other times, please. Family flowers only, please. Donations in lieu if desired to Pieta House and STOP.

Jo Googles Pieta House to discover it's a non-profit organization for people considering suicide or into self-harm.

STOP was founded by the families affected by suicide. It stands for Start Telling Others Prevent, Jo reads.

The date of the notice confirms what Jo suspected. Amy's song is her suicide note.

Jo clicks on another link returned by her search and opens a thank-you in an online RIP site to Amy:

I would like to take this opportunity to express my deep gratitude to the many people who supported me after the sudden loss of my beloved daughter Amy.

To all those who called to our home, and travelled long distances to pay their last respects, phoned, sent Mass cards and lovely, kind letters, sincere thanks from the bottom of my heart. Sincere thanks to my extended family, the many people who brought food and refreshments to my home, all those who helped manage the parking, and the neighbours and community who gave me great support, words cannot express my gratitude. A sincere thanks to Bronwyn Harris and all the staff of St Benedict's College and also Amy's classmates, who have shared so many happy memories with me. Thanks especially to Lucy Starling, who spoke so movingly about her BFF at the funeral, to those who joined St Benedict's in the guard of honour, and for the continued understanding and support shown to me at this difficult time.

Thanks to the staff and doctors and emergency services who did their best to save my darling girl. Also the Garda and A&E department in St Vincent's Hospital.

The priests who officiated at the funeral Mass and to the many priests who called to the house.

Thanks to all who joined us in Amy's funeral Mass, especially the Conquest choir for the beautiful music and hymns. A special word of thanks to Finian's Funeral undertakers for the dignity and support. I thank the grave diggers for the professional way in which they prepared Amy's final resting place.

Heartfelt appreciation to O'Brien's Hotel, who provided everyone with food and refreshments. I also appreciate the donations made to STOP and Pieta House and apologize to anyone I have forgotten, it would be impossible to thank everyone individually, but I hope that this acknowledgement will be accepted as a token of my deep appreciation. The holy sacrifice of Mass at 2 p.m. in the Sacred Heart Church, Donnybrook, on Thursday will be offered for your intentions. Rob Reddan.

A wave of sadness sweeps over Jo. She wonders how a kid so young and as talented as Amy, who had her whole life ahead of her, could have walked into a wood with a skipping rope and strung herself up from a tree. It has become the method of choice for the kids in the cluster since, as has the wood where Amy went. It's like the kids have been inspired by her. The wood too – Boley, beyond Enniskerry in the Dublin Wicklow mountain range – was a beauty spot and a place associated with family picnics, and bikers – at least before the tragedies reclaimed it as their own.

Jo wonders if Amy's father has seen her last song, and if it would be right or wrong to tell him if he has not. She recalls hearing that Amy's mother lives abroad.

Something will have to be done, Jo decides. If Rory is becoming obsessed with Amy, it might plant the thought in his head. She feels a rising sense of panic.

Pressing pause, Jo scans Amy's bedroom on the screen for something to make her stand out as different from Rory. She doesn't know what it is she wants to see – anything that sets her apart as someone with psychological problems. But the room is depressingly average. On the wall above Amy's headboard there's a poster of her namesake, Amy Winehouse. Jo's gaze travels back to Amy, still singing, her wrist stacked with leather and beaded friendship bracelets as she strums the strings steadily through her pain. The lyrics of the song are about nobody understanding her, about wanting to run away and lock herself in her room with the radio turned up so loud no one could hear her screaming.

With a jolt, Jo sits up straight at the sound of someone on the stairs.

'Shit,' she says under her breath.

She squints as she tries to find the cursor and moves her finger wildly over the mouse pad, trying to locate it. The more she clicks, the less the computer reacts. She grips the cable and walks her hands along it to the wall, all set to yank it out, but the screen has reverted back to the default home page, with about one second to spare before Rory appears in the door.

'What you doing?' he asks.

'Tidying your room – what does it look like?' Jo says, depositing the armfuls of clothes she's just swept up from the floor into his wicker laundry basket.

8

Lucy picks the bramble branch and holds it by a leaf at arm's length like dirty washing as she totters around it and continues along the remote forest track, set in a sloping valley with dense plantation on either side. She moves like someone drunk, or high, though she is neither. The buzz from the alcohol consumed earlier has worn off, and a cold slick of sobriety is oozing from her pores and leaving a sheen on her skin like varnish. Taking regular checks over her shoulder, she prays Melissa is keeping pace, right behind her, just out of sight. Lucy released the boot before getting out, just as they'd agreed. But neither of them had been expecting Red Scorpion to take Lucy for a drive first . . .

He'd been waiting for her at the entrance to the wood as agreed. He was excited, said he'd seen another man arrive at the wood earlier. My God, could she have been wrong about the troll? Red Scorpion didn't know Melissa was there, and Lucy didn't want to have to explain why. Instead, she did what Red Scorpion suggested, and got into his car. He'd driven deep into the wood, but slowly, moving at a snail's pace, with the headlights off. Melissa would have kept up with that, right? It could only have been – what? – less than half a mile, when Red Scorpion had parked up, telling her to get out. He'd told her to walk on for another ten yards or so until she came to a clearing ahead. Red Scorpion said she'd find a little shack there, and that was where the man had gone. Red Scorpion said he'd meet her there, but would take a different route to get to it, approach it from the back. He'd branched off into the forestry on her left. Presuming Red Scorpion wasn't lying, and there was a man in the hut. Presuming . . .

She wishes there was time to turn and find Melissa, to explain everything to her, but there isn't yet. Not when they're so close. She prays Melissa followed the car. But even if Melissa didn't, Lucy believes Red Scorpion will have her back . . . in a good way . . . right? She's so scared she doesn't even feel the cold, though her legs are bare. She hopes clouds will cover the moon soon. Even dark would be preferable to the light it has thrown on the tall wooden watch towers that peer over the tops of the fir trees. They're like the ones in the movie Schindler's List *where Ralph Fiennes steadied his rifle and took aim to pick off Jewish people; not as big, and made from planks of wood, but totally the same concept: with a balcony, and a ladder, and even a roof so the guy with the gun doesn't get rained on while he's trying to bump off some defenceless wild animal.*

Lucy presumes, from the hoof prints in the dirt, that this place is swarming with wild deer, and that's a magnet for the kind of guys with little knobs who like to drive big pickups with lamps across the top, cars that belong in the American Midwest. But she can also tell from the way the grass grows only in the middle of the track that you could drive all the way down here in the right kind of car, if you had keys to the horizontal poles blocking the way and secured with padlocks. She hopes it's not rutting season, when there's as much chance of ending up in the sights of a charging stag as in the cross hairs of a sniper. She shields her hand over her phone to check if the signal has come back, as she has several times since parting with Red Scorpion, but there are still no bars. Not even one in the remote little valley of trees.

The only things that are currently stopping her from turning and screaming Melissa's name while sprinting back along the spongy, pine-needled path to her mum's car parked at the entrance where she left it are the three questions going round and round her head. The first is about Amy.

Lucy cannot understand how this came to be the place Amy chose to die. Amy was the girl who pulled out of nature walks to collect frogspawn because she couldn't bear the thought of getting her pink Doc Martens dirty. Amy used her period as an excuse to get out of PE. Amy didn't do outdoors. Ever. She was, like, allergic to muck. Music was her passion, but she didn't go to festivals because they were outdoors. The RDS she'd consider as a venue, only in summer, though. Mostly, she was confined to the O2 for concerts.

But by the same token, everything Amy did was loaded with meaning. She was intense to the point of obsession. There was this one time she gave Lucy a present of a watch as a thank-you. When Lucy couldn't work out what she'd done, Amy got offended. It turned out the watch was to mark the first time Lucy asked Amy over on a sleep-over. It was Amy's way of saying, You gave me time, so I'm giving you something that symbolizes my appreciation of that. Then there was the compilation tape Amy had given her of songs that were playing in the background when they had conversations that Amy had felt were life-changing. Lucy could barely remember the conversations, and it came as news to her to learn there had been music in the background. But that was the kind of person Amy was – deep. She found meaning in everything.

Lucy had viewed Amy's YouTube goodbye, like, a zillion times trying to figure out if there was some coded explanation embedded in this place. If Lucy had had to guess a place where Amy would want to end her life, it would have been somewhere that meant something to her, like, say, Tower Records off Grafton Street, where she spent all her pocket money. Amy was the only person she knew who had an actual vinyl collection – apart from Nigel, that was. But since it would be next to impossible to pull off a suicide on one of the city's biggest streets without being seen, and stopped, Lucy would have guessed Amy was much more likely to commit suicide in her bedroom, where she'd spent half her life with her iPod earphones in, or writing songs.

Not to mention, how the hell did Amy get up here? The nearest bus went to Enniskerry village, a good few miles from here. She couldn't have walked it. Which brought Lucy to another point: Amy did not go anywhere without her guitar. Like, ever. There's no way she'd have hawked it up here.

The big problem with the second question, after 'Why here, Amy?', is that it is freaking Lucy out more than she's already freaked out: Why would the troll arrange to meet Red Scorpion here? Either the troll was a complete, like, chainsaw-wielding psychopath, or, the even-freakier-than-question-two question three: Red Scorpion just made it all up to lure Lucy here for his own dark, murdering, rapist reasons.

A loud, heart-splitting crack makes Lucy start, spin around. Lucy is a city girl, but she knows a gunshot when she hears it. There's no question. OK, this is too creepy, she's going back. She doesn't care if the troll wants to spook Red Scorpion, or Red Scorpion wants to spook her, it's mission accomplished, she's going back to the car. The Christmas-tree smell will never be something magical again. It will trigger cold sweats down her back and a desire to shit herself.

Lucy crouches on her hunkers whispering Melissa's name. She scans the trees, wondering which side of the valley the bullet came from – both sides are dense with pine trees. She will have to run, she decides, even with the heels of her boots sinking into the muck.

She looks around wildly, spots the place Red Scorpion must have been talking about through a clearing in the woods.

Lucy puts her fingers over her mouth to stop her teeth chattering. It's not the cold. It's the sight of the log cabin, or hunting hut, which is what she'd call that ramshackle little malarkey that's eerie beyond belief. Lucy loves . . . loved Amy . . . but she can't do this, not even for her, not even to save another kid's life. She's growing more and more convinced she has to save her own life now.

She peeps at the hut again. There are no bears in Ireland, but that hut would look more fitting in Canada, or Alaska. There's a shooting gallery in the front – an actual wide slit of an open window for nuts in caps to point their rifles through and take aim at whatever it is they want to shoot. Actually, that MTV real-life series about the West Virginian rednecks, Buckwild, *is where it belongs.*

Another shot rings out. Lucy's heart misses a beat. That one was louder, closer. And then a third, so near she hears it whizz. Her hand reaches up to her ear. The shot has grazed it, and hot coppery blood flows into her mouth, filling it with the taste of metal. Suddenly the hut is her only hope.

9

Nigel peers out the spyhole in his front door and stares at the driveway where his battered Volvo is parked. His wife's sports car is no longer behind it, where it should have been. His eye flicks up to the flashing neon sign on the drugs-paraphernalia shop opposite, Damm. Nigel is so pre-occupied he forgets to put on his shoes and pads out of the front door in his socks.

Nancy glances up the hall from the kitchen to see why he's opened the door, which has been left open. She sees her husband running across the street and hurries after him. A car horn blares and the motorist shouts obscenities as he swerves out of Nigel's path.

Nigel reaches the door of Damm and starts banging it with his fists. Nancy covers her face as she watches him. This cannot be happening. To them.

The lowlife they live opposite, Eric Canon, opens the door, limbs flailing, the only item of clothing he's wearing a pair of unzipped jeans. He pushes Nigel like he's made of air, and Nigel falls back on the ground. They are no match. Canon is young, and anabolic strong. Her husband is in his sixties and has never had a confrontation in his life. But Nigel is driven by a rage that doesn't feel any pain. He lurches and grabs Canon's leg, tries to bring him down.

Nancy races across the street to get her husband back

home, but Canon has him by the scruff of the neck and is slamming him against the wall of the house. When Canon sees Nancy he shouts, 'Get this lunatic away from me or I'm calling the police!' He throws him to the ground again and kicks Nigel in the ribs.

Nancy helps her husband up. She picks up his broken glasses and assesses his face. His eye will go black. Canon slams the door, and Nancy helps Nigel limp home, leaning on her like a crutch.

'Our poor little girl,' he sobs.

'Is still alive,' Nancy reminds him.

10

Lucy is gagging, choking with the smell that has filled her nose, head, a suffocating, compressed stink like a butcher's shop that a manure truck has just crashed into. It's so overpowering she can taste it. It makes the vomit particles left in her mouth taste good. It's a smell of offal and innards and an emptied bowel and fear.

She can feel, not see, the oil slick of blood all over her. She cannot tell whose it is. It might be Melissa's, but if she's that badly hurt, Lucy dreads to think. They're in Lucy's mum's car, but they're not safe yet. Melissa knows it. She's catatonic with fear. Lucy's tried shouting at her to get her to answer the question 'Did he cut you?' But Melissa cannot answer. Her shock is too deep. They escaped the hut together, they were saved from the madman in the balaclava by someone they thought was there to help him, but now the man in the mask is behind them again. Maybe the two – hunter and saviour – were in it together all along. Making them feel like they'd escaped only to intensify their fright.

Lucy can't get the car to restart. She's flooded the engine, she knows the sound from when it's happened to her parents. She needs to wait, but they can't wait. The car has bunny-hopped from the entrance of the wood out on to the road. Now Lucy can see the madman's steel-capped boots in the rear-view mirror . . .

She grabs her phone again and dials 999, but there's still no signal. Shock blocks the scream in her throat. Every fibre in her body is rigid with fear. She can't believe she's going to die after escaping the horror, because of her own stupidity. Her life has already begun flashing before her eyes, just like in the movies. Not chronologically, or in order of importance, but in a non-sequitur sequence of moments when she experienced unadulterated love: her mother wiping ice cream from her face on a beach in the sun, stretching up to reach her because her father is carrying her on his shoulders . . . A teacher telling her how clever she is, filling her life with hope and potential . . . All the little things she took for granted now washing over her in a wave of intense regret and sadness and sudden understanding: how silly, and impetuous and spoilt she has been. How blind she is to the truth, how fragile everything is, how kindness is the only thing that really matters, how much evil there is in the world outside the fold of the family, of friends. Her lungs start to feel like they have been filled with water. She cannot breathe. She can hear the shortness of her breath as it starts to trip over itself for air.

Suddenly a blinding set of headlights comes around the hairpin bend in the road and a lorry shunts towards them. Then everything goes black.

11

Nigel parks his Volvo at the wood beyond Enniskerry, the scene of the latest suicide. A bunch of kids around Lucy's age are huddled together on the opposite side of the road, watching. It's cold and blustery, but none of them has a coat or a hat. One is in a T-shirt. Another, with hunched shoulders, has her sleeves pulled down over her hands and has poked out holes for her thumbs. One minute she's crying and pointing at the wood, the next she's bending over and being spanked by one of the boys.

Nigel approaches them. His glasses are held together with Sellotape and his face is scratched.

'Heard a name yet?' he asks a spotty boy in a beanie hat and skinny jeans bouncing on a BMX.

The teens turn and look at him like he's got two heads.

'Got a smoke?' the boy on the bike replies, looking him up and down.

The boy's voice has got that four-balled just-broken echo.

Nigel shakes his head.

The kid shrugs.

Nigel puts his hand in his pocket and offers him ten quid.

'Anna Eccles,' he says. 'I heard the coppers talking.'

The girl who was getting the spanking is not impressed. She moves her fist to her forehead and indicates something growing out of it. 'You're such a dickhead, Wayne. Her family are supposed to be informed first.'

'Blow me?' Wayne grins.

The girl ignores him, and pulls some candles from the pocket in her hoodie and starts to arrange them on the path.

'They'll never light with the wind,' someone says.

Nigel walks back to his car.

'I'm the only gay in the village,' Wayne taunts after him in a Welsh accent, making even the girl in the group laugh.

Nigel keeps walking. Another child is dead. The madness has to stop. He has to do something.

12

Sexton sinks a pint of Guinness in a few well-practised mouthfuls, places the glass back on the counter, and winces at the big-screen TV as Man United go down a second goal. The camera angle shifts to a masticating Sir Alex Ferguson in the stands glaring at the new manager and pans in for a close-up of his malign stare. Refusing to let the score dampen his mood – he's invested his last €100 in a victory over Bayern Munich at 6–4 – Sexton nods to the barman topping up another pint that sits under the tap.

Taking his mobile off the counter where his newspaper is folded open on the heavily ballpoint-ringed racing page, he scrolls down through the contacts for Aishling McConigle's number.

'You awake?'

'I am now. What do you want?'

'Put Lucky Kernick in the book for me,' he says. Bets are being taken in the station on a gangland shooting earlier in the day. The killer escaped on a Segway, which means finding witnesses is not going to be a problem. The Segway's maximum speed is 10 mph. There's at least €500 in the pot already.

Sexton is nominating Lucky, a well-known young criminal. He overheard a conversation among scrotes queuing in the pub's jacks half an hour ago, but he's not about to tell McConigle that's where the tip-off came from. He wants to be in with a chance of winning the pot.

'A) What time of the night do you call this?' McConigle complains. 'And B) Lucky? He's only a kid. Is he eighteen yet? Sexton, you're in a pub. You're pissed. Next time you want to talk to someone, ring one of those chatlines. The numbers are in the back of your newspaper.'

He curls his lower lip to clear the frothy moustache. 'Have you written Lucky down yet, with a hyphen pointing to my name, or a colon – whatever you think?'

'Yeah, yeah, consider it done,' she says. 'Goodnight.'

'McConigle?'

'Yeah?'

'How did the Eccleses react when they saw Anna in the morgue?'

'How do you think?' She yawns. 'Were the kids OK?'

'No. Want to meet me for a pint to talk about it?'

'I'm in my pyjamas!'

'They're all the rage.'

'Not tonight. Goodnight.'

'McConigle?'

'Yeah.'

'Did you spot Anna's mobile among her possessions?'

'No. I handed over a watch, a butterfly necklace, some loose change. No phone, now you mention it. Why?'

'It's just something her sister and brother said. They were discussing a "How to" suicide clip someone had sent Anna on her phone.'

'What?'

''Cos if that's true . . .'

'Did they tell you about it?'

'No, I tried to ask them more about it after you'd left, but they completely clammed up.'

'The parents said Anna had been bullied,' McConigle says.

'It must be true then. Do you know what this means . . .'

'Don't get carried away.'

Sexton pauses. 'I'm not. I'm just saying.'

'And so am I.'

He rubs his forehead. 'This isn't about my wife. Jesus. What was the name of Anna's bully? Did the parents give you a name?'

'They said it was Melissa Brockle, a girl in her class. But she can't tell you anything. She's dead. She was the last one, killed herself ten days ago.'

'We need to find Anna's phone. I've been ringing it; it's still on. If we triangulate it, we could do a sweep.'

'We can bing it whether it's got power or not. It can wait until tomorrow. Goodnight.'

'McConigle?'

'What!'

'Goodnight.'

13

'Did the patient just try to open her eyes?' consultant neurologist Mr Anthony Dean asks. The surgeon's voice is muffled by the mask over his nose and mouth as he leans over the bed in the operating theatre.

A young Filipino anaesthetist moves quickly to the patient's arm and lifts it at the wrist, where the plastic tag gives her name, 'Lucy Starling', and DOB, '1999'. Frown lines melt from the anaesthetist's face as the wrist flops lifelessly back on to the bed once he lets it go. Double-checking the LCD display on the heart monitor, he raises his voice over its rhythmic electronic pips and beeps and the hiss and gurgle of the oxygen mask. 'She's still under.'

Dr Dean peers down into the patient's open head. 'There were 150 cases of accidental awareness during surgery in the UK last year,' he says. 'It'd be just my bloody luck that the single Irish case ends up in front of me. If this one got a hearing in front of the medical council, my name would be splashed all over the tabloids. It would be a case of no smoke without fire; nobody would remember whether I was found guilty or innocent of negligence.'

'Let's hope she didn't hear that then,' the radiographer ribs, as he studies a screen showing the patient's pulsing brain being filmed by the micro-camera strapped around

Dean's head. 'Or the headline will read: "Top Doc Blasts 'My Bloody Luck' during Nightmare Op".'

There is a ripple of laughter.

'You sure that isn't grey matter?' Dr Dean asks the radiographer over his shoulder. The edge of his blade appears on the screen. 'It looks like grey matter to me.'

The radiographer scans the screen. 'It's cerebrospinal fluid. Congealing.'

'How long since the car crash?' Dr Dean queries.

'A couple of hours,' the theatre nurse says, glancing at the clock on the wall. 'She had to be cut out.'

'BP?'

'Still forty-nine.'

Dr Dean blows out a spurt of air and turns his scalpel around so the blunt side is facing up. He pushes it into the girl's head and watches it bounce off the substance, then glances at the radiographer. 'What was your mode of transport when you were fourteen, anyway?'

'Penny farthing,' the radiographer jokes.

Dr Dean's face mask tightens as he grins, his gaze fixed on the image of the brain. 'Speaking of teenagers, did you see that YouTube clip of that girl from one of the schools affected by these suicides drunk in Temple Bar and going for a pee and a puke?'

On the screen, the metal can be seen making contact inside the patient's head.

'I did,' the nurse says. 'Who'd be a teenager today, eh? It's not like the old days, when only the celebrities' misdemeanours were fair game because they'd courted publicity. Now everyone's a citizen journalist. Poor kid.'

Dr Dean's rubbery finger switches the blade around and aims the pointed side at the brain. 'CSF congealing you say? OK, if you're sure.'

He puts the flat of his rubber-gloved hand out.
'Suction pump.'

Tuesday

14

School principal Bronwyn Harris is standing on the stage at morning assembly, adjusting the microphone. She is in her late forties, with a sharp bob that's thin at the side and has a heavy fringe. In front of her, the classes are organized in tidy lines – first-years on the left, sixth on the right. The gym equipment – high beam, spring boards, rubber mats – has been pushed to the back of the room. The hall is quiet apart from the occasional eruption of frightened sobs. It's like the girls are scared they'll catch the contagion claiming their pals. Nobody knows who'll be next. The class prefects, with sashes over their shoulders and tied around the opposite side at the waist, standing at the top of each class line, are red-eyed. Even the girls who haven't been briefed about what's coming know what happens next – they've been here twice already in recent weeks, last time for Melissa Brockle and Lucy Starling – two second-years.

Mrs Harris takes a deep breath. When she talks to outsiders, the only thing she can compare the feeling to are the scenes on the telly of mass mourning after the death of Princess Diana. The grief is overwhelming. The girls don't need to have known Anna Eccles personally, knowing her to see is enough. They are moved like they've lost a member of their own family.

Mrs Harris steps closer to the mic. It squeals discordantly.

She waits until the feedback subsides. 'Girls, as some of you know, I got some terrible news last night.'

The younger ones start to break down.

'We thought, we prayed, that this horrible time was over, that the message "It's OK to be sad sometimes" had got out there. We've had so many visits from so many experts who've talked to us about how to deal with our feelings, about what to do if we feel down. But on Sunday night another one of our girls, lovely, special Anna Eccles from class 2B, felt the despair that we have been trying so hard to equip you all against.'

The mention of Anna's name sets off a low keening sound from somewhere in the hall.

'Words feel so futile. I have stood here and said the same thing over and over. All I can do now is beg. Please, please, please, my darling children, if any of you feels so low or down that you are contemplating the unimaginable, seek help. Life is so precious. You are all so full of such amazing potential. You are on the cusp of everything. However big the problem in your life may appear, it is never too big. Whatever feels insurmountable now can be fixed. Death cannot.'

She pauses, and takes a deep breath. The crying is so loud she doubts even the mic will carry her voice over it.

'Anna's funeral is on Thursday. We will form a guard of honour to say our goodbyes. I am devastated by this news, as I know you all are too. There is nothing we can say that I haven't already said, except to emphasize once again, please: if you're feeling down, talk to a friend, a family member, the full-time counsellor we've appointed. Phone any of the numbers we've given you in handouts; phone me if it helps. My number is on the leaflet. It doesn't matter what time, I'm always there. I can only appeal to you again:

Don't do this to your friends and family. I promise you that whatever grief you are feeling, for the people closest to Melissa and Anna it's a million times worse. The agony doesn't go away for them. It shapes the lives left behind. Suicide. Ruins. Lives. I won't go into the statistics of alcoholism, or drug addiction, or even the suicide rates of the bereaved, but I am going, once again, to read you the letter read at Melissa's removal last week to remind you all what her mum and dad are going through.'

Mrs Harris holds up a piece of paper and begins to read:

'"Anybody's Child. Last night our daughter died. We took her cousin Beth from school and told her what had happened. Have you ever seen a heart break? Have you ever heard a heart break? It sounds like the howl from a monster. It comes up from the gut and out of a distorted face. The word 'no' is in there but you can't really hear it as the howl turns to a scream. It has another face too. One that is covered in silent tears with hair stuck to it, burrowed into a friend's neck. Hearts breaking. All at once.

'"Did we see it coming? No. Did we know of other people this had happened to? Yes. Do we know why she did this? No. This doesn't happen to us. This happens to other people. Well, it did happen to us. And it could be anybody's child lying there cold in a coffin. Why is this happening, time and time and time again? More people, so I am told, die each year from suicide than die in car crashes. Why?

'"Why is this now an option for young people? Why don't they just get drunk?

'"OK, they will be grounded and have their phone taken away, but that isn't final. Death is. Our daughter will always be fourteen."'

Bronwyn Harris swallows the lump in her throat and

switches off the mic. There is no more she can say that hasn't already been said. The worst part is, she knows from bitter experience it won't make a blind bit of difference.

15

CS Dan Mason bursts through his office door, across the corridor and into the open-plan detective unit, gripping his walking stick like he is teaching a wayward dog lead skills. The head of Dublin's Store Street station has a smashed boxer's nose, piercing midnight-blue eyes and receding hair – cut to a two-blade, contrary to regulations designed to make members of the Gardaí distinguishable from criminals. He's not long enough back from the prolonged sick leave associated with his injuries for it to have grown back. Sexton heads over to try to have a word. The chief is making a beeline for McConigle.

'Good work last night,' the chief says, jigging her shoulder. He's got a sheet with some particulars in his hand.

'If there's a suicide video involved, it changes everything. It means a harassment charge at the very least. Put together a team.'

'Yes!' McConigle reacts, giving a little victory clench. She cops Sexton staring at her and glances guiltily at him.

'I thought you went to bed early,' he says.

She turns to the chief. 'I want Sexton on my team.'

'No,' the chief states.

'What?' Sexton asks him. 'Why?'

''Cos your shrink says you belong behind a desk.'

'Bitch.'

71

'QED. Consider yourself lucky. She also says you shouldn't be around juveniles, but I'm going to have to give you the benefit of the doubt on that one, because of the pressure I'm under.'

'I'll call her,' Sexton says.

'You do that, she'll be looking for a protection order,' the chief warns. 'Don't worry, I've got something else to keep you occupied. I need a report for the Minister for Children on the exact number of cases in the suicide cluster, with biogs of each of the kids affected. We're looking for patterns – drink, drugs, whatever kids do these days for kicks – and numbers. She wants exact numbers.'

'You don't need me for that. Any rookie in the room could do it.'

'I want you to do it because of your special experience. If the press start getting lippy about your history, I can cite your sensitivity to the whole area of suicide.'

Sexton blinks. The chief is referring to the death of his wife, Maura, almost four years ago now. Not that anyone around here seems to have noticed the passing of time. Sexton is the first to admit he's let a lot of things go since, and not just his weight. But he wants to turn his life around. Things hit rock bottom a few weeks back when he had to give up driving the daytrip bus for Crumlin Children's Hospital on his day off. It was an old bus and he couldn't fit in because the driver's seat didn't go back far enough from the wheel, he'd put on so much weight. 'Morbidly obese' his GP had pronounced, quoting Body Mass Index numbers and handing over leaflets on heart disease, strokes and diabetes.

'Give up smoking first, then we'll talk diet,' the doc had said, and charged him €60 for the privilege.

Sexton needs to get his life back under control, but he won't last five minutes on a diet while he is miserable in work. If he could crack a quick murder, especially something straightforward, he'd feel like he was back again.

'Give me the Segway, Chief,' he says. 'That's a case I can sink my teeth into.'

A couple of desks away, a detective calls out, 'Here, J-Lo's after the Segway,' to the other officers in the room.

One of the uniforms sitting even closer to the spot where Sexton is talking to the chief shouts, 'He just said he wants to sink his teeth into it!'

There is a ripple of guilty laughter.

'Why do you call him J-Lo?' one of the rookies asks.

''Cos of the size of his arse!' someone replies.

Someone else taunts, 'What's the maximum weight a Segway can take anyway?'

Sexton's forearm springs up to tell them 'Up yours'. When you're a kid, being slagged means being bullied, and that's personal. When you're a man, it's a sign of endearment and a lot better than being ignored.

The chief links Sexton's arm and turns him away from all distractions. He lowers his voice. 'Do you have any idea how many officers I've had to take off the roster to visit the schools in our district on the "Talk About Your Feelings" programme?'

'Four,' Sexton answers. He should know – he's one of them. 'Can we talk about the Segway murder, Chief? I prosecuted Lucky Kernick for a drug deal a while back, do you remember? I mean, it was small by his standards, but I got a conviction and I could call on a couple of the touts who helped me back then to see if I can get an early lead . . .'

The chief stared. 'Have you been listening to a single word I just said? I want you on the suicide report because you have the *right* experience.' He lowers his eyebrows in a way that said 'Fill in the blanks.' 'You can start by interviewing the principal at the school where the latest kid died. Her name's Bronwyn Harris and the school's St Benedict's on the Green. There have been a few other suicides there. Get her to give you the list of names.'

The chief eyes his secretary, Jeanie, sauntering across the room with his coat slung over an arm. She's got that Imelda May war-style thing going on since returning from a sabbatical she'd taken after her maternity leave ended.

Standing behind the chief silently, Jeanie holds the coat up behind his back for him to put on.

Sexton can smell her spicy perfume. He wonders if Jo knows Jeanie is back.

The chief holds his arms back and lets her slide the coat on to them. He glances over his shoulder at Jeanie. 'Still raining?'

'Cats and dogs,' she purrs.

He turns back to Sexton, jabbing a finger. 'Tell you what, you have the report sorted by tomorrow morning, and I'll consider you for the Segway. I can't say fairer than that.'

There is a roar of protest from the room as the detective nearest them, who has overheard, relays the update.

As the chief heads back towards the corridor, Sexton gives his colleagues a wink and rubs his thumb off his first two fingers: he'll be rolling in it when he wins the money for cracking the case.

16

Jo is doing what everyone thinks best and taking the first step in getting back to work. If she's honest with herself, she's glad of the distraction. She wants to think about anything other than Rory and the constant threat she has felt under since teenagers started to die. She and Dan have been walking on eggshells around him ever since the death of Amy Reddan. They have gone to countless parent information sessions in the school, the essence of which is not to treat the kids' problems like they don't count or matter, because, even if they're not huge in the scheme of things, they are to the teenager. Jo doesn't necessarily agree with the experts. She thinks it's postponing the problem, setting the kids up for a fall in adulthood. Life isn't all roses. You have to learn that the hard way, that it doesn't matter when things don't go your way, things hurt, but you get up, you brush yourself off, and you keep going . . .

She hears the footsteps of the woman she's interviewing returning from the hotel-lobby bathroom. She's Esther Fricker, Sexton's mother-in-law. Jo is looking into the circumstances surrounding Sexton's wife Maura's death, just as she promised him she would, before her sight failed.

Maura's mother is a well-preserved woman in her seventies. They'd met before, at Maura's funeral, and remembering a conversation they'd had about her home in

Belfast, Jo had phoned her this morning. As it happened, Esther was in Dublin and Jo had got a taxi to meet her for coffee in her hotel, the Radisson on the N11, a few miles from the cemetery where Maura was buried.

'You were saying?' Jo prompts.

Esther sniffs. 'Just that Maura had everything to live for,' she says. 'That she wasn't the type. That she didn't suffer from depression. That Gavin is right.'

'Tell me about her,' Jo says, squinting, aware that Esther's hair is white but unable to make out any other details apart from distinguishing her heavy perfume as Anaïs Anaïs, one Jo's mother used to wear. 'She never came with him to any of the station's socials.'

Esther blows out a long breath. 'She was one of life's happy people. You know what I mean? I never had to worry about her. She wasn't academic in school, but she always had friends. People loved having her around because she was a problem solver. She didn't suffer from stress. She just ebbed and flowed, and nothing really got to her. She was a hippy in the best sense of the word.'

The waitress comes over with the coffees. 'Latte?'

Jo motions to Esther.

'And an Americano,' the waitress says, clinking the second cup down in front of Jo. 'And your scones, ladies.'

'Thanks,' Jo says, holding the chit up to her face to make out the cost. She hands over a note.

'It's true she owed money,' Esther continues. 'Maura was useless with money – impulsive, reckless even. If she saw something she wanted, she got it, end of story. The fact that she couldn't afford it was lost on her. But it was never material stuff, you know what I mean? Not clothes or cars or the like.'

Jo sips her coffee. 'What did she spend it on then? She owed €15,000, didn't she?' Jo asked.

'And the rest,' Esther says, 'when you add in the interest she was being charged. She'd borrowed it from loan sharks. Those animals pick their interest rates from the sky, as far as I can see. She owed more than €100,000 when she died. She was spending it on the next phase of her life.'

'I don't understand,' Jo says.

Esther leans in and lowers her voice. 'Maura bought her own headstone. When Gavin asked me about it, I had to pretend I didn't know anything about it, because I knew that's what Maura would have wanted.'

Jo tilts her head. 'What?' Maura's suicide note had been signed off with the name Patricia, which was also the name on the gravestone, which had been commissioned by an unknown party, adding to Sexton's suspicions about her death.

'Maura paid for it herself,' Esther says.

'Why would she do that?'

'Patricia was her middle name. She'd been using it because the banks wouldn't touch her. She was trying to dodge the Irish credit-check searches to raise more funds. She'd created a whole new identity for herself.'

Jo blows the coffee in her cup. 'But why buy a gravestone for herself?'

'She was going to fake her own death . . . for the life insurance,' Esther says. 'She'd told me all about it. She was going to leave Gavin, but she didn't want to hurt him. If you'd known her well, you'd understand. She didn't do confrontation. That's how she'd hidden her debts for so long. She found it easier to construct this whole alternative scenario she was going to give him, involving her dying, which would allow her to leave him without a big row. She'd bought a memorial stone. When the time came, she wanted me to have it erected to give him a sense of closure. But because she'd paid for it from her Patricia Sexton account, the inscription was messed up. The stonemason rang me when it was ready for collection and I asked him to have it put on her grave. I didn't see it before it was erected or I'd have stopped it.'

'But Sexton said you didn't know anything about it.'

'If I'd told him, it would have felt like a betrayal of her.'

'Maura is gone,' Jo says crossly. 'Don't you think it would help Gavin?'

'She didn't want him hurt, that was her last wish.'

'But he has been hurt, terribly. If Maura had it planned, it changes everything.'

'She couldn't fake a hanging,' Esther snaps. 'She was going to leave a note, drive to Howth Head and leave her clothes on the cliff. That was her plan. She wanted that baby so badly.'

'Yes, Sexton did too,' Jo cuts in. 'He only found out Maura was expecting after the post-mortem.'

Esther nods rapidly. 'They'd been trying for so many years and nothing had happened. She knew, if Sexton found out about the pregnancy, he'd be in her life for ever.' She pauses, before adding bitterly, 'Ironic, isn't it, that everyone thinks she did it?'

'I have to tell him,' Jo says.

'He'll never forgive me,' Esther says.

'He needs to know. And I think you need to accept the possibility that the stress of everything was getting to Maura. She must have been a little unhinged to have come up with the idea of faking suicide in the first place. And suicide has become . . . so common. Look at all the kids doing it at the moment. It's an epidemic.'

'What do kids these days know about anything?' Esther asks. 'They think life is something you can throw away in a fit of pique. They haven't lived long enough to appreciate life. Maura wasn't serious about it. She was a grown woman. She was about to have the baby she longed for. She thought she was getting a second chance to start again.'

'Did you ever think it's possible that . . .' Jo starts.

'I'm in denial?' Esther finishes. 'Of course. But I knew my own daughter. She wanted to live. She had a hair appointment on the day she died,' Esther says. 'Do you really think she'd have bothered to book if she was thinking that way?'

Jo shakes her head. 'I just don't know. One other thing. Why are you telling me all this now, when you didn't tell Sexton all this time?'

Esther leans across the table and clutches her hand. 'I heard about that man he attacked. I want him to let Maura go before anyone else gets hurt.'

17

St Benedict's College is located on St Stephen's Green. Sexton walks past groups of girls in uniforms – navy tartan skirts, V-neck jumpers and white shirts – and into the head-mistress's office.

Bronwyn Harris's white shirt has that blue glow that comes with a first wear and she plays with a string of pearls hanging over her ample breasts as she speaks.

'We're all devastated by events, as you can imagine,' she says, pouring Sexton a cup of tea from a china set that her secretary has left on a tray at the edge of her desk. 'It's a total nightmare. Sugar? Milk?'

Sexton shakes his head.

'Something like this throws a shadow over the whole school. Did you notice how many girls are still outside? We didn't even have classes today, but it's as if they're afraid to leave each other in case . . . well. You can't go through the day without passing at least one huddle bawling their eyes out together. It's awful. It's the worst thing I've ever experienced in my life, and I've lost two sisters to cancer.'

Sexton takes a sip and keeps his eyes on the principal.

'It's hard to explain to people outside the school. But for many of the kids it's their first experience of death. The fact that it's a tragic, entirely preventable death adds to the intensity of the grief, which is just flooring them. The most terrifying thing about it is that the energy in this wave is like a tsunami. It keeps building as it moves. If we thought it was over, we could try to get on with it, but we're constantly waiting for the next one. We're barely coping since we were last hit, and now this – it's horrific.'

Sexton mutters the cardboard condolences she is waiting for. He's always been useless at polite civilities uttered for the sake of it. Of course, he's sorry about the deaths. You'd have to be made of stone not to be sorry.

'We're on high alert, of course, as is every school in Dublin,' she goes on, apparently not noticing his discomfort.

'We've a counsellor available 24/7. We are keeping the school open tonight so if young people want to be together they can. We're doing everything we can think of, and more. We've had meetings with journalists to appeal to them to stop publicizing the deaths in case the publicity is giving the impression that suicide is something heroic, or something that makes you famous, but the teenagers have their own way of communicating through the Internet. A lot of them don't even read newspapers. We've also had meetings with the social-network providers about how to cut off access to Facebook and platforms, but you're talking about taking their smartphones, computers – it's just not workable in today's world.

'The terrible reality is that we believe, based on the experience in Bridgend in Wales, that it's only a matter of time before this thing spreads to other counties. Twenty children have taken their own lives in sixteen weeks . . .' Her façade cracks. 'I'm sorry. It's just too much to bear. Most of the time anger keeps the tears at bay. I am so bloody angry with them for being so reckless, for doing this to the others.'

She knits her fingers around her cup and regains her

composure. 'Our school is not the worst hit, believe it or not, and we've lost four girls.'

'Can you give me their names?' Sexton asks, lifting his pen over his notebook.

'Amy Reddan was the first. She died in November. She was fourteen. As a matter of fact, all the girls were fourteen, they were all in the same class – 2B. Melissa Brockle and Lucy Starling were next, they're the two I mentioned from ten days ago. Lucy survived, but only just, after stealing her mother's car and crashing into a truck. And the latest one is poor Anna Eccles. Gone.'

'What were the girls like?' Sexton probes. 'Did any of them have any history of mental illness or drug taking?'

Bronwyn takes a deep breath and sighs heavily. 'Nothing that doesn't go with the teenage territory. Just Lucy. She had OD'd shortly after Amy died.' Another sigh. 'Amy was the most withdrawn of them; she wanted to be a songwriter. Lucy had lots of friends, but would have self-harmed in the past. It was her second suicide attempt – parasuicides they call them, a cry for help – she took her mother's car and crashed it. Melissa was a talented singer too, and the most strident personality. Of all of them, she was the least likely. Anna was still more girl than woman – I doubt puberty had even started, she was just a child. She was shy, but always smiling, and had lots of friends. She wanted to be a journalist and had written an excellent review of a musical for our school newsletter.'

She pulls open a drawer in her desk and takes out an annual with the school's crest on the front. Flicking through the pages, she stops at one and bends back the spine, pushing the book across the desk.

'This is the class of 2B as first-years,' she says, of a group of thirty-odd girls standing in three staggered rows. A red nail points out the faces of the dead. 'That's Amy . . .' she continues, indicating a girl with a big mane of hair and hunched shoulders. Her finger moves to a girl with blonde hair, dark at the roots, who's standing beside her. 'Lucy,' she taps. Her finger slides to the front row. 'Here's Anna . . .' she sniffs, pointing to the petite girl with wispy hair. She sighs, and points to a pretty girl in the back row, 'And this is Melissa . . .'

Bronwyn turns to a bookshelf and selects another annual, turning the pages and then showing Sexton. 'This is the class shot this year. Amy is gone. In next year's shot we'll be missing Lucy, Melissa and Anna, and who knows who else . . .'

She blows her nose into a tissue and pulls herself together.

Sexton studies the most recent picture. There is something sadder about the whole class; few of them are now smiling. Melissa looks like a cancer patient, Sexton notes.

'Was Melissa sick?'

'No, that's alopecia.' She hesitates. 'It struck late last year. They do link it to stress.' She takes the annuals and closes them, putting them back in the drawer together. Sexton senses she's holding back on him.

'Can you tell me more about Melissa?'

'I've been advised not to, I'm sorry.'

'Advised? What does that mean? Do you mean you've taken legal advice? Hang on – has this something to do with bullying? The Eccleses mentioned it. Was that why Melissa was so stressed her hair was falling out? Had she spoken to you, or any of the teachers, about being bullied?'

Bronwyn puts her palms up. 'It's a very sensitive issue. It could have a major impact on enrolments. Our numbers are already right down.'

Sexton slaps a hand on the desk. 'Yeah, well, four girls

killing themselves might impact your cash flow too. Answer the question, please. Now: Was bullying a problem in the school?'

Bronwyn fidgets with her necklace. 'It's such an abstract word, you see, and so loaded. But, to answer your question: Yes, Amy had complained to me about being bullied.' She looks relieved.

'Amy?' Sexton pushes.

'Just Amy,' she states. 'She said Melissa was targeting her.'

'But I thought Melissa was the one suffering.'

'Yes, because of what had happened since. But Melissa was no wilting lily. She was a force of nature, for want of a better expression. I had spoken to her about it, especially after Amy's death, for the sake of Amy's father, but to tell you the truth, given the speed of developments, and the rate of suicides hitting schools, I became very reticent to pursue it. I was too frightened of the repercussions for Melissa, all of which did come to pass, as it happens.'

'In what sense?' Sexton asked.

'After Amy died, the girls blamed Melissa, and there were incidents at her home – the windows were broken and several times the emergency services were sent to her door falsely. An undertaker was sent once too, in a horrible and poorly veiled threat. I have tried to keep a lid on this, but Melissa was the author of some vile Ask.fm questions that were sent to Amy before her death. The IP address came back to the school and I was able to trawl through the CCTV footage to pinpoint her on the computer at the specified time. It probably seems Big Brotherish to you, but we keep the room under surveillance because it's our only way of completely protecting the girls and the school.

'So Melissa was the bully turned victim?' Sexton asks.

Bronwyn nods. 'Yes, that sounds so harsh, given that she's

the one lying cold in the grave now. But the truth of it is that nobody ever bullied Melissa, at least not before Amy died. It was jealousy, you see. Melissa was very interested in music and was talented in her own right, but, compared to Amy, she couldn't compete. Amy was in a league of her own.'

'What about Anna? If she was reviewing musicals, maybe she fell foul of Melissa too?'

'I never heard about there being any incident.'

'Ever hear anything about a suicide "how to" video being circulated? I understand one was sent to Anna. That would suggest she was being bullied.'

'What?' Bronwyn is appalled. 'I've never heard anything about it. But if you know something, please tell me . . .'

'It may just be an urban myth,' Sexton says. 'But perhaps you could make some discreet enquiries and get back to me.'

'Of course.'

'OK,' Sexton says, 'so Amy's the shy musician . . . Melissa is the confident singer . . . there is jealousy, rivalry . . . how am I doing?'

'That's it in a nutshell.'

'Melissa bullies Amy to intimidate her,' Sexton goes on. 'Amy takes her own life and then Melissa is bullied and she takes her own life. And Anna shares an interest in music with both the girls. What about Lucy?'

'Lucy was Amy's best friend, but she was a different kettle of fish, not the most academic but certainly someone who seemed to enjoy life, a little too much sometimes, admittedly . . .'

'What does that mean?' Sexton cuts in.

'This isn't for anything official, right?' Bronwyn asks.

'It depends on what it is,' Sexton says impatiently. 'We may need to return to it when I take your statement.'

'Then perhaps I shouldn't say it at all.'

'We need all the information at our disposal . . .'

Bronwyn puts up her palms. 'Fine, I just wouldn't want her parents to suffer any more than they have. Lucy was, shall we say, a lot more grown up than her years. One of the teachers spotted her in a nightclub she was attending herself. The teacher said she seemed inebriated. She'd also started to answer back in the classroom. It's a very difficult age. And, as I said, prescription drugs were found in her system when she tried to OD. Her stomach had to be pumped.'

'Any idea what kind?'

'Serozepam was mentioned.'

'What's that?'

'An anti-anxiety drug, like Xanax, I believe. Serozepam is a drug that makes the hairs on the back of my neck stand on end, detective. We've made several seizures from girls in the school.'

'What happened to hash, space cakes, or magic mushrooms?'

'It's a different world for teenagers today, Detective. You have no idea.'

'Still, seems an odd friendship,' Sexton comments. 'Why was a worldly girl like Lucy drawn to someone who sounds introverted and withdrawn, which, if I'm taking you up right, sums up Amy?'

Bronwyn sighed, 'Yes, that's about the sum of it. Amy was an introverted girl who found it hard to make friends, and Lucy hardly knew anyone. That's what they had in common.'

'What do you mean?'

'Well, as you've gathered, Amy hung back when it came to joining in; she was on her own a lot. When Lucy joined the school, she didn't know anybody. I presume it was easier to befriend a girl like Amy than take on a group. Lucy only joined the school a little over a year ago, you see.'

'What secondary had she previously been in?' Sexton asked. 'Was there some issue in her leaving?'

'If there was, I'm unaware of it. The family had moved over from Wales, and that's why she joined us. From the get-go they said the school wasn't ideal for them in terms of their faith, but they wanted somewhere with a strong moral code and a convent school was the closest they could get to that. Lucy was determined to defy all that, at least that's the way I see it . . .'

'I'll get on to her previous school myself. You said they lived in Wales – any idea what part?'

'Yes, actually,' Bronwyn said, giving him a funny stare. 'Bridgend. Horrible coincidence, isn't it?'

18

Lucy is lying prone in the high-dependency unit, with an oxygen mask over her mouth and a nurse entering her vital statistics on a chart at the end of her bed. Nancy sits on a chair beside the bed, holding her daughter's hand. Nigel stands behind the chair. The nurse taps Nancy on the shoulder and hands her a leaflet.

Nancy stares at it for longer than it takes to read the words printed large on the front: 'Coping With Suicide'.

'It was an accident,' Nancy says.

Nigel puts his hand on Nancy's shoulder and gives it a comforting nudge.

'It's an epidemic with teenagers,' the nurse says softly.

Nancy snarls. 'My daughter is still alive.'

In the bed, the once-spirited teenager now looks like a stroke victim. Her head is tightly bandaged.

The nurse raises her eyebrows in an 'Excuse me for living' expression and slips the leaflet on the pine-effect bedside locker.

The consultant neurologist Mr Anthony Dean appears, followed by a gaggle of student doctors, some carrying clipboards. The females are dressed as if they're about to go down a catwalk. The surgeon has traded the surgical robes for a white coat, and a stethoscope hangs from his neck.

Nancy barely acknowledges him; she's too busy

whispering reassurances in Lucy's ear.

Mr Dean speaks to his students: 'Patient presented with cerebral oedema following a car crash.'

He moves to the foot of the bed and pulls back the sheet, revealing a set of glitzy toenails, completely incongruous against the starched white.

Mr Dean runs a plexor along the sole of one of Lucy's feet. He pauses then does the same to the other foot. The students watch closely.

Neither foot moves.

Nigel brushes away a tear.

'The condition's commonly known as "Talk and die" syndrome because of the speed with which concussion can suddenly cause death,' Mr Dean drones. 'Intercranial pressure punctured dura as a result of the impact.'

He stops because Nancy is interrupting: 'No, no, no. A subdural bleed developed between the brain and dura, causing hypertension.'

Mr Dean gives a knowing look to the students. 'Mum's a doctor. MRI shows activity but the patient is unresponsive, uncommunicative, has complete paralysis.'

'Wrong again,' Nancy pipes up.

She turns to her daughter in the bed and squeezes her hand. 'Show them my darling. Blink once, if that tickled,' she says, full of love.

Everyone stares as Lucy's disarmingly long lashes blink. The nurse gasps.

'This is Locked-in syndrome,' Nancy states categorically. 'I'm taking her home. She's better off with us.'

Mr Dean is flustered. 'You can't,' he blusters. 'We will need to do tests . . . monitor her progress. A diagnosis like that takes months.'

Nancy locks eyes with her husband. 'Try and stop us.'

19

Sexton walks with the headmistress from her office to the musty gym hall downstairs, already packed with concerned parents about to be briefed by a psychologist attached to the Department of Education.

'One of the dads has just arrived,' Bronwyn whispers, twisting away from the door and mouthing exaggeratedly for Sexton's benefit, 'Amy Reddan's father.'

She turns back and Sexton follows her gaze to the broad, pale-faced man who looks like a lost soul, in an Aran-knit cardigan and a denim shirt buttoned up incorrectly. He appears completely and utterly distracted, as if he's not connected to the present at all.

Sexton puts a hand on Bronwyn's before she can sweep off 'to see how he's doing'.

'I could do with an introduction,' he says.

She drags air through her teeth as if she can't face it, but then gives a resolute nod. They cross the room together, but Sexton hangs back as she invades the man's body space, watching as she takes his hands and goes through the motions – the pitter-patter of condolences mingled with comforting chin-up talk. Then she sweeps an arm towards Sexton.

'Rob, I want you to meet Detective Inspector Gavin Sexton, from Store Street. He's compiling a report on the girls, and the pressures they were under. If you feel up to it, he would like to . . . Well, he can probably explain it better himself.'

Sexton puts out his hand. 'I'm very sorry for your troubles.'

'Thank you,' Rob replies.

Parents arriving into the room put hands on his back and shoulders as they pass, touch his arm, offering him a sad face, which disappears the second they have moved on, relieved to have escaped anything more in-depth.

'Can we talk about Amy and the issues she had before she died?' Sexton asks.

'Of course . . . if there's anything I can do to help . . . You know about the bullying, I presume.'

Sexton gives a nod.

'You want to know the ironic thing,' Rob says. 'As terrible as it was, it was no worse than what Melissa went through afterwards. Amy was such a sensitive girl. She took it to heart.'

'I'd like to find out if Amy was taking any drugs – prescription or otherwise?' Sexton says.

'Not that I ever knew,' Rob says. The psychologist comes over and asks him if he's ready.

'Can we talk after?' Sexton asks Rob.

Rob puts his hand in his pocket and hands over his card. 'I can't today but ring me any time. Today would have been Amy's fifteenth birthday, you see. That's the only reason I'm here. I said I'd contribute to the talk. Afterwards, we're going to release fifteen lanterns in Amy's memory.' He points to the card in Sexton's hand. 'Call me, I'd like to help. I've also done a lot of research since Amy died that you might find useful.'

He checks his watch and says he has to get started. Sexton thanks him and tells him he will ring soon. Bronwyn gives

Rob a hug, or tries to, but his arms stay stiff at his side and his back straight as a pole, despite the tears that have welled up in his eyes. It's as if what's happened has drained him of every last resource. Sexton remembers how gutting it felt when his father died. He can't imagine what it must be like to bury a teenage child. Finding out Maura was pregnant when she'd died nearly killed him as it was. He scans the room for a free seat and finds one right at the back of the hall.

The crowd consists of an even split of mothers and fathers – some clutching each others' hands, many gripping tissues. They lean in to each other, exchanging worried whispers, and when they spot Rob, brace themselves before heading over to give him long hugs, waiting for the lecture to get underway.

At the top of the room an attractive brunette in her thirties, wearing a just-below-knee navy skirt and matching tailored jacket, points a remote control at a projector and runs through the order of beaming pictures on a large screen behind her, before turning them off to lead Rob up to the podium.

Sexton stretches out his legs and makes himself comfortable as the shrink raises her voice to introduce 'a very special guest speaker'. There is a thunderous round of applause, and Rob looks uncomfortable as he puts a hand up to make them stop. After clearing his throat, he begins. 'Amy was three years old when we watched *Toy Story* on DVD. There's a part in the movie when Woody causes Buzz to fall out of the bedroom window and all the toys think he's trying to murder him because Buzz has just become Andy's favourite toy. When this happened, Amy became upset and cried that Woody hadn't meant it, when even Woody himself didn't seem too sure. That was Amy. All her life she had a built in sense of right and wrong, even as a little girl.'

Rob adjusts himself, and Sexton watches him swallowing hard. 'There has been a lot of anger since my daughter died. A lot of people rushed judgements, and it's human nature to want to have someone to blame. I certainly did. But it needs to stop now. Enough children have been lost. My daughter would have hated that anyone else felt compelled to take her own life too. Even when things were very tough for Amy, she was willing to give Melissa the benefit of the doubt. If I'm honest, I wanted to go and talk to Melissa, to go and give her a piece of my mind, but Amy said we didn't know what was going on in Melissa's life.' He takes a breath. 'That's the way Amy was all her short life. Her heart was too big. Anyone who heard her sing knows she felt things more deeply than most people. Even those people carrying clipboards who stop you in the street looking for your bank-account details for charity, people I'd go out of my way to avoid, well, Amy never let me pass one without agreeing to donate something. "It's only ten euro, Dad," she'd say.'

There is a quiet murmur of laughter in the room.

Rob sighs, and his eyes stay lowered. 'I kept all her things – the little band they put on her wrist when she was a baby in the hospital with her name and date of birth, the umbilical-cord clip that snipped her from her mom and made her dependent on the universe. Every shoe she ever wore, I have, even ones with holes in the toes, because every step she took in them mattered. Maybe I always knew she was too good for this earth, and sensed that I was always going to lose her. Her giant heart saved the life of another girl, all her organs were donated; she didn't have one drop of bitterness or guile in her body. Please let the lesson of Amy's life be compassion.

'My heart is broken, but every time another kid follows

Amy's way they diminish her a little more. Please tell the kids not to let the bullies have the last word, but also that bullying back is never the answer. Thank you very much.'

Rob swipes an eye and finds a chair in the crowd as they applaud him again. The shrink turns her projector on and ignores a collective groan that emanates in response to the first detail she delivers – that some twenty-five people between the ages of fifteen and twenty-eight killed themselves in Bridgend within two years of January 2007.

'I want to say from the outset, I'm here not to scare but to inform,' the psychologist states.

All the suicides occurred within a ten-mile radius of the town, and all but one were by hanging, she goes on.

The shrink clicks her control stick and the face of a Goth-eyed teenage girl with dyed black hair replaces a damp-looking town that could have been anywhere in Ireland.

'Suicide epidemics are rare, but not unprecedented,' she continues. 'And the gender breakdown is interesting. Whereas, here, we have an exact 50:50 ratio, in Bridgend it was a largely male phenomenon at first. Within a month of the first female and fifteenth in the Bridgend cluster, Natasha Randall, hanging herself in her bedroom, four more hangings followed, three of whom were girls.'

Females tend to overdose or slash their wrists, she says, because often they are more interested in self harm, and issuing a cry for help than dying, and these cases are referred to as parasuicides.

'There has been speculation that the victims might have belonged to an Internet suicide cult.' She indicates a map of the Welsh town on the screen which has interpreted the clusters as darkened shades of red. 'This was because of the speed with which Bebo pages eulogizing the dead went up on the Web. Sometimes the people leaving messages were themselves found hanging weeks later.

'But true Internet suicide cults – in which strangers meet online and agree to die together – are most common in Japan, a country with the worst suicide rate in the world, perhaps because of the cultural association of suicide being honourable, from the Samurai military nobility of pre-industrial Japan to the kamikaze pilots of the Second World War. To put it in context, in 2003, more than 34,000 people died by suicide in Japan.

'Of these, only around thirty-four died in Internet-linked group suicides, but that figure has been rising steadily ever since. So many young Japanese people have now killed themselves by inhaling fumes from household cleaning agents, or burning charcoal in cars and taking sleeping tablets, that it's no longer even considered newsworthy. Every night across Japan, hundreds of people meet online, looking for strangers to die with.

'The Internet messages are all variations of this, typically: "I want to die . . . anyone die with me? Let's die together."'

A sudden bang makes her stop and Sexton sees Rob bolt from the room. His chair has overturned in his haste to get away. One of the mums runs after him.

The speaker waits for a second then clicks the screen, and a snapshot of a chatroom exchange appears. 'This one is called the Suicide Club,' she resumes slowly. 'And this message says, "I've got a car and a charcoal briquette and medicine, everything. I'm a 22-year-old man and I want to die with six other people."

'There are thousands more equally sincere messages about despair and wanting to die. A guidebook on the best places to do it and describing the pros and cons of various methods has sold over a million copies.'

She pauses. Sexton notes how quiet the room is.

The lecture continues: 'There seems to be a reassurance for people in the idea of dying together. The reason why these pacts between strangers should hold any appeal is as mysterious as the cases of the Bridgend deaths, where victims tended to know each other, and so, in some cases, the domino effect of multiple deaths might be attributable to unresolved grief.

'In Bridgend, some experts have put the cause down to Gilbert Grape syndrome – where bored, impulsive teenagers with nothing to do in a backwater town consider infamy an achievement. Suicide became something cool to do.'

There is a collective intake of breath.

'But the Japanese believe,' the shrink goes on, 'that the problem is the Internet has created a new generation of *"hikikomori"* – recluses who never leave their room and use computers to socialize, to communicate and as their only source of entertainment. They believe online suicide pacts are ultimately kids trying to find friendship.

'We must not underestimate the role of the Internet in Bridgend either.' She stretches a pointer to the screen as a graph appears showing the number of Bridgend victims with Facebook accounts. It looked like almost all of them.

'The teenage years are turbulent for every generation, but since the advent of the Internet we have seen the demise of face-to-face discussions, leading to a greater sense of alienation and inability to communicate feelings anywhere other than on the Internet.

'Internet clubs are not confined to Japan. In Oregon, a suicidal man posted a message on Valentine's Day with the tagline: "Suicide party – you want to join it?"

'Ultimately, though, it's too easy to blame the Internet, cults, pacts, video games. At the end of the day, today's youth are more sexually active, and more likely to experiment with drugs at an earlier age than ever before. This, combined with the impulsiveness that comes with such a hormonal stage of life, has turned out to be a deadly cocktail, as we know to our own cost in this country.'

She reaches for a glass of water and sips slowly.

'I think it would be helpful to try to understand what's going through the heads of the suicide survivors, and I'd like to read what one near-suicide victim said after her head accidentally slipped through a noose she had made from her belt and she was found by her mother.'

The psychologist puts on a pair of glasses, reaches for some cue cards and, angling them into the light of the projector, reads:

'"It's something that developed in my mind. I started to think death is not the bad thing I was taught to think, I got this feeling I wanted to be with the others, that they understood me more than the people around me. I felt miserable being here and thinking there's got to be a better place. I don't believe in heaven, God, or none of that.

'"I was thinking about suicide since I was thirteen and I knew some of the others were hanging themselves. When I was twelve, my family fell apart and my mother took up with this man and I didn't get along with him. I've had a lot of people betray me and I find it hard to trust people, friends as well. I did try to kill myself when I was fourteen. I took an overdose of painkillers. I suffer from severe headaches and carried them in my schoolbag, but I got scared of what I done. We were at school and I told the nurse and she got me to the hospital in time.

'"A lot of people said it's selfish what these people done. But to me the only selfish people are the ones that drove them to it. It's been a month since I tried to do it. I can't really remember much about it, but I was feeling unhappy with life, sitting alone in my room. My mother was in the house. At the time I was mad at her. My head kept telling me to do it because everything was going to be OK. So finally I tied a couple of belts and jumped off the stairs, but my head slipped through the noose. It only held me for a split second. My mother came. I fell to the floor really shaking, and got up, sitting and crying. I still haven't recovered, to be honest."'

The psychologist pauses after putting down her notes, recognizing the sense of horror in the room. Everyone assembled is the parent of a teenager, Sexton presumes. It isn't hard to imagine what might be going through their minds.

'There is a psychodynamic explanation of suicide, that it's 180-degree murder. The victim really wants to kill somebody else, possibly an abuser, but instead they eliminate the abuse by killing the self. You kill the abusee instead of the abuser to send – excuse my French – a "Fuck you."'

There is a murmur of discomfort in the room. Sexton uses the opportunity to take his phone from his pocket and read a text. It's from Jo: 'I need a favour. Would you call over and have a word with Rory about how hard it was when Maura took her own life? Tonight. It's important.' Sexton puts the phone back in his pocket.

'Oh, for God's sake,' comes a voice from the crowd. 'It's our fault, now is that it?'

'Not at all,' the shrink answers. 'It might be more helpful if I just go straight to some more examples, to help us see the world through the eyes of depressed teenagers.' She clicks through slides showing the brain and a lab.

She stops when the stunning doe-eyed girl with the white face, heavy black eyeliner and jet-black hair from the start of the presentation reappears, staring blankly back. 'Angeline is another Bridgend victim. She was eighteen when she died. She had tried to take her own life twice before she succeeded. Angeline's Facebook profile said, "I don't like myself, but hey, who does?"

'Angie was a Goth, and some of you here might well have been Goths too in your teenage years.'

There are grunts of recognition from the crowd. 'The Goth subculture started in the eighties but it never disappeared through the nineties and noughties. It's that phase teenagers go through – dressing in black because of a sudden sense of the morbidity of life. Goths are influenced by the horror and romance of nineteenth-century literature. And today's teens, who devoured the *Twilight* series about vampires, and the *Hunger Games* about teenagers battling to the death, are not such a big leap away.'

The shrink clicks and the faces of two girls standing side by side appear.

'In Australia in 2007 these two sixteen-year-olds, Jodie Gater and Stephanie Gestier, also made a horrific pact.

'They were part of a musical subculture known as "Emo" after a type of music characterized by emotion and a confessional tone.

'Their online messages were "F*** this world/ Don't ever judge me."

'And in many ways, all teenagers are Goths and Emos, even the ones playing the soundtrack from *Glee* in their bedroom. It helps when we know them to see: they're the kids in black T-shirts, skinny jeans and sneakers, who hide their faces behind straightened hair. Their sleeves are pulled down over their sore wrists, and they wear lots of eye make-up. They've got the weight of the new adult world on their shoulders. Their iPods are blazing in their ears and when a parent asks them to do something they act like condemned prisoners. They think adults don't understand them, and, in many ways, we don't. We've been there ourselves, but we've come through, so we know what they're feeling is a phase, but to them – trapped in the time and space – their problems are life-and-death stuff. They're becoming adults, and it's an utterly changed world. They're trying to get to grips with it, and so should we.'

She flicks off the projector and signals for the lights to go on. 'Does anyone have any questions?'

Sexton squints against the brightness and puts his hand in the air.

Other hands started to lift, but he stands before the shrink gets a chance to choose.

'Yes, the man at the back, go ahead.'

'Have you been to Bridgend yourself, in the course of your research?'

'Yes,' she answers.

Parents are twisting around to look at Sexton.

'I just wanted to ask what drugs are used in the treatment of depression,' Sexton says. 'To be more exact, I want to know if Serozepam, specifically, was used.'

The shrink shakes her head emphatically. 'Actually, studies have shown us that Serozepam is a major inhibitor of serotonin. Which, in medical terms, means it contributes to depression, and doesn't cure it.'

20

Sexton goes back to the station to try to find out more about Lucy Starling, the only survivor in the suicide spate. Since she's the only one still alive, she might be able to fill him in. Maybe she got sent the vile video.

Nothing shows up on the computer records under Lucy's name, which is interesting. He'd thought, given her impulsiveness in taking her mother's car, which Bronwyn Harris had mentioned, it was possible she'd have been cautioned for something. Teenage tearaways get lots of chances before things ever go to court, but all warnings and Anti-social Behaviour Orders (ASBOs) are logged on the system. He'd half suspected some previous form, because it seemed unusual to graduate straight to joyriding without testing other waters first. There's absolutely nothing. He spots the asterisk beside her address linking the file to another, and clicks on it. One 'Nigel Starling' made a number of calls to Gardaí complaining about his windows being broken . . . tyres slashed . . . and . . . Sexton winces . . . dog poo being shoved through his letterbox. Sexton can see from the file that Nigel didn't accuse anyone directly, so the job wasn't actioned. In other words, nothing was done. He can see from the dates that the last complaint was four months ago. Things must have calmed down for Lucy's dad – if that's who Nigel is – he decides. The address is the same as the one he's got for Lucy.

He logs out and runs a couple of searches using her name in Google. Lucy crops up on Facebook and Ask.fm. He signs in to Facebook with the phoney details he'd set up on a compulsory social-networking course a couple of years back.

He glances up from the computer as McConigle enters the room.

Sexton goes back to the screen. There are loads of Lucy Starlings on Facebook, but only one living in Dublin. In her avatar, she's wearing a pair of low-slung jeans and a vest top; her midriff is bare in between. Her hip is cocked to one side and she's sticking her tongue out. Her hair is up in a pony-tail. If he didn't know otherwise, he'd have said the heavily made-up girl looking back at him was eighteen or nineteen. With a pair of beer goggles on, he'd have been willing to put her at twenty. That thought makes him shudder.

In 'About', her profile reads: 'Sexy bitch gagging for it.'

Sexton clicks on Lucy's photo albums. She looks like a hooker in every one of the pictures. All the shots were posed in her bedroom in negligee tops and panties, or skimpy dresses. Sexton's eyebrows go up a notch. She is pouting and strutting provocatively at the camera in all of them.

He goes back to the search and clicks on the Ask.fm link. It's a Latvian-based company which has got a lot of stick in recent months in the newspapers because of the kids' deaths. Its anonymous Q&A format has enraged parents' groups. Users – mostly teenagers – get sent questions from nameless people in a forum anyone with an account can see. The obvious question is why does anyone sign up, or even respond to vile questions? – but it is only ever asked by people from Sexton's generation, or older.

The issue is that while most social-networking sites are forcing users into giving their details to hold them accountable, Ask.fm is doing the precise opposite, and it's trading on the notoriety. He can see how the controversy will appeal to teens. Up until around five years ago, Facebook was doing the same. Internet police – anything associated with being responsible – put kids off.

Lucy's profile picture on the Ask.fm site is one of her trademark barely there outfits. Under her name, and photo, her biog reads: 'Fuck me!'

He reads:

You going to Back Gate 2moro nite?
You bet ;)
I'll finger ya at it so
Fuck you
You wearing your thong, it's so hawt?
Course, ye :D
i <3 ur ass ;)
Thats good, :) ha:L
bra colour ?
Red :L
Things id do to your arse
:L
did you give Billy a hand job
nopes?
so you would consider having my cock up your ass
NO:L
fancy my cock in your ass
not really :L:L
you're a desperate heuuur
you'd know, swear :L:L

He jots down the weird symbols that punctuate the sentences.

'Oi, that's my desk,' Fred Oakley says, heading over.

The DS is a heavy-set former rugby player who's managed to get Jo Birmingham's goat up because of his sexist attitude towards answering to women. The job Oakley signed up to is under siege in another way. One hundred stations have closed in order to slash departmental costs in recent years, and the knock-on effect, combined with the directive on logging every tea break, was that desk space was now at a premium.

'Fuck off,' Sexton tells him.

Desks are only ever claimed on a first-come, first-served basis.

'It's illegal to download anything that brings the force into disrepute,' Oakley sneers, peering over Sexton's shoulder, ogling Lucy's profile shot.

Sexton pushes against the desk, making the chair wheel backwards and into Oakley.

'I would, though.' He winks at Sexton.

'One of these days I will be waving at you through the bars in the Joy, you know that?' Sexton smirks.

'How come girls like that didn't exist when I was growing up?'

'Oh, now you've grown up, have you?' Sexton retorts. 'What age is your kid anyway?' he asks, to remind him that he is the father of a girl not much older.

'Which one?' Oakley asks.

'The teenager.'

'Which one?'

'I thought you only had one!'

'What, with this aim?' Oakley reaches for his nuts and gives them a Michael Jackson shake.

Sexton shakes his head. 'You're a sad bastard.'

'Yeah, but at least I'm getting some.'

'Yeah, if you roll Vera over.' Sexton has a thought. 'How are you on those weird symbols kids use?' He holds out his notepad to show him what he's written. 'Give one of your kids a ring for me, will you?'

Oakley plucks the pad off him. 'Don't need to. Every text I get is full of this. If I didn't know it meant I'd be collecting her from ballet when I should be picking her up from swimming, if you get my drift.'

'Just translate . . .'

Oakley points to one with his finger. 'This one "<3" means "love".'

Sexton frowns. 'A greater-than symbol and the number three? How do you make that out?'

Oakley tilts the pad. 'It's a love heart, see? And this colon followed by a capital "D" is someone laughing heartily . . . this one's a wink, this is a snigger, as in a cheeky joke. "L" means Loser, and the "P" after a colon is supposed to be the shape of a tongue in a cheek under a set of eyes. Unless . . .' Oakley angles the pad another way. ''Course, it could always be . . .' He makes a pumping motion with his wrist at the side of his face and pokes the opposite cheek out with his tongue.

Sexton grabs his pad off him. 'That image is going to stay with me for the rest of the day.' He sees McConigle is on her own and takes the opportunity to approach her.

'Did you get a phone number for Anna Eccles?'

'Not yet.'

'Well, have you organized to have the wood triangulated?' She stares at him blankly.

Sexton shakes his head. 'Do you even know the provider yet? They could give us the phone's history.'

'Don't worry, I'll put Oakley on it.'

'Oakley?' Sexton glances across the room at him. 'I

wouldn't trust him with a cup of tea.'

'You don't have to,' she reminds him.

'How many has the chief assigned you for the case?' he presses.

'Oakley, and three uniforms,' she admits.

'A team of four! For fuck's sake!'

'And Foxy is keeping the jobs book,' she argues.

Most gardaí retired from the force by the age of fifty-five, but the station's bookman – Sergeant John Foxe – had joined the force later than most and, at sixty-five, was due to retire at the end of the week.

'Listen, you need me and you know it. Let me interview a parasuicide in Anna's school. Her name's Lucy Starling and she's still alive. I could ask her if she knows anything about that "How to" video.'

McConigle shakes her head. 'The chief was pretty clear . . .'

Sexton curses and starts to walk away.

'But, if you have to interview the student because of the report you're compiling, I'm sure that would be extremely useful,' she adds.

21

The Starlings' house looks nice enough, but it's in a shit location. Rutling Street has a block of notorious, drugs-ravaged flats at one end, and a chefs and sparks college around the corner, meaning most of the accommodation has been converted for students. Sexton stares as he spots a surgery sign on a separate entrance at the side.

The woman who answers looks too old to be a fourteen-year-old's mum. She reminds Sexton of that hairy angel whose album he bought for his mum one Christmas.

'I'm Detective Inspector Gavin Sexton,' he says, holding up his ID. 'The juvenile liaison officer for the area. Can I have a word?'

Heavy eyebrows shoot up behind a pair of horn-rimmed glasses. 'Oh. OK. Come in. I'm Nancy Starling. Is this about Lucy?'

Sexton nods and follows her down the hall to the kitchen, where she holds the kettle under a tap. He calculates that a woman who doesn't look a day under sixty would have been forty-six at the time her daughter was born.

'How can I help?' she asks. Her accent is more mid-Atlantic than Welsh, he notes.

'I'm working on a report on the recent suicide cluster,' Sexton explains. 'To try to build a picture of what's going on with the kids . . . what's happening and why.'

'Why does everyone think Lucy was trying to kill herself?' Nancy snaps.

'You don't believe she was?' Sexton asks.

'I'll tell you exactly what I think, once I've explained to Lucy what's going on. She'll have heard the bell and be wondering. She's always been the most curious little thing. You should have seen her when she was a toddler. She used to follow me everywhere, afraid she'd miss something.' Nancy stops, pushes her fingers under her glasses and rubs her eyes quickly.

'Have you got children?' she asks, pulling herself together and taking her glasses off to clear steam spots with the hem of her camel-coloured polo-neck, before sticking the glasses back on.

Sexton shakes his head.

'You're still young, plenty of time. Stick the tea on.'

She heads off.

Sexton pulls open presses until he finds the one with mugs, pulls out two. He drops a teabag in each, yanks open drawers to locate cutlery, drops a spoon in each mug, and helps himself to a couple of gingernuts left on the workbench.

'You could do with cutting back on snacks between meals,' Nancy tells him as she returns. 'At your age and weight, you're asking for trouble. If you're having sugar cravings, I'd be prepared to bet you've got diabetes. It's a lot more common than you think.'

They move to the kitchen table and sit.

'You're the GP, I take it?' Sexton asks, taking out his notebook.

'Yes. My husband Nigel's a homeopath. Or he was before we moved here. We lived in Bridgend, in Wales, where all the children died before. We thought we were getting away from the horror. Sod's bloody law, eh? I've phoned Nigel to tell him you were here, and he's on the way. What is it you need to know for your report?'

'I'd like to find out about the circumstances surrounding Lucy's . . . accident,' Sexton says. 'Establish whether she's one of the kids affected.'

Nancy sighs. 'I was working. My practice is in a couple of rooms at the side of the house. I run a Methadone clinic once a week, or I used to. I'll have to cut back on everything now, obviously. Or close. I am the only GP in a five-mile radius willing to dispense Methadone, so you can imagine the amount of patients I have to see on a Friday night. I insist they all give me a fresh urine sample when they come in, to make sure it's their own. It's very time-consuming.'

'Were any of the teenagers who died seeing you, as a matter of interest?' Sexton asks. He wants to know if he's found the Serozepam dispenser.

She shakes her head and looks at him curiously. 'No, thank God. I wouldn't want that on my conscience. I've enough to deal with as it is.' She studies her hands. 'I'll have to live with the guilt of not being there for my daughter for the rest of my life.' She pauses, pulls herself together. 'Lucy told her dad she wanted to go to a concert. Nigel offered to give her a lift, but she's always been very wilful.' She glances up quickly and corrects herself. 'They all are at that age; Lucy was no more wilful than most. Have you written that down? I'd like to change it if you have. "Wilful" is the wrong word. I mean "impulsive", a typical teenager in other words.'

She rubs her forehead, stressed.

Sexton looks up from his notes, motions a hand for her to keep going.

'We didn't notice my car was gone until a good hour after she'd left,' Nancy continues. 'We tried calling her, but the phone was diverting straight to her mailbox.'

She starts to sob. 'A moment of madness, that's all it was. One that's going to define the rest of Lucy's life. I'm sorry,' she says. 'God works in mysterious ways, I suppose. Without our faith, we'd never get through this. But, sometimes, it's just so hard to understand why.'

Sexton shifts on the chair. 'Can you give me Lucy's number?'

'Sure,' she says, reeling it off.

He jots it down. 'I'd like to have a look at the phone, if you don't mind.'

'That will be more difficult. We don't know where it is. We never got it back after the crash. It only occurred to us afterwards, but it didn't seem to matter at the time, given everything else going on. Why?'

'It doesn't matter,' Sexton says. 'What time did Lucy leave the house?'

Nancy wrings her hands. 'Around six thirty, I think. Nigel will be better able to answer you on this.'

'Where was the concert on?'

'The Phoenix Park.'

Sexton looks up. 'But wasn't Lucy's crash at the Scalp in the Dublin mountains? I checked the log before I left. She was miles away from the Phoenix Park.'

Nancy shrugs helplessly.

'Lucy will be able to clarify, I'm sure,' Sexton says. 'Can I talk to her? Is she here?'

Nancy looks at him strangely. 'Weren't you told? Lucy can't move.'

Sexton glances up. 'I'm sorry, I didn't realize she was paralysed.'

'Paraplegics can sometimes move their heads, some can even walk. Lucy can't even swallow, Detective. The only thing that she can move is her eyes. She can communicate though – incredibly. It's a testament to her character. She's a tiny little thing – only four foot eleven, but she was always so . . . strident.'

They both turn at the sound of the front door crashing open and footsteps thundering down the hall.

22

Nigel Starling storms into the kitchen like a man possessed. He paces over to Sexton, too close, invading his space, poking a finger into Sexton's chest.

'You make me sick,' he blasts.

Sexton wipes drops of spittle from his face and pushes him off. 'What's the matter with you?'

Nigel steps back into the space. 'Lucy's fourteen! Don't you have any real criminals to find, or can't you resist an easy target? What kind of man are you?'

Sexton crosses his arms. 'What?'

'Are you planning to prosecute her? Is that what this is really about? What are you going to do? Adapt her prison cell? She's already locked in without you ever locking her up.'

Nancy forces herself between him and Sexton, facing her husband. 'Stop!' she tells him.

'Why is he really here? What's he going to do? Charge Lucy with joyriding . . . causing an accident? Teach her a lesson? Will that make the streets safe so she won't do it again? She won't do it again!'

'Please, darling,' Nancy implores. 'He's only doing a report, that's all.'

'She's fourteen years old. She made a mistake. We all did at that age. She's going to pay for it for the rest of her life. If she's put through the ringer of a court case, found guilty and the judge recommends a custodial sentence, what then? She needs round-the-clock care. Everything would have to be adapted. The prison isn't even equipped to deal with able-bodied people from what I read everyday in the newspapers.'

Sexton opens his mouth to speak, but Nigel isn't having any of it.

'The lorry driver Lucy crashed into walked away without so much as a scrape or a bruise, but because Lucy was un-insured and had no licence, Tim McMenamy is suing us. It's not enough for him that Lucy was the only one hurt by what happened. He wants his pound of flesh. We could lose our house and Lucy her only chance of some comfort at this stage in her life. And here you come wanting to charge her with a crime.'

'That's not why I'm here,' Sexton says.

'Why else?' Nigel asks.

'If you give me a chance to get a word in edgeways, I'll explain,' Sexton clips.

Nigel shuts it.

'It's just a report,' Sexton explains. 'Just a round-up of cases so we get an idea of what's going on.'

Nigel shoots his wife a puzzled look. 'We've been completely paranoid,' she admits. 'The law seems so unforgiving these days. We kept thinking about that old bachelor in the papers from Wicklow who shot his brother for not obeying their mother's last wishes not to be buried with her husband. Remember him?'

Sexton gives a delayed nod.

'Cecil something or other,' she says. 'He had Parkinson's disease and it was a crime of passion, in as much as he was in the full throes of grief when he fired that shotgun, I remember.'

Nigel puts his hands out. 'What he did was terrible – I'm not condoning it – but it was understandable. The poor man had to be wheeled in and out of court every day and he couldn't even speak his own name. Even after he was acquitted of murder in the Court of Criminal Appeal, the state arranged for a second trial. It brought him back to his nursing home to wait for the day they could put him through it all over again. I can't bear the thought that Lucy might be prosecuted for what happened, on top of everything else.'

Nancy whispers something in her husband's ear.

'I'm sorry, Detective,' he says, offering his hand.

Sexton shakes it, wondering how Nigel got the bruise on his cheek.

'I shouldn't have flown off the handle. It's just we're determined to care for Lucy in her home so she doesn't end up doped up to the eyeballs in some home, or in prison. We love her so much. And when we learned this week that we're being sued by that lorry driver, I thought he might want a criminal prosecution to help his civil action.'

Nancy nods her head. 'We're going to fight off McMenamy's despicable attempt to turn Lucy's accident into his personal windfall . . .' Her voice cracks, but she continues, '. . . Lucy was the miracle baby we'd given up hope of ever having, you see. We had her later than most. She was a blessing from the day she was born.'

Sexton jangles the loose change in his trousers pocket. 'I'm very sorry for your . . .' He looks at his feet.

'Troubles?' Nigel reacts. 'Lucy's not dead, far from it. We're glass-half-full people. We see ourselves as the luckiest people alive that Lucy has survived. We'll have her back with us properly yet.'

Nancy cuts in. 'That's why it's so important to us we keep

our daughter here, with us, where she belongs.' She looks at her husband lovingly, as she goes on: 'If we lose our home, Lucy is the one who will suffer. This is where she belongs. Lucy is everything to us. Our only child. We're the best people to look after her. We love her so much.

'We weren't the perfect family. Lucy's adolescence was becoming . . .' she pauses '. . . problematic. In the year prior to the crash three months ago, she was finding it more and more difficult to manage the tidal wave of feelings that come with the transition to pubescence. But there was as much love in this house as any. We'd have got through it. Together. We will get through it together. This is her home. We've had to fight tooth and nail to convince the hospital we could care for her full-time ourselves. Tim McMenamy is an opportunist. If Lucy's guilty of anything, it's of being over-zealous in taking my car out for a spin that day, that's it. We have to try to prevent whatever kind of comfort the money we've made could have given her, whatever we could have invested in research, from ending up in McMenamy's pocket. If she can avoid criminal charges, that will be one less battle we have to fight. It will help us concentrate all our energies on her.'

'Lucy made a mistake,' a sobbing Nigel tells his wife.

Nancy holds him close, her head on his chest. 'I know, love, I know.'

'What happened to your face?' Sexton asks.

Nigel puts his hand up quickly. 'This? It's nothing. Just a run-in with a neighbour.'

'What about?'

Nigel shrugs. 'I asked him to stop depositing his waste in my wheelie bin. You pay by the weight of those things.'

'Did it have anything to do with the problems you'd reported to us – someone broke your windows and slashed your tyres, didn't they?'

Nigel looks surprised. 'No, nothing at all,' he says quickly. 'That was just some kids getting drunk and messing about.'

Sexton turns to Nancy. 'You said Lucy can communicate.'

She sighs and steps back from her husband, holding him at the upper arms. 'You sure you're OK, love?'

'Yes, love.' He nods.

She takes his hand and they lead Sexton to Lucy's bedroom.

23

Sexton stands, stares and jigs a leg. The gurgling sound of the pump is grotesque, and the smell of disinfectant mingled with bodily fluids is one he has only ever picked up in hospitals. He walks his tie down a couple of inches and opens a shirt button.

Lucy Starling, lying in the bed with spittle drooling out from one side of her mouth and a rag perched under her chin to catch it, is one of the sorriest things he's ever seen, especially since her eyes have followed him since he's entered the room. He's never seen as many tubes coming out of anyone. She's only fourteen. The fact that the room is like a shrine to the teenage rite of passage makes her near-vegetative state even more depressing. The wall facing her is entirely covered with posters. He scans them, recognizing Chris Brown because of the controversy over a tattoo of a supposedly battered woman on his neck – he wouldn't have recognized his music. He knows Professor Green too, but only because one of his superiors in the station had gone mental when the station's social club had raffled tickets for one of his concerts. 'Green' was a thinly veiled reference to hash. That was it. Sexton didn't know anyone else.

'You can sit there,' Nancy says quietly, pointing to a chair beside the bed.

'Bet you've never heard of The Verve, or Oasis?' he says to Lucy, still standing.

'Sorry?' Nancy cuts in.

'I was just telling Lucy how old I feel,' Sexton says.

He glances at a crucifix nailed to the wall directly over her bed, wondering if it's a form of torture for Lucy.

The heat in the room is stifling. Sexton picks his shirt off the damp spots on his skin.

'Aren't you going to sit down?' Nancy asks.

He shifts his body weight to the other leg and turns to Nancy. 'Shouldn't she still be in hospital?'

'Lucy gets more medical attention here than she would in any hospital,' Nancy says. 'And her personal happiness will have a huge bearing on her recovery. I'm convinced of that from almost forty years in the job. Where there's life, there's always hope,' she says, as much to herself as to him. 'And stem cells are revolutionizing medical research . . .'

'Yes,' Sexton says. 'Are you sure she can do this?'

'Yes, if it will help, she can do it. But it's exhausting for her, so if you could keep it brief. You need to confine your questions to answers that require yes or no answers. Lucy blinks once for yes, and twice for no.'

24

Rihanna Canon races down Rutling Terrace into her dad's shop, Damm. She sweeps past 'Gok', the Chinese man who works there fixing iPhones. Grabbing either side of her bell-shaped communion dress, puffed out with several layers of netting and lace, she clumps up the narrow, uneven stairs at the back.

Eric Canon is out cold on a mattress on the floor of the dim box room, which stinks of sweat and booze. There is no other furniture in the room. Only a couple of cans remain in the slab of Dutch Gold on the floor beside him; crushed empties are scattered all over the floor.

Rihanna pushes her ringlets out of her face with her satin fingerless gloves, grabs his T-shirt and shakes him hard.

'Da, wake up! Come on, Da, wake up now!'

Eric doesn't move.

She grabs his hair and yanks. 'Da, there's pigs across the street.'

Canon opens his eyes wide, sits up straight and pushes the child out of the way. He has a red goatee beard in a fleshy face that is permanently pink. He staggers over to the window in his grey towelling socks. He puts a hand to his head as he moves.

'Don't!' he roars at the child, jerking away from the window as she switches the light on.

It goes off again.

He tousles her hair, reaches for a pair of binoculars perched on the sill and peers out. 'How long are they there?'

'Don't know. I was down the flats collecting my money.'

'Anyone downstairs?'

'A man in from the hostel, but he'd no money and Gok kicked him out.'

'And how long since you went to the flats?'

'An hour. They definitely weren't there when I went out.'

Eric puts the binoculars down. 'How much did you get, in anyway?'

'Seventy-nine euro.'

'Scabby fucks. Did you get your breakfast off your ma?'

'No, I'm saving any money I make for a pair of Heelys, remember?'

'What the fuck is going on over there?' he mutters, pre-occupied again by the presence of the squad car at the Starlings' house.

She shrugs and smoothes the ruffles in her dress.

'Did you get any dinner?' he asks, bending to pull up a corner of the heavily stained mattress.

'I had a bag of chips,' she says.

'Want to go to McDonald's?' he asks, sliding out a Glock 9mm semi-automatic and tucking it in the back belt of his jeans, pulling his T-shirt on over it.

'Get the usual for me, princess, and whatever you're having yourself. Good girl. How's your ma, in anyway?'

'She's a dope,' Rihanna says, pulling a crooked face that makes him laugh.

He holds his hand up for her to high-five it. 'Here's fifty euro for your skates. Don't let your mother see it.'

Rihanna nods and starts to totter off towards the stairs.

Canon calls after her, 'Here, have you called over the

road and told them you made your communion yet?'

'No, you told me to stay away from there.'

He follows her and looks down at her on the staircase as she looks up. 'I'll go with you. We'll do it now. What's the only way to get rid of rats?'

'Smoke them out, Da,' she says robotically.

25

Sexton manoeuvres through the wires and oxygen tank and monitors that are humming and beeping in Lucy's bedroom. He pulls a Kleenex from a box perched on her locker to soak up the sweat beads breaking out on his forehead.

'We've ordered equipment that will allow Lucy to spell out entire words by just glancing at the letter of the alphabet,' Nancy says.

'As long as Tim McMenamy doesn't empty our bank account first,' Nigel adds.

'Do you know how Jean-Dominique Bauby came to write *The Diving Bell and the Butterfly?*' Nancy goes on. 'He would spell out words by blinking a number to indicate which alphabet letter he needed. We've come a long way since then. We don't want to go back.'

Sexton turns to Lucy. 'I should have introduced myself to you earlier, Lucy,' he says, checking over his shoulder that he was doing it right.

Nancy nods.

Sexton turns back to the bed. On Facebook, Lucy had been a ringer for that Hollywood actress Drew Barrymore, but now there is no similarity at all. 'My name is Detective Inspector Gavin Sexton and I'm attached to Store Street station. I'm here, as you know already, to investigate the circumstances surrounding, well . . . what happened to you.'

Lucy blinks once through her dead stare. Yes.

Sexton is astonished. It is unmistakeable. A big grin breaks out on his face. His heart has stalled and surged in pity and amazement.

'I need to ask just a few basic questions so I can put together my report and then I'll leave you in peace to concentrate on more important things, such as your recovery,' he says.

It wasn't meant as a question, but her Bambi eyelashes are batting again – twice this time. He wonders why she is indicating 'no'. Maybe she means 'no', as in 'Don't leave'? Then again, maybe Lucy means she doesn't want to recover. He presumes she is as depressed as fuck in there, trapped, powerless, claustrophobic. He takes his pen out.

The doorbell goes and Nigel moves to the window to peer out. 'It's him,' he tells his wife. 'I'll get it.'

'Let's start with what was going through your mind at the time of the crash, and then we can get into the detail,' Sexton says as Nigel leaves. 'Were you down . . . low . . . did you want to end your life?'

Sexton is conscious that Nancy has followed Nigel into the hall, where they are talking out of earshot, but he keeps his gaze fixed on Lucy.

She blinks – once, twice. He is about to make a note of her answer – no – when he realizes she is still blinking – three, four – perfectly paced blinks. There are nine in all in the sequence.

He opens his mouth to call Nancy back to ask what nine blinks mean, but he doesn't get a chance, because Lucy has started blinking again, and he counts eight perfectly paced blinks.

'Did you see that?' he asks, as Nancy returns to the room. 'Lucy blinked nine, and then eight times. What does it mean?'

'That she needs to rest,' Nancy says categorically.

'What?' Sexton asks vaguely, because he is concentrating on counting again: nine times again. After a beat, Lucy's off again.

'I think we've been too hasty,' Nancy says.

Sexton does not take his eyes off Lucy, afraid he'll lose count. He puts a hand up to tell Nancy to wait. At eighteen blinks, Lucy stops. He makes a note. He realizes she's off again and adds five blinks to the list.

Nigel arrives back in the room, asking Nancy for her wallet. She directs him to the kitchen, where she's left her bag.

'Four,' Sexton writes.

Nancy moves to the opposite side of the bed to try to get Sexton's attention. 'I want Lucy to sleep now . . .'

One.

He holds his palm up again to silence her so he can count. Lucy blinks eight times. A pause. Nine. Another pause, during which he didn't so much as breathe in anticipation, and then she starts talking again through those eyes, a desperate staccato Morse code to tell them: she's in there. He writes '20' on his list as Nancy leaves the room to consult her husband. When she comes back a couple of minutes later, the numbers 13, 1, 1 and 14 are on his pad.

'Have you any idea what this is about?' Sexton asks, once he's sure the blinking is over.

'Maybe she wants to do the lottery,' Nancy jokes nervously.

Sexton looks at her to see if she's serious, but she has begun clattering in a metal press behind him. Sexton notices the word 'Love' cut into Lucy's arm in healed scars. Nancy moves to the bedside.

'We'd hoped for too much for tonight,' Nancy said.

'Come back tomorrow, Detective. I don't want her upset.'

With a couple of steps Nancy reaches for Lucy's arm, turns it over and twists the plug on a cannula. She inserts a hypodermic syringe filled with fluid.

'Just your medication, darling,' she says gently. 'This is not normal for her,' she tells Sexton. 'It's too soon. She's worked up. You should go. She's asleep,' she adds.

Sexton looked from the series of numbers on his page to Lucy.

'Can I use your bathroom?' he asks.

In the pokey space he stares at the numbers on the page: 9-8-9-18-5-4-1-8-9-20-13-1-14 and begins to count up to the corresponding letter with his fingers. As the words appear on the page, he realizes exactly why Nancy and Nigel wrapped up the interview and are so anxious at the thought of a criminal prosecution. They weren't worried about a dangerous-driving charge at all. Sexton stares at the words on the page: 'I hired a hitman.'

26

Nigel and Nancy are waiting for him when he emerges from the loo. Nancy hands him his coat.

'I need to ask some more questions before I go,' Sexton says.

They are surprised.

'But Lucy is asleep,' Nancy says.

'I need to talk to you two this time.'

He sees the distrust in Nigel's face. 'It's just procedure,' Sexton explains.

They lead him back to the kitchen.

'I don't mean to be rude, but is this going to take long?' Nancy asks. 'I'm due on a call-out to a patient.'

'I wanted to get some more things straight in my head before I go,' he says, returning to the kitchen chair he'd been sitting on.

'Such as?' Nigel quizzes.

'You said that Lucy's teenage years were becoming problematic, difficult. I wondered how bad relations were right before the crash?'

Nancy shoots Nigel a puzzled look.

'What's the point of a question like that?' he asks.

Nancy touches his arm, keeping her eyes trained on Sexton. 'Great, we were all getting along great. Lucy was . . . is . . . lovely.'

Nigel turns his face away.

'But you already told me her adolescence was an issue,' Sexton reminds Nancy. 'I could see for myself signs she was cutting herself. And the principal told me about her overdose.'

Nigel shakes his head. 'Lucy had her moments, like all teenagers do. But it was nothing we couldn't handle. We were getting on great right before the crash. As a matter of fact, we'd never been happier. Isn't that right, Nancy?'

Nancy gives a series of little nods.

'But she must have been acting up to have taken the car without your permission at fourteen years old?' Sexton presses. 'Things must have been strained? I mean, you've already admitted that much yourselves, right?'

'She was —' Nigel hesitates. '— is our angel.' He stands and walks across the room to a dressing table, pulls open a drawer and removes a photo album.

'I never got lured into this generation's obsession with the digital,' Nigel says, opening a page and smiling. 'Remember this one?' he asks his wife, carrying it over and pointing out a photo.

'How could I forget?' Nancy asks.

Sexton leans over and sees a pretty little girl, aged about eleven, sitting on a pony, grinning under her riding cap in that big-toothed way pre-teens have and pointing at a rosette pinned to her jacket.

In another shot on the page, Lucy is singing on a stage in what looks like a school play. Another image shows her practising piano.

'Do you mind if I have a look?' Sexton asks.

Nigel passes the album over.

Sexton turns the pages and glances at the images of a red-cheeked little girl on a bicycle; more of her in a paddling pool. Here she's blowing out seven candles. There are numerous pictures of her throughout the years, starting with her first day at school, but he can't find any up-to-date ones. He flicks back through the pages to double-check. Another thing that occurs to him is that Lucy's extracurricular schedule must have taken up every spare minute. There's a picture of her dressed in a white tutu, with her back arched, standing tiptoe in pointed ballet shoes, the ribbons criss-crossed up her calves, her arms stretched up over her head. In another, she can be seen concentrating on a sheet of music so intently as she plays the violin that she looks furious. There's a shot of her running cross-country, even her face lathered in muck as she nears the finish line. Sexton realizes what it is that's wrong with the photos: not only are the teenage years missing, but there aren't any at all of Lucy lounging on the couch or lolling about. He spots a picture of her in a wetsuit standing on a beach, her hair dripping with water. He taps it.

'What age is she in this one?' He guesses it is relatively recent, based on the spots breaking out on her skin.

'Twelve,' Nigel answers.

'She was clearly an over-achiever,' Sexton remarks, handing the album back to them.

'She was good at everything she put her mind to, always,' Nancy agrees.

'Very determined,' Nigel says.

There is a trace of weariness in his voice, which Sexton picks up on.

'Did she ever threaten you?' he asks.

Nigel splutters as a mouthful of tea goes down the wrong way. 'What?'

'Of course not.' Nancy is indignant. 'Why would you even ask something like that?'

'I'm trying to establish if things were tense between you, if the acts of rebellion might have got worse? If she ever' – he picks his words carefully – 'threatened you, or made you feel unsafe?'

'Absolutely not,' Nancy says, standing.

Nigel carries his cup over to the sink, and keeps his back to them.

Sexton looks at Nancy. 'I need to know if Lucy had any dealings with criminals?'

Nancy blinks. 'Criminals! Lucy had been an A-student up until last year, when other distractions just proved too tempting. She was also a gifted athlete. She excelled in everything she did. She was even starting to talk about which university she wanted to attend.'

'Was it the first time she'd taken your car without your permission?' Sexton asks.

'She was fourteen,' Nancy reiterates. 'Of course it was the first time she'd taken the car. Lucy had never even had a driving lesson. She was too young to drive.'

'Is that a yes?' Sexton asks, not waiting for a reply. 'She'd also lied to you about where she was going, told you she was going to the Phoenix Park, but had headed in a completely different direction. Look, it's what adolescents do. I presume she was rebelling as they all do. I need you to talk to me if we're going to help Lucy.'

Nigel cracks his fingers. 'Lucy was a very kind-spirited girl. She'd probably organized to pick someone up.'

Nancy nods. 'Yes, that'll be it.'

Sexton runs a hand through his hair. 'Who?'

Another pregnant pause.

'Did she have a boyfriend? Was that the distraction you just mentioned?'

'Of course not,' Nancy says. 'She was still just a child.'

Sexton scratches his jaw irritably. 'One of her friends then? Can you give me a list of their names?'

'Actually, she preferred her own company,' Nancy says quickly.

Sexton puts his notebook and pen down on the table. 'You mean she was a loner?'

'That's a loaded word,' Nancy replies.

'How would you describe her then?'

'Kind, sensitive, talented, for starters,' she says.

Sexton puts his cup on the pristine glass table and pushes it forward. 'In other words, the perfect daughter?'

'She had her moments – who doesn't?' Nigel says. 'Look, we indulged her, no question. But Lucy was a sensitive girl. If we were too lenient it's because we were worried she might . . .' His voice trails off.

'Do you think that's why she crashed?' Sexton pushes. 'I thought your wife's view was that Lucy was not trying to kill herself? But she had overdosed before . . .'

'No, no, no!' Nancy snaps. 'Lucy took some drugs, OK? But it wasn't a proper suicide bid. It was a cry for help. She didn't really mean it. If she'd meant it, she wouldn't be here now.'

'So she could have had criminal contacts,' Sexton says. 'Where else would she have got the drugs?'

'Not those kind of drugs,' Nancy says. 'She took pills from the surgery.'

'Like Serozepam?'

'Yes, among others. She OD'd on Benzodiazepines . . . anti-psychotics.'

'So Lucy was lying, joyriding, self-harming and stealing drugs from you. In other words, she was totally out of control?'

'You're twisting our words,' Nigel says. 'If you must

know, a girl with whom she was friendly had taken her own life . . .'

'Amy Reddan?'

'Yes. Lucy was so upset . . . she stopped thinking straight.'

Nancy chips in. 'A lot of the schools have been affected by this blight. We're not the only ones.'

'Did Lucy take anything else from you apart from your car, the drugs that she shouldn't have . . . ?' Sexton probes.

'Such as?' Nancy asks.

Sexton decides to take a punt on the hitman angle. He shrugs. 'Money? A lot of money?'

Nigel shoots a worried look at his wife. Sexton clocks it.

'That's a very specific question, and it suggests you already know the answer,' Nigel says, his voice breaking.

'Shut up,' Nancy blurts.

'Even if he's bluffing, he can find out with one phone call,' Nigel says, tears welling up.

Sexton's phone trills to life. He sees Jo's number and declines the call. It goes to message. Sexton leans back in the chair. 'How much, and when exactly?' he asks.

27

The *Channel 4 News* jingle is playing on the box when Jo elbows Dan, who has nodded off on the couch, to answer the front door.

'I didn't hear anything,' he says.

'Someone definitely rapped,' she tells him. 'It's probably Sexton, I asked him to call.'

'Why?'

'Sorry, love, I haven't had a chance to tell you about what I found on Rory's computer. He was looking up . . .'

A loud rap cuts her off. 'I'd better get it before that lunatic rings the bell and wakes Harry,' Dan answers, heading for the hall.

There is a murmured conversation at the door before Sexton arrives into the room. He walks past Jo and heads straight over to the fire to warm the backs of his legs.

'It's freezing out,' he says stiffly. He has come straight from the Starlings', after a conversation with a little girl in a communion dress waiting by his car. She must have asked him forty questions.

'What's wrong?' Jo asks. 'You usually give me a kiss on the cheek.'

'Will someone tell me what's going on?' Dan cuts in gruffly.

'I asked Sexton to come over to talk to Rory about what

he went through when Maura died.' She indicates Dan should close the door in case Rory overhears.

'What about Maura?' Dan asks.

Sexton throws his hands up. 'Don't mind me.'

'What's wrong, Gavin?' Jo asks.

'Both of you, actually. I've said it numerous times, but I'll say it again, because nobody seems to be listening. I do not believe Maura committed suicide. Dan, you think I've got the right experience for a report on suicides, because of what happened to Maura, but as I'm the only one in the station who doesn't believe she topped herself, you couldn't be more wrong.

'And Jo, at one stage, I thought you might actually believe me. You offered to help me investigate the circumstances surrounding Maura's death, do you remember? But clearly you were just humouring me, stringing me along, because that never happened, and now you want me to counsel your son.'

Sexton swallows.

'Gavin, that's not true,' Jo says.

'Which bit?'

'I couldn't investigate anything when my sight went. But, as a matter of fact, I'm looking into it now.'

A tickle starts up in Sexton's throat and makes him cough. He thumps his chest. 'You're what?'

'I'll go water the plants, shall I?' Dan says, heading out.

'There's no need to look into Maura's case any more. I've moved on. But for the record, Maura did not commit suicide!'

'Well, that's what I'm going to establish once and for all, and the reason I met your mother-in-law today.'

Sexton's temper rises. 'You've no right to do something like that without clearing it with me first.'

'What are you talking about? You asked me to look into it, and Esther happened to be in Dublin. Why the sudden change of heart?'

'What did she say?'

Sexton looks around, heads over to the drinks cabinet, examines a bottle of Scotch, twists the lid and reaches for a glass. He knocks back a drink and pours another.

Jo decides against telling him what she's found out when he's this animated. He's got a track record of flying off the handle. 'Now isn't the time to go into it. I need to check on a few things first, if that's OK with you.' She pauses, waiting for a reaction from Sexton. He sighs and shrugs, which Jo takes for a reluctant yes. Jo changes the subject. 'I'm sorry for asking you to talk to Rory. I should have been more sensitive. It was a bad idea.'

'You driving?' Dan asks, re-entering the room.

Sexton taps his nose. 'We need to talk about the bullying case. There's been a development.'

Dan sighs and paces to the hall door, which can be seen from the room, and holds it open. 'I told you, I'll see you in the morning.'

On his way out, Sexton passes Rory padding down the hall in his socks while eating from a bowl of cereal.

'Hey, kid,' Sexton says.

'Dude,' Rory says, not stopping.

Sexton glances at Jo, who has one hand on her neck, which she is rubbing and rolling.

'Could we have a word, in private?' Sexton asks Rory.

'There's no need,' Jo cuts in, stepping into the hall.

Dan puts a hand on her back. 'Let them talk.'

28

Rory leads Sexton into the kitchen and closes the door.

'Story, mate?' Rory asks.

Sexton glances at the door and lowers his voice. 'I need to find out if you ever heard of a kid called Lucy Starling. She's a teenager. One of the kids involved in this suicide business. Your mum mentioned you knew one of them. I just wondered if you knew her. Lucy.'

'My mum what?' Rory asks, outraged.

Footsteps in the hall outside suggest someone in heels is very close to the kitchen door. Sexton pulls a face for Rory to go along with him. 'I need some help translating "Teenager" into English,' he says, louder than necessary.

'What?' Rory asks.

'I can't keep up with the lingo on Facebook, it's like double Dutch to me, all the poking and stuff,' Sexton continues, still talking to the door. He clicks his fingers. "P-M-S-L", for instance?'

'Pissing myself laughing,' Rory answers flatly. 'I know of Lucy. I don't know her personally.'

Sexton put a finger to his lips, and points at the door. '"P-A-L?"' he spells out.

'Parents are listening,' Rory answers, throwing his eyes up to heaven. 'Why do you want to know about Lucy anyway?'

'"R-O-F-L"?' Sexton practically shouts at the door,

135

lowering his voice to turn back to Rory and adding, 'There's a suicide video doing the rounds. Do you know anything about that?'

'Rolling on floor laughing,' Rory says. 'No, that's the first I heard of a video.'

'"Y-O-L-O"?'

'You only live once,' Rory replies.

The footsteps outside move away from the door.

'"S-A-D,"' Rory states. 'As in sad. My mother's such a head fuck.'

'She's just trying to protect you.'

'My old dear thinks I'm going to put my neck in a rope like Amy, is that it?'

Sexton takes a deep breath. 'Where did that come from?'

After a pause, Rory says, 'Lucy was in a coma, last I heard.' He clicks his tongue. 'Imagine the nightmare of ending up like that when life was so bad already you wanted out.'

'Were you close to her friend, Amy, the one who did manage it?' Sexton asks, studying him closely.

'Look, give me a break, will you? I barely know you, dude. I can't believe my mum told you about this. She might have sent you to do her dirty work, but it doesn't mean I'm going to let her get away with it.'

'Jo's heart is in the right place,' Sexton says. 'She thinks I'm in denial about Maura, but we do agree on one thing: it's a stupid waste of life.'

Rory is indignant. 'How come they think it's OK to kill yourself if you're in physical pain, but not mental? How come it's called euthanasia if you want to put yourself out of physical misery, but if it's mental you're not in your right mind . . . you're stupid, adolescent, petulant?'

Sexton crosses his arms. 'You know, for a couple of years

after Maura died, all I could think about was following her. Only I knew that I'd just have been passing my problems on to someone else.'

Rory is defiant. 'So how far did you go with it when you were thinking about it? Did you drink bleach? Slash your wrists?'

Sexton puts a hand on Rory's shoulder to make him look up. 'Would that make you respect me more? Is it a badge of distinction to want to die now? Something to look up to?' He pauses. 'Human beings are the only species that commit suicide, did you know that?'

'You don't think bison stampeding off a cliff, or whales beaching themselves, indicates some form of melancholy?'

'Touché. You've thought about this a lot, haven't you?'

'Did you ever hear of Amanda Todd?' Rory asks.

'Nope.'

'She's like this fifteen-year-old Canadian girl who uploaded her suicide note on YouTube explaining with flashcards why she was about to do what she was about to do. You should look it up if you want to get your head around what's going on. It's had like a million hits or what-ever. She'd met some stalker video-chatting on the Internet. He made her flash her boobs. And after that she was basically bullied to death. She killed herself last year. If you want to understand someone who was in so much pain that ending it all was easier than living, Google "Amanda Todd".'

'OK,' Sexton says. 'You said you know of Lucy?'

Rory sighs. 'The girl I knew, Amy Reddan, she was my mate Darren's girlfriend and palled with Lucy. But I know Lucy better since she became one of the living dead than I did when she was alive, if you must know. There was a dis-cussion online about whether Lucy had tried to kill herself or not. Amy hanged herself in a wood. Some people want to turn it into like this suicide forest in Japan where everyone goes. They're saying that's where you should go if you're going to do it. I think it's kind of cool . . .' Rory's voice trails off.

'Where are they saying this?'

'A chatroom.'

'Jesus. They think it's cool! Really? Do you know how many kids died in Bridgend in Wales?' A beat pause. 'Neither do I, but it was needless, unnecessary stuff that caused an untold amount of grief for the families and friends. I think you should talk to someone.'

'Not you as well!' Rory blasts. 'Christ! I don't want to die. But if I do, that's my right. I'm just interested in what's going on, that's all.'

'So how did you know of Lucy anyway?'

'You mean apart from through my friend, Darren? She's in a private school; so am I. We're all just a degree of separation.'

'How does that work in a city this size?'

'We're into the same sports, for starters . . .'

Sexton cuts across him. 'You mean like lacrosse and polo?'

'Ha, ha, very funny. I mean like rugby versus GAA, and netball versus basketball for the girls. We all go to the same discos. When you think about it, the chances of me not knowing someone who knew her are slim. The parents' associations even organize socials to keep everyone inbred in the same little golden circle. They don't want anyone seeing someone from the wrong side of the tracks, so they have these classist get-togethers. It sucks. Anyway, Lucy's not one of the suicide club.'

'Club?'

'Relax, it's just a word, not an actual Masonic group or anything. You need to take a step back, man. So does my mum.'

'I prefer the word "cluster".'

'Fine. My point is, Lucy wasn't part of it.'

'How do you know that?'

'She didn't do it in Amy's Wood. It's kind of the unwritten rule in the club, or cluster, or whatever you want to call it. Amy was her best friend. If she'd really wanted to die, that's what she'd have done. No question.'

Wednesday

29

Next morning, the chief listens with a frown as Sexton fills him in on developments, up to a point. McConigle is there too, because her enquiry into the bullying aspect is dovetailing with the report Sexton is compiling on the dead kids, and because she hopes what Sexton has established will help her convince the chief to assign more officers to the case. Sexton tells them everything the headmistress, Bronwyn Harris, has told him about the girls and their relationships to each other. He does not mention anything about the message Lucy Starling has communicated to him. He believes Lucy has suffered enough for the mistakes she's made. If she is guilty of soliciting a killer to murder someone, Sexton will find him. He doesn't want the chief and McConigle deciding that she should face very serious charges now that the investigation has changed gear and there are suggestions of incitement and harassment. He believes this is why Lucy's parents were so jumpy, and so intent on winding up his interview with her once they realized she was communicating with him. He believes they were protecting her.

McConigle is animated by the news that the principal was concerned about bullying and is pacing up and down the room. 'Maybe Lucy Starling can tell us more,' she tells Sexton.

'Unlikely. She's completely paralysed,' he snaps. 'She's got Locked-in syndrome.'

McConigle is surprised. 'Poor kid. Who found her anyway? Did she do it at home? Try to hang herself?'

'No, Lucy crashed her mum's car,' Sexton says.

'Oh. Where?'

He hesitates. 'A country road.'

McConigle crosses her arms tightly. 'A country road where?'

Sexton knows the more he tries to resist, the more she'll probe. 'In the Dublin mountains . . . Near Boley Wood.'

'But that's where the other girls died,' McConigle blurts. Her eyes narrow. 'When exactly did Lucy crash?'

'January the eighteenth,' Sexton replies, avoiding her glare.

'You know bloody well that's the night Melissa died,' she says, turning to the chief, who looks unconvinced. 'What time did Lucy crash at?' McConigle presses.

'Dunno.'

'How about morning, noon, or night?'

'Night.'

McConigle sighs heavily.

'I'll find out,' Sexton says.

'You do that.'

McConigle isn't finished, but the chief cuts in. 'I'm not prepared to allocate more resources until you give me something more to go on. Anna Eccles has not been buried yet. Is the Prof doing a post-mortem?'

McConigle shakes her head. 'Just an external, like the others.'

'Organize a post-mortem on her body and then come back to me with something more – defence wounds . . . Rohypnol . . . something. Potentially, we could be talking about having twenty kids exhumed, if he finds anything. I want more proof that something more sinister is involved. Otherwise we are putting the families through the horror of a virtual second death.'

The chief looks past Sexton at the sound of a rap on the door and barks, 'Come in.'

Jeanie, dressed in a belted white shirt and tight black pencil skirt, appears with a stack of paperwork. She walks over to Dan's side of the desk and places a sheet in front of him, pointing at the spot where he is to sign. The chief gives it a glance and reaches for his pen.

Sexton turns to McConigle. 'Any idea who a little red-haired girl in a communion dress on Rutling Terrace might be?' he asks McConigle.

'Sounds like Rihanna Canon,' she replies. 'Based on the fact that she made hers last year, is permanently playing truant, and on her mother's drug problem. When did you see her?'

'Last night, when I was interviewing some parents for my much anticipated report.'

'Her dad's that scumbag. Eric.'

Sexton knows the name. Eric Canon is a small-time street dealer in the Rastas gang in the city.

McConigle purses her lips. 'Rihanna's a little jade, suspected of setting her national school on fire a couple of times just for days off. We think she's behind the bomb threats too, though we could never prove it. I think the mother has full custody, but she's an out-and-out junkie. I'm pretty sure that Eric's only allowed supervised visits. What was she doing so close to her dad's place?'

'Just hanging around.'

'Maybe Rihanna's sick.'

'Didn't look like it.'

'You should log it,' she says. 'Or let the lads know. They might want to do something about it.'

'I might want to do something about it,' Sexton says.

'Somebody's time of the month,' McConigle mumbles.

The chief continues to rant as he scribbles.

'I heard that,' Sexton tells her.

'You needn't concern yourself with doing any investigation you haven't been assigned to,' the chief warns. 'And don't think I'm not still expecting your report today.'

'I need Sexton on my team,' McConigle argues.

'He's otherwise engaged,' the chief answers categorically. He points to Sexton as he uses his walking stick to get up. 'Today.'

30

Sexton paces out of the chief's office, reaching into the breast pocket of his shirt for his mobile phone, which is vibrating. He reads the text that has just beeped in: 'The customer has no credit but would like you to call them.'

Sexton doesn't recognize the number. He heads into the stairwell and leans against the wall to make room for people passing on the stairs. Despite the constant traffic up and down, it's the quietest place in the building apart from the john, but nobody wants those background noises during a conversation.

He hits redial; it's Rory who answers.

'I got your number off my mum's phone,' Rory says. 'I've been doing some digging online. I found out some more stuff about Lucy. She's not safe.'

'What?'

'I joined another thread on one of the boards discussing Amy and asked if anyone knew of Lucy. It turns out some-one does. She said Lucy's father's a pervert,' Rory continues. 'I thought you should know.'

Sexton puts a finger in his ear. 'Nigel Starling? What makes you say that?'

'Lucy hated him. Sorry, hates.'

'What exactly did she say?'

'She told my . . . source that he'd been spying on her. Her own dad. It's disgusting.'

'What do you mean, spying?' Sexton probes.

'I mean totally invading her privacy, dude. I mean violating her basic civil and human rights. I mean . . .'

Sexton rolls a crick in his neck. 'Yeah, but are we talking spying as in cameras in rooms and holes in ceilings?'

'No, spying as in monitoring her texts, hacking into her email and even reading her diary.'

'Oh,' Sexton answers flatly.

'You don't think that's weird?' Rory is angry.

'At my age, I think it's good parenting.'

'OMG, it's so offside, dude.'

'OK. Let's agree to disagree on that. I need to talk to this girl. Your source. What's her name?'

'Sorry, no can do.'

'Why not?'

'Because I told her I wouldn't.'

Sexton sighs hard. 'Well, did she say if there was any touchy-feely pervert stuff involved? Or was it all just "My dad's a freak," "My dad's a perv"? In other words, did Lucy tell this girl if Nigel actually *did* anything . . .' Sexton stumbles for a word, '"inappropriate", or is it possible Lucy was just being a drama queen because she craved attention?'

'Lucy told this girl her dad used to wait for her to see her coming out of the shower,' Rory says. 'She said he'd be standing there watching. Dirty old fart. Happy now?' He waits for Sexton to react.

'It still could have been innocent, and how do you even know this girlfriend isn't just making it up? Did your source give her real name?' Sexton says.

Rory sighed. 'It's a chatroom. Nobody gives their real name, but this girl knew, like, things about Lucy she couldn't unless they were around her. Like her school, where she lived and stuff.'

'You could get that on her Facebook page,' Sexton states. 'Or in news reports about the crash.'

'OK,' Rory says, like he's working up to something big. 'So Lucy told this girl she found her knickers in Nigel's drawer. That's, like, sick. Incest . . . paedophilia, what does it take to convince you, dude?'

Sexton shakes his head. 'I need a name, or at the very least the address of that chatroom. Otherwise it could just still be a laundry mix-up.'

'Forget it. She'll never give it, and if I start asking for them she'll just disappear off to some other site. There's millions of them,' Rory said. 'Oh, and so you know, Lucy called her dad Nigel.'

'So? I bet you don't call your old man Daddy.' Sexton pauses. 'What do you call him, as a matter of interest?'

'Prick,' Rory admits.

Sexton grins.

'Seriously, she said Lucy was really upset because Nigel used to talk about her boobs developing and stuff,' Rory says. 'It grossed her out. What are you going to do about this?'

'I'll call over and have another chat with him.'

'A chat? Aren't you going to get Lucy out of there? You can't just leave her there. It's like being left in a morgue with Jimmy Savile. She can't do anything to defend herself.'

Sexton listens. 'You care a lot, considering Lucy is some-one you didn't really know.'

'Just because I didn't know her that well doesn't mean I don't know what she was going through. Lucy Starling's dad should be charged with something.'

'That's a big leap without any foundation. Why are you taking this so personally?'

'Look, I know you need proof and all that, but I have a radar for lies, and this girl is not lying. And . . .' he pauses, takes a deep breath '. . . you know the way Lucy was a friend of Amy's?'

'Amy, who inspired all the copycats? Sure.'

'I wouldn't put it like that, but yeah, that Amy.'

'Why do kids want to copy her anyway?' Sexton asks.

'Because she was so beautiful, and talented, but she was, like, bullied by jealous haters. As soon as she was old enough, she was going to enter *The X-Factor*. But now, all that's gone. Nobody can touch her. She's more than famous. She's an inspiration. She gave her life to stop bullies. She's immortal.'

Sexton thinks Rory might be crying. 'You OK, kid?'

'Poor Lucy,' Rory goes on. 'No wonder her friends were such knackers. Some people should not be allowed to have children.'

'How do you know about her friends?'

'That's what I've been trying to tell you. It turns out I did meet her once. I told you Dublin was small.'

'Where did you meet her?' Sexton asks. 'What was the story?'

'It was just a party. Kind of more like a Remember Amy party than an Eat Space Cakes, Get Sloshed party. I got introduced to Lucy, but I never really chatted to her properly because she was bragging about being pals with a real scumbag.'

Sexton guffaws. 'Hey, I thought you didn't subscribe to the snob-school ethos. "Classist", you called it last night.'

Rory pauses. 'I've no problem with people who've no money, Gavin. I've a big problem with people who want to rob to get it. Lucy was waving around this *Sunday World* article about her mate. He had one of those mad nicknames they give criminals, like Mr Dick or something, a bar over his eyes and this huge tattoo of a scorpion on his arm. She said he was in the Real IRA and he was extorting money from drug dealers. She said he killed someone.'

'Can you remember his name?'

'Nope. It was an old article and it said they couldn't name him for legal reasons. But you know when you get the feeling that someone would kill you for looking sideways at them? Well, that.'

31

The sixteen-year-old girl's dyed black hair and smudged eyeliner give her a heroin-chic look. She storms down the sideline of the rugby pitches of Doolin College in south Dublin, scanning the faces on the pitch as she paces. Her clothes and nails are black; the only white part of her that's exposed is her head – her hands are permanently pulled into her sleeves. She bounds up the steps to the school and troops past groups of kids stopping in their tracks at the sight of a girl in the building. There are plenty of female teachers, but never any girls. Her arms are stiff at her sides, making her fast walk look more like a march.

'Where's the canteen?' she asks a young kid in a blazer, and he points, open-mouthed.

She heads for the door, both arms still at her side along the corridor of lockers, when she spots Darren – Amy Reddan's ex. His uniform hangs off him like a grunge outfit. When he sees her, he breaks into a sprint – in the opposite direction. The girl takes off after him, ignoring a teacher's shout to stop.

Darren gets out into the grounds but at the bike shed where a couple of older boys are having a smoke she lunges and gets him to the ground. He's face down, with one cheek in the gravel. His long blond hair has fallen out of its clasp and covers his face.

The girl has straddled his back and twisted his arm so high up he's yelping with pain. The lads are laughing, and a crowd builds around them to clap and chant, 'Fight-fight-fight!'

'It's all your fault,' she screams. 'I'm going to cut your balls off for Melissa.'

'I had nothing to do with it! Let go! You're mad!' he says.

'Fight-fight-fight . . . !'

She flicks open a Swiss army knife.

The chanting stops as suddenly as it started.

'If Lucy dies, I'll be back to cut your head off.'

He screams and she grabs a clump of his hair at the scalp and starts to cut.

The teacher who'd followed them into the yard sticks his hands under her armpits and reefs her off him. The girl kicks, wrestles and screams and drops the knife.

Darren slides out from under her and runs for his life.

The girl's face is red and sweating as she screams after him, 'You're a murderer!'

'Who are you? What's going on?' the teacher shouts at her. When she doesn't answer he asks the lads watching: 'Who is this?'

'Beth Brockle,' one of them answers. 'She's Melissa Brockle's cousin.'

Beth spits at him and then starts to sob black-tracked tears.

32

Sexton is frustrated. He had failed to coax any more information about the chatline out of Rory. Then he couldn't find a free desk to sit down at to begin his report. To top it all, McConigle has been like a hen on an egg, convinced he is hiding something. He heads back to the Starlings', determined to talk to Lucy again.

He is pulling on to Rutling Terrace when his eye is caught by the flashing neon sign directly across the street from her house. Sexton has done a lot of crosswords to pass the time in dingy pubs, and anagrams come easy. He knows Damm is an anagram of MDMA, the chemical code for the love drug, ecstasy. He grabs the sandwich of battered chicken and the can of Diet Coke he picked up for lunch from the passenger seat and gets out of the car, crossing the street to investigate. He wonders if it has any links to Eric Canon and, for that matter, if Nigel's run-ins with the neighbours have anything to do with him. He presumes living opposite a head shop might have been a source of concern to Nigel, given that Lucy had been rebelling to such an extent before the accident. He walks with his hands in his pockets, feels a bookies' chit, which he takes out to check on an accumulator in the Down Royal. He'd inherited a house from an aunt but had sold it for much less than expected thanks to the property crash, and had since blown the lot. If he doesn't start recouping some of his losses, he is going to lose the shirt on his back. That filly had owed him ever since it had fallen at the first at Cheltenham – over a year ago now. He scrunches the chit up and kicks it to touch.

'They say if you nibble at these things,' he tells the Chinese man behind the Damm counter, holding up his sandwich, 'slowly, you give your stomach a chance to fill up, never finish, and actually manage to lose weight in the process. 'Course, if they didn't taste like cardboard, that would be a big help.'

The man glances up but goes back to what he was doing – reassembling the parts of at least ten broken-up iPhones spread out on the desk.

The pokey space is packed floor to ceiling with lava lamps, glass bongs and pipes, weighing scales, wind chimes and novelty gifts in boxes with pictures of cat's-eye contact lenses on the front.

'They made head shops illegal, didn't you hear?'

'It's gift shop,' the Chinese guy says.

'Funny how you never see "drugs paraphernalia" on a wedding-gift wish list these days,' Sexton says, looking around.

'It's gift shop,' the Chinese guy repeats automatically.

Sexton reaches for one of the sachets from a shelf and reads the product description. The Space Devil is a 'little acrylic beauty that tucks away nicely in the living room behind a couple of books'.

Sexton moves towards shelves and starts to read the labels on the items: Laughing Buddha; CH9 Afghani Milk; CH9 California; LSD; Top Dog; Amnesia Lemon; Super Haze; Top Dawg; G Bomb; Moonshine.

'You didn't answer my question,' Sexton says. 'About head shops being illegal.'

'We sell seeds, not chemicals. What you want?'

'To see whoever's in charge. Hey, I'm talking to you. What's your name?'

This time he has his attention.

'Gok Wan,' he states defiantly.

Sexton holds up his ID. The Chinese man glances to the stairs at the back of the room, looking away quickly and then checking to see if Sexton had spotted it. Sexton turns to see a weird UV glow.

'Didn't see anything on your signage about a tanning shop upstairs,' he says.

With a sudden jerk, Gok has vaulted the counter and is bolting towards the stairs. Unable to sprint after him, Sexton grabs the can of Diet Coke from his pocket and lobs it at Gok's head, missing by a mile. Gok is up the stairs, shouting in a pronounced Dublin accent, 'Get the fuck out,' as he goes.

Sexton's bulk has some use, and with one sideways step he blocks the exit and waits. Something flashes and thuds and he realizes there's a man in a pair of boxers lying on the street. As he groans, and tries to get up, Sexton pulls open the door and grabs him by the scruff of the neck.

'Hello, Eric,' he says.

33

Canon is slumped in a hard plastic chair in the station interview room. He moans to Foxy, who sits like a statue in a chair beside the door, 'This is police brutality. I need a doctor. Me leg is definitely broke.'

Sexton admires a tray of planting pots with seedlings about the size of watercress perched on the small square table between them. He'd found them upstairs after the commotion on the street. He doesn't know what they are yet, but the fact that they've grown at all has given him grounds to make an arrest.

The seedlings weren't the only thing he found in Damm. There was the rotting carcass of a stag in the yard out the back. The stink was off the olfactory scale, and if it hadn't been especially cold, it would have been buzzing with flies and gnats. Because of the time of year, it was only rodents that had got at it.

'Do we have any Baby Bio?' Sexton asks Foxy. 'Little blighters could do with a feed.'

Canon groans and tries to reposition his leg by lifting it with his hands.

Sexton zaps a remote control at a blue light in the corner. The room is hot-wired like a *Big Brother* set with videos and tapes, but because digital recordings can be doctored, only the first-hand testimony of an eyewitness will count in court.

Only the bloody remote isn't working. He shakes it at the light.

'Batteries are gone,' Foxy says. 'Give me a go.'

'Make him a cup of tea, will you?' Sexton tells him impatiently, as the light finally flickers to red.

'Milk, sugar?' Foxy asks Canon.

'Skinny, and five,' Canon replies, not looking up.

'None for me, thanks,' Sexton says.

As soon as Foxy is out of the room, Sexton reaches for the remote again and turns the recording off. He holds up a photograph of Lucy which he's had printed from her Facebook page.

Canon doesn't even glance at it. 'Never saw him in my life.'

'It's a she, and your daughter called to her house last night, you toerag. What dues were you collecting – extortion money, protection?' Sexton asks.

'You got that all wrong, mate. My little one made her communion, that's all.'

'Rihanna, isn't it?'

Canon looks surprised, 'Yeah, that's right. Very good, you'll make the special branch at this rate.'

'How's your custody battle been going?' Sexton asks. 'Sad, isn't it, that the kids always get caught in the middle. It doesn't matter what the mother's parenting skills are like, they always win, don't they?' He gives the plants a doleful look. 'Still, not going to help your case growing these in a drugs shop, is it? My guess is cannabis. But really, what next? Heroin arriving into the docks in containers marked "Poppy Products"?'

Canon shrugs.

'Explain this to me,' Sexton goes on. 'The stag I found in your back yard . . . what was its part in the plan? Smuggle the gear in for you, did he?' He uses his index fingers to indicate he has horns on his head. 'Knock on your door with an antler and say, "Special Delivery," did he? Or were you thinking of getting into the venison trade? See, I just am not seeing you in your tracksuit and trainers up to your neck in muck, shouting, "Pull".'

Canon clears his throat and gobs at Sexton, who jerks out of its path. The spit misses his face and rolls down his coat. He pulls a tissue from his pocket and dabs it away, his stare boring through Canon.

'A Daddy's girl, is she?' Sexton asks. 'Rihanna. Did you name her after the singer? Was it like David Beckham calling his son Brooklyn 'cos that's where he was conceived? Maybe you poked your old dear under an umbrella at the time – what do I know?'

Sexton keeps the pressure on him. 'Has anyone got in touch with Rihanna's mother, by the way? She might have a view on her kid hanging around dead animals, or want to know if Eric keeps suncream in his grow-house. Redheads need an extra-high factor, don't they?'

'I already told you, I know nothing about the plants,' Canon hisses. 'I only lease the downstairs part.' He is shivering so much that his teeth have started to chatter.

Sexton stands and walks to the window, taking a puff of his electronic cigarette.

'What the fuck is that?' Canon asks, waving away the vapour cloud.

'I've never had a problem with pot myself,' Sexton says, almost to himself. 'They should legalize it, if you ask me. Nicotine's more addictive than weed, and kills more people. As for alcohol, that's a real mood-altering substance. It's involved in nearly every domestic murder.' He moves to the table, puts his hands on it, studies Canon. 'Here's another thing I can't work out. Why, if you are trying to build a drug business, is the doctor across the road getting on your tits? You've got a steady supply of custom. The words "bees" and "honey" spring to mind. *You* should be the one dropping *her* payments, the way I see it.'

Canon's lips tighten. 'I don't know what you're talking about.'

Sexton straightens. 'Pull the other one. Someone's been slashing the Starlings' tyres and smashing their windows. Have you been sending them presents after your bowl of Weetabix? Are they one of your rackets? They're bleeding hearts – did you give them a sob story? Or was it Lucy who was the soft touch? Did you come to some arrangement? Did she solicit you to do something for her that's going to turn your possession of drugs with intent to supply charge to one that means a mandatory life sentence for you?'

'What you on about, copper?' Canon grins. 'What's life anyway now? Eleven years, is it? Be out in seven for good behaviour. You got nothing on me.'

'Is that why you jumped out of the window?'

'I fell.'

'Here's what it looks like, Eric. The kid right across the road from you, the middle class kid in a posh school with a future, sees you every morning and last thing at night when she wakes up and goes to bed. Maybe looking at you puts crazy thoughts in her head.'

Canon shifts his weight in the plastic chair. 'I want to stress, for the record, that I have no idea what you are on about. The grass is not mine.'

'See, I was right,' Sexton says triumphantly. 'I knew it was cannabis. Did Lucy's money get you started in your new business? Ten grand, wasn't it?'

'Give over. This is a fit-up, you bent, fat bastard.'

Sexton kicks the legs of his chair, sending it sprawling. Canon lands on his back with a yelp.

Foxy appears in the doorway with a cup, which he puts down before running over to grab Sexton's shoulders. 'That's enough.'

Sexton puts up a palm to tell him he's finished. He leans close to Canon. 'I'm going to be at every family court hearing you're up on from here on in telling the judge Rihanna belongs at home with her mum, that you're not a fit parent.'

Canon rubs the soles of his squeaking feet against the linoleum floor. 'Where's my brief?' he shouts. He names a solicitor widely regarded as bent, as he only ever represents the guilty.

Sexton lifts the chair and smashes it against a wall.

Foxy shouts at him to stop.

'You're a fucking looper,' Canon retorts. 'Get away from me. You want to know why the kid is throwing money about I suggest you check out her email. Starlinglucy589@hotmail.com. Password is her initials and date of birth. Then come back to me and tell me I have a case to answer.'

'How do you know all that?' Sexton asks, astounded.

'Gok fixed her iPhone.'

34

Jo peers closely at the list of transactions, holding each sheet inches from her face. She's in Sexton's bank, where she has been given access to the records on the joint account he shared with his wife. She does not have Sexton's permission or blessing for this. She needs neither at her rank if she's conducting an investigation. She sits at a desk examining their spending habits immediately before Maura Sexton's death. In a foolscap pad, she first makes a note of all the direct-debit and standing-order reference numbers, then locates the letters from the banks identifying what each one is – car, house, life insurance. She riffles through the paperwork to find some €100,000 would have been paid in the event of Maura's death occurring within ten years of the policy's start date. Jo chews the top of a ballpoint as she notes in the small-print Terms and Conditions at the back – which she needs a magnifying glass to see – that suicide is not covered.

'Term policies will not be paid out if death is caused by a medical condition you were aware of when you first applied for cover but did not disclose, or in cases of suicide,' Jo reads.

It occurs to her that since the verdict at Maura's inquest was 'open', that may have created a loophole.

Licking an index finger, she goes through the documents, sucking air through her teeth when she spots a handwritten letter dated six weeks before Maura's death. It's a letter seeking to clarify whether the policy covers suicide, and it's signed by Maura. The answer from the bank states: 'Suicide is covered only if it occurs thirteen months after the policy has been taken out.'

Jo's eyes move back to the date Maura took out the policy and establishes that her death occurred exactly thirteen months after the policy was set up.

She glances at the section naming the beneficiary, and blinks in surprise. She can't make out the name written there, which has been blacked out, and a note added: 'See amendment as per accompanying letter.' The letter is stapled to the back. Sexton had come into a €100,000 windfall as a result of his wife's death.

35

After taking a bollocking from Foxy reminding him that the heavy gang had been decommissioned, Sexton looks around and sees there's still no free desks in the detective unit. He settles down in the peace and quiet of Jo's office and enters Lucy's email details in the computer. It is highly possible, he realizes, that if Eric Canon has Lucy's password, her account has been compromised, and that Eric may have even typed the messages and sent them from Lucy's phone himself. It is also possible that, since Eric Canon has Lucy's details, the dogs on the street could have it and could also have sent phoney emails in Lucy's name. But the undeniable fact is that the tag on the top email has the ring of truth as having been sent by a teenager and not a two-bit criminal like Eric Canon. There are only three emails listed, making him even more suspicious about this account, particularly as all were sent to an account under Amy Reddan's name. He scrolls down to read them in chronological order:

RE CAN'T BELIEVE YOU'RE GONE
Hi Amy,
   I know, I know . . . it's nuts emailing you now you're gone, right, Babe? I'm still not ready to let you go yet I feel so alone ☹ Can't believe you're not around . . . Feel sick every time I think how alone you felt . . . Cry myself to

sleep every night and burst into tears at any stage during the day . . . Can't concentrate on anything . . . Nothing matters . . . The pain gets so bad, I try convincing myself it's just a bad dream and when I wake I'll remember you are backpacking around the world and staying in this amazing hostel and hanging out with amazing guys and smoking wacky baccy and singing your songs . . . But then the truth just makes the pain worse and it makes me so angry . . . Put my fist through the window the other day . . . it helps when I bleed, can see the pain is real and not in my head . . . Just cannot keep in the feelings ☹ Want to kill someone . . . Wish you'd talked to me about how bad she made you feel . . . We were so busy talking about what happened with me before you must have felt that you couldn't burden me . . . The worst bit is waking up and for a split second everything's good and then am hit by the dread when I remember how bad things were for you . . . How did you get the courage BTW? The woods you went to are becoming a legend . . . It's somewhere kids go to like worship you, or it was until parents found out that some were going in tents and staying the night . . . They're saying on the chatrooms they couldn't decide what to do but found peace there like you're talking to them . . . See you are an angel . . . I heard people can't get in now cos the parents set up patrols . . . You would not believe how many kids want to go there now . . . They've even given the forest a name – The Everlasting Wood . . . Kinda corny but I love it . . . I was always scared of the woods, but if I'm going to go that's where it'll be . . . Had an accident when I took pills to numb the feelings, took too many and didn't wake up . . . If I'd died, I wouldn't have been sorry if it meant seeing you again . . . But couldn't even do that right . . . I'm such a loser . . . When I woke up I was glad

even though my parents were the first thing I saw . . .
Please don't hate me ☹ I don't want to die . . . You
shouldn't have had to either that's the point . . . Why
should the troll be allowed to live after everything they did
to you???!? . . . They're like a murderer . . . Someone has
to stop them . . . Remember you said about the butterflies
batting their wings in the forest over there and how the
ripples come all the way around the world to us . . . well
the butterflies must be going crazy!!! OK, I never could
keep a secret from you so here goes . . . I'm meeting this
guy I met on the chatroom who said he can help . . . He
calls himself Red Scorpion but he's like this really cool guy
. . . He says he knows how we can ID the troll and he
wants to help. We've been chatting a lot. He understands
everything. He doesn't judge me, he just accepts how I'm
feeling and doesn't tell me it will pass, or I don't have the
perspective to put it into context. He knows how sad I am
and he says it's OK. He says he can make the troll pay for
their crimes and he wants to meet me to discuss it ☺ I
really like him . . . We've talked about EVERYTHING . . .
Send me a sign if you can, baby doll, I miss you so much
. . . See you on the other side if I can find a way into the
Everlasting Forest . . . Love ya . . . <3 BFF 4ever xxx

The next email is dated one week later. It reads:

MELISSA ADMITS EVERYTHING
Amy,
This link will show you who the troll is. I'm so sorry,
sweetheart . . .
Miss you babe
<3 xoxoxooxxxxxxxxxxxxxxxxxxxxx

Sexton clicks the link, which leads to a YouTube video of a teenage girl in a short dress in a pizza parlour with the caption: 'Melissa Brockle eats scraps, abuses fellow diners and rants about how "powerful" she is.' Sexton watches as a very drunk, or drugged, girl, who looks sixteen – based on the heavy orange make-up and short skirt – staggers from the ladies' toilet in her bare feet with a length of toilet roll stuck to the sole of her shoe. She sits at a bench and sloppily pulls a scrap of pizza from a diner's plate.

Underneath all the make-up, Melissa would have been a nice-looking girl, Sexton notes. She looks very different from the vulnerable face Bronwyn Harris had pointed out to Sexton in the most recent school photo. Things kick off in the video when Melissa realizes she is being recorded on a camera phone. She jumps to her feet and starts abusing the stranger whose pizza she's just pinched.

'You fucking loser,' she slurs.

Whoever recorded it has focused on the fact that her short skirt is hitched so high it leaves nothing to the imagination. If he was this kid's mother, he'd have grounded her for a year. Melissa is really animated, trying to smack the phone out of the holder's hand. 'Do you have any idea who I am? You are going to be so sorry, loser. You've heard about the troll, right? They're, like, a god deciding who lives and who dies. Just checking you've heard of them, because I promise you, you're going to find out soon enough. You are nothing.'

With that Melissa finally made contact and the phone goes black and has clearly, by the sounds of things, just hit the floor.

Sexton scrolls down to the last email's tagline, which reads: NO GOING BACK.

My darling Amy,
What happens next is for you, and all the other lives that
will be saved and not the loss of my own soul. Am meeting
Melissa tonight, and taking her to the wood, where Red
plans to teach her a lesson she will never forget.
There's no going back.
Lucyxxxxxxx

Sexton starts as McConigle leans her arms on Jo's desk
and studies the screen.

'What's this?' she asks.

'Nothing,' he says, closing the email.

'Get your coat,' she tells him. 'I want someone with me at
Anna Eccles' PM in case I pass out.'

Sexton nods, and as she heads for the coat stand he deletes
all the emails that incriminate Lucy. Bullies lie, bullies hide,
they cower. Lucy has owned up to her wrongdoing. He
doesn't want McConigle and everyone else closing in on a
girl who cannot defend herself. Everyone makes mistakes in
their teenage years. Lucy has suffered enough.

36

After getting Sexton to sling his hook, Jo takes a seat back in her office, pulls Maura Sexton's inquest details from her bag and starts reading the section relating to the cause of death, holding it a couple of inches from her face. Foxy sits in the uncomfortable chair on the far side of her desk, which she keeps for visitors, complaining about Sexton being a loose cannon.

'He's not himself,' Jo agrees, more determined than ever to get to the bottom of Maura's case. '"Compression of carotid arteries causing cerebral ischemia",' she reads in a puzzled voice.

'Good to have you back,' Foxy says.

'If Maura was hanged, as against strangled, there'd be no damage to the hyoid bone in the neck, because the ligature typically misses it when the pressure is here,' she goes on, drawing a line around her jaw, 'but a pair of hands is much bigger and causes more damage.'

'Hands . . . you mean she was strangled? There was no evidence of any bruising, was there?' Foxy asked.

'No,' Jo says slowly as she scans. 'But if the hyoid is damaged it backs up Sexton's theory that maybe Maura was killed before she was strung up.'

'Any defensive wounds on the arms or anywhere else to back that theory up?'

'No,' Jo says. 'But there wouldn't necessarily be, if, hypothetically, she knew the person or people there.'

'What about the headstone?' Foxy asks. 'Who paid for it?'

'She did,' Jo says. 'Long story – she was leaving him. Apparently faking her own death was easier than telling him. She was hoping to cash in on a life-insurance policy. Sexton was the beneficiary.'

Foxy pulls a face. 'Have you spoken to him?'

Jo shakes her head. 'Not yet.' She flicks the page. 'And why do some coroners keep recording suicides as "open" verdicts?'

'Out of sensitivity to the families who don't accept death was the intended outcome,' Foxy says.

'I know that, but what about sensitivity to the Central Statistics Office?' Jo snaps. 'How can we ever know how widespread a problem it is if they're deliberately cooking the books?'

'We already know things are bad. It always tops the toll on the roads,' Foxy says. 'And some of them don't want to deprive families of their life-insurance pay-outs,' he adds.

Jo tosses the report on her desk, 'Tell me about it. You know they've had to rip out and refit Rory's school with anti-ligature devices?'

'What does that mean?'

'Basically, rounded cornered partitions, sinks with no taps, toilets with no seats. No hooks.'

'You sound worried.'

'I am . . . this craze is putting ideas in the kids' heads. It's like a cult now. I mean, I look back on my teenage years, and they were the worst in my life without question. I lost Dad. I blamed myself, and I thought I'd never get my sight back. But suicide never occurred to me, it wasn't an option. If it had been as common as coffee back then, I just don't know.

Your hormones are all over the place, little problems become huge, you've no perspective on life and—'

'Rory's a smart kid,' Foxy cuts in.

'They all are, or were. Read the papers. Watch the news. The parents are all saying the same thing – they had no warning, they had no signs. It's not vulnerable kids who are doing it any more, it's anyone it occurs to. I think they see it as romantic, or tragic, or something. Those vampire books have a lot to answer for, if you ask me. Dead kids coming back more powerful to avenge themselves on the living. In a way they're right. Just the threat of it does give them power. When I was growing up—'

'Back in the day—' Foxy says.

'Yeah.' She appreciates his attempt to lighten things, allows herself a grin. 'In prehistoric times, in my teens, I realized that, as I had no money, no power, no space and was completely at Mum's mercy, the only thing to do was to build a life for myself, and that's why I went to Templemore.'

Jo had met Dan in the Garda training college and had become pregnant with Rory while still in her teens herself.

Foxy glances through the glass to the detective unit, where Jeanie is crossing the room. He hopes Jeanie will not come in.

'If you're a teenager, all you have to do is threaten suicide and you can get whatever you want. The whole order of things is messed up,' Jo continues. 'The next generation will have no respect for authority.'

'You're not really worried about Rory?' Foxy asks.

'He's under a lot of pressure with his exams this year, these other kids' cases have freaked him, and' – she puts her head in her hands – 'he Googled "carbon-monoxide poisoning" last night. You don't have to say anything, I know it could be innocent, but equally . . .' She draws a breath. 'Some of the parents are so freaked out in the schools they're talking about sectioning their kids.'

'Putting them in asylums?' Foxy asks, astonished.

'Anyway,' Jo says, reaching for the report again, 'it's back to square one. I'm going to try and find out who Maura had borrowed all that money from. Did I tell you what she was going to use it for?'

Foxy shakes his head. When Jo didn't pick up on the prompt, he says, 'No.'

'A one-way ticket to Australia.'

'What do you mean? What about Sexton? They were having a baby, weren't they?'

'I told you, she was leaving him, wanted a new start. Maura's mother has never told Sexton.'

'I thought they were happy.'

'Nobody ever knows what goes on behind closed doors . . . I should know.'

'And me,' Foxy agrees. His own wife, Dorothy, had left on the birth of their daughter, Sal, who had Down's. Sal was a teenager too. He wouldn't have changed a hair on her head, and would never have to go through what the parents of so-called 'normal' adolescents were going through. Since Sal was a tiny baby, she'd had heart problems. 'You going to tell Sexton?'

'Yes. Eventually. He wanted answers. I'm going to get them for him. Where is Sexton anyway?'

Foxy shrugs. 'I'm really worried about him. He wanted to kill that scrote, Canon, earlier. He's supposed to be putting together a report for the chief, but based on what he just did, I'm not sure what's going on any more.'

Jo reaches for the ringing phone on her desk.

'What's the story with your sight?' Foxy asks.

'How long you got?' she replies, putting the handset to her ear.

Foxy stands to leave. He's only got as far as the door when Jo slams the receiver down, saying, 'Shit.' She starts knocking things over in her haste to get out from behind the desk.

'What's the matter?' Foxy asks, alarmed.

Whoever had been on the phone could only have spoken to her for ten seconds, max.

'Rory didn't show up for his exam this morning. They don't know where he is,' she says.

37

Rory is standing at Lucy's front door with a bunch of wilting, garage-bought carnations. Nigel opens, and stares, his hands held away from his body like a surgeon, because he's got a pair of yellow rubber gloves on.

'These are for Lucy,' Rory says, thrusting his arm out.

Nigel hesitates, and then takes them. 'Are you a friend?'

'Sort of.'

'What's a sort of a friend?'

Rory lowers his hoodie. 'We met at a party.'

Nigel stares. 'Lucy is too young to go to parties. When exactly was this?'

'I'm not sure, Mr Starling. There was nothing, like . . . I mean, we didn't . . . I wouldn't want you to think . . .'

'I believe "make out" is the phrase you're looking for.'

Rory scratches the back of his head. 'I was going to say "talk for long", because I wouldn't want you to think we became close friends, because that would be a lie. I just wondered how Lucy is doing, Mr Starling. I was really sorry to hear about what happened. I'm Rory Mason.'

Nigel peels off a rubber glove and stretches out his hand. 'Lucy's on the mend, thanks for asking. Come in.'

Rory shakes and follows him in to the house, wiping his hand on the back of his jacket.

'Shouldn't you be in school?' Nigel asks, leading them into the sitting room.

The furniture is shabby, but the room pristine.

Rory shrugs. 'Yeah, technically. But they sent us all home because ... because ... it's a teacher-training afternoon.'

Nigel kneels on a sheepskin rug at a spot on the floor near some scattered fire irons, a rag and an open tub of Brasso. He lifts a poker and starts to shine. 'Sit down,' he directs, without looking up.

Rory has his hands in his pockets, and he keeps them there as he takes a seat on an armchair.

'Not that one,' Nigel says sharply.

Rory stands up quickly.

'That's where Lucy used to sit,' Nigel says.

Rory steps sideways and reticently takes the couch. His phone is ringing for the zillionth time, but it's set to vibrate. It sounds like a trapped insect in his pocket.

'So you met Lucy at a party?'

'Right,' Rory answers.

'Would this have been around New Year's? Lucy didn't come home one night back then, and she said she was staying with a girlfriend.'

'I'm pretty sure she was there with a girlfriend,' Rory says, glancing at his buzzing phone, peeping out of his breast pocket. It's only his mother again.

'And what did you talk about?'

Rory shrugs. 'This and that. How is she?'

'We're going to need a miracle. Do you believe in the power of prayer, Rory?'

'That would be no. I'm an atheist.'

'You don't believe in anything? What's the point of anything, in that case?'

Rory clears his throat. 'I just don't think, if God existed and was loving, kind, and forgiving like he's supposed to be, he'd leave so many people in the world starving, and have so many little kids getting their arms and legs blown off in war. You said Lucy is getting better?'

Nigel bends down and picks up a J-cloth. 'Man causes hunger and war, Rory, not God. When you have God in your life things that seem mundane suddenly have meaning. Things that would try and test you to the limit become bearable. If it weren't for Him, we'd never be coping right now.'

'Can I see her?' Rory asks.

Nigel looks up, surprised. 'I'm afraid Lucy's not well enough for visitors.' He pauses. 'Are you hungry? I make a mean triple-decker sandwich.'

Rory shakes his head.

Nigel sighs. 'Oh, all right, you can see her for a quick minute.'

He leads him to the room where Lucy is sleeping.

Rory stands in the doorway looking appalled.

'She's sleeping a lot at the moment,' Nigel explains. 'We found out about a pioneering new medical project that needed volunteers. There are new drugs that could change everything for Lucy, but they haven't been tested yet. It just might give her the boost she needs, but we won't know about progress until she finishes the course.'

An alarm starts to beep from the kitchen and Nigel excuses himself. 'That'll be the roast. I'll be back in a second. I just need to turn it off.'

When Nigel returns to the room a minute later, Rory has gone. He hears the front door close and walks over to Lucy to make sure she's warm enough before pulling her blankets up a little higher.

'Breaking hearts even still, princess,' he says lovingly, tucking a strand of hair behind her ear.

38

The post-mortem on Anna Eccles takes place in a prefab in Marino – the city's temporary morgue for over a decade. The facilities – or rather, lack of – make a joke of the abiding principle engraved in the coroner's court, which Sexton is reciting for McConigle to make that exact point: 'Show me the manner in which a nation cares for its dead and I will measure with mathematical exactness the tender mercies of its people, their respect for the laws of the land and their loyalties to high ideals.'

By way of agreement, McConigle springs up and down on her insteps to show how bouncy the floor is. 'Couldn't even stretch to tiles,' she says about the linoleum-covered floor where the body fluids will sluice once the post-mortem begins. On cue, Professor Michael Hawthorne, the state pathologist, arrives, gowned up in the same white polyethylene suit as Sexton and McConigle are wearing. An aide wheels the body of Anna Eccles in behind him. It has been in storage in one of the horizontal cooling units set in the next room.

'Morning, campers,' Hawthorne says cheerily. 'Anyone want to tell me what this is about? I haven't had time to read the notes. I was in Kerry yesterday following a house fire, and in Galway the day before following a house party . . .'

Sexton crosses his arms and focuses on anything other

than Anna's face. She's only a kid, covered for the moment, with a sheet up to the neck.

'Anna Eccles is fourteen, Prof,' McConigle explains. 'She's supposedly the latest teen suicide victim.'

Hawthorne picks up on the key word. '"Supposedly", eh?' He moves to one of Anna's hands and lifts it at the wrist, turning it over to both sides before leaning across the body to do the same with the other. 'The psychologist Sigmund Freud held a conference in the 1920s on clusters of teen suicides, because it baffled even him. He, by the way, himself committed suicide. It happens to be the third leading cause of death in 15–24-year-olds in the States, did you know that? There have been major incidents in Germany, Japan, Canada and the United States. Plutarch wrote about an epidemic among young women in ancient Greece, which was stopped after a threat to drag their naked corpses through the streets. Appearance apparently matters to girls even after death.' Hawthorne looks up from his rambling. 'There's no sign of any bruising.'

He begins to scrape underneath Anna's fingernails and to deposit the contents into an evidence vial. 'They say girls tend to overdose or slash their wrists rather than hang themselves, out of consideration for their appearance at their funerals,' he continues. 'What do you think of that?'

McConigle glances at Sexton protectively.

He bristles. He's got a thick skin, except when it comes to pity. That always gets to him, puts him on the defensive.

'I think that's bullshit,' he says.

'Not at all,' Hawthorne argues, oblivious to Sexton's fury. 'It's the human condition. All copycat behaviour can be explained by the "contagion effect". One person does something and, suddenly, something previously taboo becomes acceptable, like a bunch of pedestrians suddenly getting brave and following a jaywalker across the street.

'The adult population has had plenty of experience of being sucked into suicide cults over the years,' he goes on, lowering the sheet and examining Anna's skin closely, taking the tip off a felt marker with his teeth.

'Jonestown, Guyana, 1978 . . .' He circles bruises on Anna's knees. 'More than 900 members of the People's Temple died from a cyanide-laced drink, more than 300 of them children. An audiotape was recovered from the scene in which the cult leader, Jim Jones, can be heard stating, "We committed an act of revolutionary suicide protesting about the conditions of an inhumane world."'

McConigle snorts. 'You know a lot about it.'

'Did my thesis on it, fascinating stuff,' he explains. 'Then there was the Order of the Solar Temple, which sprang up in Switzerland and Canada to prepare for the Second Coming and unite Christian and Islamic faiths. The order ritually sacrificed a three-month-old boy in Canada in 1994 because he was identified as the Antichrist. Some forty-eight adults and children were also found dead.

'Then there was Marshall Applewhite, leader of the Heaven's Gate Cult. In Santa Fe in 1997, his followers asphyxiated themselves with plastic bags. Thirty-nine people died in order to evacuate earth, which they believed was about to be recycled, so as to get on board an alien space-craft following the comet Hale-Bopp.'

McConigle shoots Sexton a look of bemusement.

Hawthorne hasn't finished yet. 'The Waco siege in Texas of 1993 ended when seventy-six Davidian cult members controlled by David Koresh died in a fire set inside their compound after the FBI tried to gain entry following allegations of child abuse. Twenty-four of the dead were children. David Koresh never met his father. His mother lived with a violent alcoholic and at four, David moved in with his grandmother. His nickname was "Mr Retardo" in school. In his twenties he became a born-again Christian and in 1983 began having a sexual relationship with the 76-year-old leader of a splinter group of the Seventh-day Adventist church. After his aging girlfriend claimed that David was the chosen one, Koresh would annul the marriages of couples joining the group and have exclusive sexual relations with the women, and the underage girls whose parents had joined the cult. Remember?

'It's important to keep suicide cults in mind even when we are dealing with a seemingly random copycat case, because of what they tell us about the human condition and how suggestible the mind is. And so the consideration of appearance post-mortem is not as far out as you seem to think, Detective.'

Sexton rubs his hands over his face to revive himself. The sight of Anna – her skin is so thin at her joints that the bones look set to burst through – is going to rank up there with the most depressing things he's ever seen.

'Anorexic?' McConigle asks, reading his mind.

'By the looks of it,' the Prof comments, as he positions a scalpel at the top of her breastbone. Sexton puts a fist to his mouth and takes a step back, glancing away. There is scented Vaseline smeared in his nostrils but it's the sight and sounds that get to him most. Bones creaking and vital organs being scooped out and slopped into stainless-steel trays. The Prof stops suddenly, distracted.

'Ho hum, what's this?' He places the blade down and traces his latex-covered fingers along Anna's mottled neck. An imprint of the rope's weave can clearly be made out between the lividity patches.

McConigle moves closer. 'What are they?' She peers at the

two circular brown marks on Anna's neck which Hawthorne is pointing out.

'I saw a set just like this after a death-in-custody case when I worked in Northern Ireland,' he says. 'Care to venture a guess?'

'A vampire?' McConigle jokes.

Sexton is fixated by the marks. He steps forward, staring at them. 'It's a bloody Taser,' he tells McConigle. 'Someone used a stun gun on her.'

39

Sexton uses queasiness as an excuse to escape the autopsy early. He has to get away, but not because he's revolted by the body on the slab. If some psychopath had used a Taser on Anna, the weapon would have hijacked her body's central nervous system and, with a zap of electricity, flooded her nerve endings with a pulse to override the brain's signals, completely disabling her muscle control. Could it have had anything to do with what Lucy told him about hiring a hitman? Someone used an overwhelming force to disable Anna, and now she's dead. He needs to meet the one person who might be able to tell him exactly how Lucy came to crash her car.

After phoning Foxy to get Tim McMenamy's number, he makes a hasty arrangement on the phone to meet the lorry driver Lucy smashed into. If anyone can tell him if Lucy had a death wish, or was just an inexperienced driver, it will be him. Something else has occurred to Sexton that he wants to rule in or out. Perhaps Lucy hired a hitman because she had failed in her first suicide bid. Perhaps his target was his own client, Lucy, and his job to make sure she died. Perhaps this is the reason for the car crash. It's a long shot, but if it is the case, whatever McMenamy witnessed will be crucial. And Sexton has no other leads.

Parking up in Dublin Port, he watches the small, wiry

man in his forties with a shock of frizzy hair, and a neck brace that doesn't impede him in jumping from the cabin of an 18-wheeler like he is Frankie Dettori on one of his flying dismounts. Tim McMenamy is wearing faded jeans, steel-capped boots and a hoodie with a tight-necked T-shirt underneath. When he climbs into the passenger seat of Sexton's squad car, the support on his neck doesn't prevent him twisting to face Sexton either.

'Drive,' McMenamy states as he pulls the door shut.

'What's wrong with here?' Sexton asks, looking around.

'The guys are trying to kip,' McMenamy says. 'You'll make them nervous.'

Sexton surveys the containers on the vehicles. 'I'm hardly Customs and Excise.'

'Nah, it's not that,' McMenamy says, nodding his head to the left.

Sexton looks past him and sees a middle-aged woman in a very short red skirt and pair of white stilettos mincing off towards a Portaloo. He guns the engine and steers back out on to the quays, driving to a spot where he can pull in next to the Liffey.

McMenamy has lit a roll-up in the meantime and is puffing away. Sexton pops his e-fag in his mouth and inhales the tobacco smoke, making the passenger guffaw. 'Like I told you on the phone, you're lucky you got me at all,' he tells Sexton. 'I'm on my way to the Chunnel.'

'Truck not badly damaged in the crash then,' Sexton answers.

'It'd take a tank.'

'I need to know exactly what you saw the night of the crash,' Sexton explains. 'Was she driving erratically, or did the car suddenly spin out of control?'

'Where do you want me to start? She was on the wrong side of the bloody road for one. I just came around the corner and she was there, no lights on or anything,' McMenamy says, straightening his back and reaching into his bum pocket to take out a set of battered cards, all with solicitors' names and numbers on them. They all have some variation of 'specializes in personal injuries – no win, no fee' along the bottom. 'Do I need any of them for this? They've all been in touch.'

Sexton shakes his head. 'I just wanted to chat before things get too formal, find out how you're doing, but clearly there's not a bother.'

'Life goes on. I still have to pay the bills . . . Doesn't mean I'm not in agony . . . going to need injections for the pain.'

'You should see Lucy.'

'Who?'

'The kid you crashed into,' Sexton says flatly.

'Am I supposed to feel sorry for her? She could have killed someone.'

'Yeah, well, it's a pity she didn't,' Sexton says with conviction.

'What does that mean?' McMenamy asks.

'Maybe *she'd* be better off dead.'

McMenamy shrugs. 'Shit happens.'

Sexton pushes his door open and paces around to the passenger door, which he pulls open. Grabbing McMenamy by the neck brace, he reefs him out and slams him against the side of the car. He picks the cigarette from the trucker's mouth and flicks it away, holding him under the chin so his face is twisted against the force.

McMenamy groans.

'"Shit happens," is that all you can say?' Sexton hisses.

'She's fourteen years old and she can't walk, talk or wipe her own arse any more. You make me sick.'

McMenamy knees him in the balls and Sexton winces, hunching over. McMenamy repositions the brace. 'It's not about the money. I don't want anyone's blood money. I'm going to donate anything I get to charity, if you must know.'

Sexton's grip loosens.

McMenamy jabs a finger into Sexton's chest. 'You want to know why? I had a six-year-old kid once, Leah. I could tell you about her mother, but that's a whole other story. All you need to know is that for six years it was just me and her – a team, a family.' He starts to cough to stop his voice wobbling. 'She was never any trouble . . . ate like a bird . . . tiny little portions would fill her . . . Full of energy she was, always dancing and playing. We were in the park on her last day. Her ball flew over the railings and on to the road. I told her I'd get it, but she squeezed out between the rails. She was mown down by a drunk driver. Three months my angel spent in intensive care before they made me turn the life support off. They told me from day one there was no brain-stem activity but I just wanted to keep her warm for as long as I could before they put her in the ground.

'The driver was a woman, married to some rich business-man, someone told me. She staggered out of the car in a fur coat, looked at my baby lying in front of the car and said, "I'll pay you whatever you want not to call the Gardaí." I can still smell the drink from her.'

He makes a gagging noise, and then continues to talk through the tears and snot as he wipes them on the back of his sleeve. 'It didn't make any difference that I didn't take Lady Muck up on her offer. The case never went to court.

Nobody ever told me that the case had stopped, let alone why. My baby's life was worth nothing, as far as the system was concerned.

'You want to know why I'm still driving the truck? I got to keep going so I don't start thinking. That girl – Lucy – she was too young to be behind a wheel. She was wearing too much make-up and was dressed like a tart. She thought rules were for the rest of us. And yeah, she stank of drink too. Like I already said, it was a miracle the only person she hurt was herself.'

Sexton exhales. 'Lucy didn't kill your daughter, mate. It's touch and go as to whether she will make it too.'

'She could have killed someone.'

'Maybe she wanted to kill herself,' Sexton says.

'Wearing those clothes? In that car? Not on your Nelly. She was just a spoilt little rich kid showing off in front of her pal. Well, I'm not letting her get away with it.'

Sexton tilts his head. 'A pal? Was someone else in the car?'

'Yeah, there was a girl in the passenger seat.'

'Can you describe her?'

'That's easy. She was bald as an egg.'

Melissa. Sexton draws a deep breath. 'Where did she go?'

McMenamy looks confused. 'What do you mean?'

'Lucy was the only one taken to the hospital. Are you sure you saw the other girl?'

'Yeah, I looked in on them. They were both unconscious, but looked like they were OK. I left them to try and get help because I couldn't get a signal on the phone. It took me a few minutes to flag down a car – nobody wanted to stop – but when a motorist eventually did, we had to drive for ten minutes before we could get the phone to work. I didn't go back to the scene. The controller told me to wait where I was for the ambulance.'

'Melissa must have legged it then . . .' Sexton says. 'Back to the wood.'

40

Sexton glances at a text from McConigle as he arrives back at the station. He's five minutes late for a case conference she organized for after Anna's autopsy. He knows he will have to tell her that Melissa and Lucy were together in the car on the night of the crash. But Lucy's blinked message he still wants to keep to himself. The kid's in enough trouble. She and he have a lot in common. The force is full of people who can't think outside the box, the P.C. brigade who think all 't's' have to be crossed and all 'i's' dotted. It's bullshit. Sitting in front of a complete stranger telling her intimate details about yourself, because she has certain qualifications, and you fucked up, is not natural. Neither is prosecuting a kid who fucked up. It's what kids do. It's what human beings do.

But Sexton is worried about Lucy more since talking to McMenamy. Why would Melissa have fled from the car after the crash? Why would she go to the wood and take her own life, having survived the smash? But if someone brought her there, it meant the investigation should be ratcheted up to a full-scale murder inquiry. It's the only explanation for her fleeing the scene and not waiting to see if Lucy, who was so badly hurt, had survived. What, or who, had Melissa been running from? Did she have the same marks on her neck as Anna? And were the girls being chased when Lucy crashed?

Sexton stops in his tracks to watch the chief's son, Rory, being helped out of the back of a squad car by a uniform, who does not let go of the top of his arm as he walks Rory inside.

'What's that about?' Sexton asks Foxy once he gets inside. 'Skateboarding on the pavement, was he?'

Foxy is behind the public counter. 'The father of one of the kids affected by the suicide spate rang to say Rory had arrived on his doorstep, inveigled his way in and taken some of her possessions. Rory denied taking anything when we found him nearby.'

'Which kid?' Sexton asks.

'Lucy something or other,' Foxy says. He looks at Sexton from under his eyebrows. 'The chief is addressing the conference upstairs, by the way.'

Sexton checks him out to see if he means what he thinks he means, registers his expression and then hurries for the stairs. If the chief is sitting in, it means he's going to allocate more resources, which must mean there's been a big development.

Upstairs in the detective unit, twenty-odd officers have gathered in front of the chief, who is in mid-flight.

'As a result, the Minister has asked me to widen the investigation, and that's what I intend doing . . .'

Out of breath, Sexton nudges the arm of an officer standing alongside, whispering, 'What's this about?'

'They think there might be something more sinister about the kids' deaths.'

'What?'

Sexton strains to see the chief. He notices Rory in the door of his mother's office, watching through the glass, and Jo is there too – her back to them – speaking on the phone.

'Good of you to join us, Sexton,' the chief says, deadpan.

'As I was saying, Melissa Brockle's parents made a criminal complaint that their daughter was being bullied. They noticed that clothing Melissa was wearing at the time of her death was covered with animal hairs, and they sent it for analysis, because Melissa would have had no reason to be around animals. She was, apparently, allergic to dogs and cats. The lab the Brockles contracted also noted the presence of some minute blood stains on her clothing, missed at the time of her death, or she'd have been given a PM. As the blood did not correlate with any injury on the body, although she had suffered some bruising around her ribs . . .' – From the crash probably, Sexton realizes – 'We've been in touch with Melissa's parents, who are adamant this is information of significance. The Justice Minister wants us to rigorously pursue it in case there is something else involved in these deaths, in case we are talking about some kind of cult ritual.'

'Yeah, 'cos it's his constituency,' someone shouts.

'That's your cynical mind,' the chief says with a grin. 'In any event, we now have two members of the Cabinet taking an active interest in this case between Sexton's report for the Minister of Children, and now this. We need to find out if there is some sinister aspect to what is starting to look like a suicide club,' he adds. 'McConigle, if you'd like to take over from here.'

McConigle walks over to the chief and turns to face the team, looking grave. She crosses her arms. 'If there is a reason why these children have been taking their own lives, we need to find it. If someone has been using force – mental or physical – or influence of any kind to overpower them, or overwhelm them, it is going to give the parents some answers, where now they have none . . .' She becomes distracted by the sound of her phone, which has trilled to life.

'Sorry, I've got to take this. It's the Prof, probably with some toxicology results.'

As she puts the phone to her ear, the officers start to discuss Monday's football match.

Sexton doesn't take his eyes off McConigle. The Prof has come up with something of interest. He can see it in the way her back has tensed.

'What does it mean?' he lip-reads her saying over the din. After a pause, she nods and thanks the pathologist, ends the call and sticks the phone in the back pocket of her jeans. Her expression changes as she tries to get the lads' attention, but their spirits are too high now. Then McConigle shouts, 'Oi!', which gets their attention.

'There was a case in Canada that I think we can learn from.' She paces over to her desk and riffles through some paperwork until she finds what she's looking for. 'It's an extract from a blog by the father of a seventeen-year-old girl – Rehtaeh Parsons – from Nova Scotia, who took her own life in April,' she says, glancing from a sheet of paper to the assembled. 'The kid was gang-raped by four teenage boys at a house party. The boys photographed her being raped and vomiting while it happened, and posted the images on Facebook. The rapist can be seen giving the thumbs up to the camera at the time. The victim was bullied, called a slut, and her life made unbearable as a result.'

Sexton crosses his arms as he listens.

'Her father has an online blog which I think makes some important points. He says about the boys: "Why is it they didn't just *think* they would get away with it; they *knew* they would get away with it? They took photos of it. They posted it on their Facebook walls. They emailed it to God knows who. They shared it with the world as if it was a funny animation.

'"How is it possible for someone to leave a digital trail like that, yet the Royal Canadian Mounted Police don't have evidence of a crime? What were they looking for, if photos and bragging weren't enough?

'"Numerous people were emailed that photo . . ."'

McConigle looks up. 'The point I'm making is that teenagers today, whether in Nova Scotia or here, are digital freaks. We need to shift our focus from a search for finger-prints, footprints, fibre, DNA to IP addresses. We're looking for someone in cyberspace, in the ether. Every kid nowadays has a Facebook page. That's how they communicate and how we're going to crack this case. Any questions?'

Sexton's finger springs up. 'What kind of animal did Melissa come into contact with?'

McConigle looks at the chief. She doesn't appear to know yet either.

'Oh,' the chief says, taken unawares. 'It was a deer, I think. Why?'

Sexton shrugs. 'Just wondered.'

41

Sexton makes his way to Jo's office. He needs to breathe. Rory's face distracts him from the revelation that's left him spinning as he enters the room – that deer in Eric's bloody back yard! The teen is engaged in some serious eye wiggling to indicate there's something on his mind that he doesn't want to tell Sexton in front of Jo.

'What is it, kid?' Sexton asks him.

'What's going on?' Jo asks.

'Rory's just back from a visit to one of the girls linked to the suicide circle,' Foxy says, arriving in behind them.

'He what!' Jo gasps.

'Actually, Lucy's not one of them,' Rory states. 'Lucy crashed. You have to hang yourself in the wood to be in the club, it's kind of a rule . . .'

'Jesus,' Jo says, putting her head in her hands.

'Did you talk to Lucy?' Sexton asks. 'Did you ask her questions? Did she blink back?'

Jo pads her way towards them using the edge of her desk as a guide, and reaches out. Her hand lands on Rory's dreadlocks. She moves it to his back and says, 'Come on, we're going home. Now.'

'Hang on,' Sexton pleads. 'I need to find out what Rory knows. Go on. Good lad,' he coaxes.

'Lucy was out cold,' Rory says. 'She could be dying, for

all I know, and if she is, it's because you didn't get her out of there when you had the chance.'

'I don't believe this,' Jo says, pushing him on both shoulders.

'Mum,' Rory moans, resisting.

'Go and wait for me in Dad's car,' Jo tells him. 'And as for you,' she tells Sexton, 'I'll deal with you later.'

Rory zips down his hoodie and pulls out a handbag, which he tosses over to Sexton as he heads for the door.

'It's Lucy's,' he says with a grin. 'And her journal's in it.'

Sexton studies the bag from arm's length and looks from it to Rory. 'Where did you get this?'

'I pinched it from her bedroom,' Rory replies.

'Good God,' Jo says, shoving him out the door and turning back for a last word. 'You haven't heard the end of this,' she tells Sexton.

Sexton sits down in Jo's seat and opens Lucy's handbag, turning it upside down and shaking it. Straight away they both see the flash of metal foil.

'Bubblegum flavour,' Sexton says, after picking one up to double-check it is a condom.

He rummages through the make-up tubes, sticks and powders and plucks a medicine vial from the items. Pushes off the white lid with his thumb and empties the contents into the palm of his hand. He examines the white tablets with little heart shapes in the palm of his hand.

'Serozepam,' McConigle says, arriving in the room. 'They've replaced Chardonnay as the number-one preference of bored housewives.'

'Thought that was Valium,' Sexton says, trying to scrape the pills back into the container.

'Too addictive, and a lot cheaper than Xanax. I take those babies for flying. They zonk fear, block all anxieties, worry, self-doubt.' McConigle stares at Sexton. 'I hate flying . . . So whose are they?' she demands, hands on her hips.

Sexton reaches for the heart-padlocked journal. 'I need you to give me long enough to read this, and if I can't convince you, or myself, by then, that it took great courage for the person who owns them to come clean and tell me what she did, you can presume whatever you want.'

He knows McConigle won't let it go now, but he's out of choices, because he can't get something out of his head, a reason why Lucy could have crashed the car that night. And ever since the thought struck him, he's known that he's going to have to let McConigle know exactly what Lucy said she did. If Lucy did hire a hitman because she wanted to end her own life, presumably the killer has to finish the job in order to be paid the balance.

'What are you talking about?' McConigle demands impatiently.

'I'm talking about the one characteristic bullies never have,' Sexton answers. 'Courage. The one thing the person who owns this stuff has in spades.'

42

'What's a bucket list?' Sexton asks McConigle, flicking through the diary.

McConigle glances over his shoulder. 'It's a list of things you want to do before you die.' She taps a foot. 'Who wants to die? Why won't you tell me?'

'What does this mean?' he asks, showing her the page.

'It's a hashtag. It's sort of a way of summarizing a concept, or shortening things. What exactly did this person want to shorten?' She scans the diary, and reaches out for it.

Sexton backs away. 'So it says here on the bucket list,' he reads: '"Pitch my matching wellies and tent concept to *Dragon's Den* so nobody ever need lose their way back during Oxegen or Electric Picnic again cos everyone will be able to signpost you home."' Sexton makes bunny ears with his fingers. '"Hashtag minted."'

'Hashtag greatidea,' McConigle answers. 'What's going on?'

'It says,' Sexton reads, 'that if she can persuade her mother to pay for a six-week blow-dry, she'll be saving her the same amount in unused GHD electricity.'

'Hashtag the kidsgotsavvy,' McConigle says. 'I presume it is a kid, even if she is sexually active and on drugs.'

'And also,' Sexton continues, 'she is trying to persuade her father to buy her a home-spray-tan kit, says she could do

197

her friends for a fee, pay him back and make a profit. Is it just me, or is she obsessed with making money?' he asks.

'Money's the bane of every teenager's life. Phone credit, make-up, concerts, it all costs spondulicks. Now are you going to start filling me in?'

'They told me she'd no friends,' Sexton says aloud to himself. He looks up. 'Does this sound like a girl with no friends?'

'The opposite,' McConigle says. 'She sounds popular.'

'Which bullies aren't,' Sexton points out.

'Who is she?' McConigle demands.

Foxy enters the office with his jobs book. 'Who do you want to take the Brockles' statement?' he asks McConigle.

Sexton shoots her a puppy-dog look.

'Forget it,' she tells him, turning to Foxy. 'Put Oakley on it.'

'Sexton,' McConigle says impatiently. 'Are you going to tell me who owns that diary and those drugs voluntarily, or am I going to have to organize the relevant paperwork?'

'No need to arrest me, it's . . . Melissa Brockle's stuff,' Sexton lies. If McConigle is prepared to choose Oakley over him to interview the Brockles, there's no point in giving her the full picture yet. Sexton is still Lucy's only hope. He holds the diary up. 'And since I now know exactly the way her mind was working, I'm the one who should interview her parents.'

'Fine,' she says dismissively, putting a hand out.

Sexton clutches the diary tighter. 'It's all yours . . . once I'm finished talking to them.'

43

The Conquest Church is located in a squat prefabricated warehouse in an industrial floodlit park off exit 10 for Ballymount on the M50.

Eric Canon is sitting in the car park behind the wheel of his gleaming, 5 series, 131-registered BMW, waiting for Nigel Starling to emerge. Beside him, Gok's seat is almost fully reclined. His eyes are closed, but every now and then he opens them to shoot Rihanna – in the back – a murderous look. She is twiddling her thumbs madly on her Nintendo DS, apparently oblivious to the *bip-bip* noise that's driving Gok mad, and taking regular glances up, to scan the scene outside.

'How the fuck can they call that a church, in anyway?' Canon asks Gok, staring straight ahead. 'There's no steeple, for one. No bell, for two. There isn't even a window in that yoke . . . you need stained glass. You go into a church, you expect certain things – like Frankenstein, for instance. Am I right?'

'It's frankincense, Da.'

Gok grins and stretches his arms out zombie fashion.

Rihanna yelps.

'Whatever,' Canon goes on. 'The point is if they brought you in there you'd be more likely to come out in meat packs than a coffin. Am I right?'

Gok doesn't answer. An overweight woman with large glasses in a floral skirt and fussy white blouse emerges. Her hair is scraped back in a severe hair band. She is wearing frilly ankle socks under her shoes.

'And another thing, how come you never see trendy Opie Dopies?' Canon continues.

Gok turns his head. 'What's Opie Dopie?'

'You know, the funny handshake crowd . . . Opus Dei . . . like in the Dan Brown book? And how come, no matter what the church, they all look like they should be playing a tambourine or a triangle? Also, how come you never get women who look like strippers arranging flowers?'

'Da, there he is,' Rihanna says.

With a sudden movement, Canon leans across Gok's legs and pulls open the dash, reaching in for the 9mm Glock automatic. He flicks the magazine release with a thumb, catches the released cartridge and jams it back in, all in a second.

'Back in a sec,' Canon says. 'Mind her.'

Gok opens his eyes sleepily to register Nigel Starling walking across the car park towards his Volvo – and then closes them again.

Nigel glances up and starts to run towards his car.

Canon takes off after him and within ten paces has twisted his arm up behind his back and slammed him against Nigel's own car. He tucks the gun in the waist of his jeans.

'Give me the keys,' Canon says. 'We're going for a little drive, buddy.' He reefs them from Nigel's balled fist. 'What did you tell the cops?'

Nigel thrashes but can't connect. 'I told you this already: nothing! They were there because of Lucy's crash.'

Canon uses his full weight to keep Nigel pressed against

the car as he zaps the key fob. The car's indicators flash.

'What are you doing? Where are we going?' Nigel asks, frantic.

Canon doesn't get a chance to answer.

'Get off, you animal,' a woman is shouting.

Canon has to use both his arms to fend off the blows from an umbrella that are raining down on his head. One lands an inch from his eye, making him drop the car keys. It turns out the heavy-set woman from earlier has one hell of a swing.

Rihanna sprints over from the car and bites the woman's arm. Gok runs after Rihanna, grabs her by the waist and tries to pull her off, but she holds like a terrier.

Canon is screaming for everybody to calm down. When that doesn't work he fires a shot in the air. The commotion stops, and Eric stares in disbelief as he realizes Nigel is speeding off in his car. He raises his arm to shoot at it, but with a jab the umbrella knocks the gun out of his hand.

44

Jo bites the inside of her cheek for most of the car ride home. Much as she wants to talk to Dan about what has happened, Rory is in the back of the car. She knows she will say something she regrets when her emotions are running this high, so it's better to say nothing. But by the time they get home, she's still bloody furious with Sexton for encouraging Rory's obsession. She leaves Dan to organize dinner with Rory while she bathes Harry. The little lamb had fallen asleep in the car but is wide awake now, and she kisses her young son's angelic face. Rory was this size only yesterday. Where have the years gone? He is independent and a man now, but her instinct to mother him is as strong as ever. In her mind Rory is always going to be her baby, and she knows she will have to let him go or she will lose him, but she needs to make sure he's ready before she does that.

After drying Harry and getting him into his jimjams, she brings him to Dan to feed and heads into the study.

Jo closes the door behind her. How dare Sexton involve her son in the city's suicide-cluster probe? It was a mistake to ask him to speak to Rory. She has been trying to undo his interest, not widen it. Nobody can afford to be arrogant and think this horror will not happen to them, because of the rate it is happening to families just like Jo's. Every expert is saying, and Jo agrees, that kids are under too much pressure to grow up ahead of their time these days. The stress on kids Rory's age is relentless. At least, when Jo was growing up, kids could escape a difficult home life when they went to school, or a difficult school life when they got home. But for the Internet generation, there is no escaping peers, or the pressure. Popularity is measured in numbers of Facebook friends. Humiliations happen in public. If you are bullied, it is in front of the world, not just the schoolyard. Bullies thrive on the Internet because they can hide behind anonymity or fraudulent identities.

Jo gathers up her paperwork on Sexton's wife's case and methodically spreads the documents of note across the desk. The answers are in here somewhere . . .

'Dinner?' Dan calls down the hall.

'Not tonight, love,' Jo calls back. She goes back to work, mumbling, 'I'd choke on it.'

45

'What happened to your eye?' Sexton asks as Eric Canon opens the door of Damm.

The gangster attempts to slam the door shut, but Sexton wedges his foot in the gap and the pair wrestle on either side of the door.

'You've been holding out on me,' Sexton says breathily as he pushes. The door gives and he pins Canon to the floor. 'You were there, you bastard. In the wood on the night Melissa Brockle died. She had deer blood all over her clothes. If I find a Taser in your house, I can put you there with Anna Eccles too. You live opposite Lucy Starling, which I expect you're going to tell me is purely circumstantial. That's three of them – how many more were there?'

Sexton sees the way Canon's eyes flick behind him, but doesn't have time to turn before someone knees him in the kidneys and gets the crook of an arm around his neck. He has to move with the arm holding him, and its owner is pushing him inside, where Canon delivers a blow to his solar plexus that makes him cough for air and his eyes water.

'Get some rope,' he tells Rihanna.

'We can't keep him here,' Gok says behind Sexton's back.

They all freeze at the sound of a siren, and suddenly the air is flashing blue through the curtains on the street outside.

Sexton is as surprised as they are, but he doesn't show it. Rihanna runs to the curtain and peeps out.

'Let him go, Da. It's his backup.'

'What were you going to do?' he asks. 'Take me to the wood, like the others?'

There is a pounding at the door, and a shout of 'Gardaí, open up!'

Rihanna opens the door, and holds her hand up to McConigle to be high-fived. 'All right, Inspector?'

'It's past your bedtime,' McConigle tells her.

McConigle stares at Sexton in the middle of the room. 'I've got a search warrant,' she tells Canon, gaze still fixed on Sexton.

'Since the conditions of his bail for operating a grow house have just been revoked, you can also arrest him,' Sexton says, adding, 'And him, for assault,' about Gok.

As officers pace into the room and cuff the pair, she takes Sexton aside. 'You've got some explaining to do.'

'How did you find out?' Sexton asks.

She speaks slowly, as if she's trying to work something out. 'Foxy decided to play back the tape of your interview with Canon to find out what it was that led you to snap this time. He thinks you can still be helped, but the jury's out on that, as far as I'm concerned. I saw you try to turn that recording off. Why didn't you pass on the information about the deer? And what are you doing here? You are supposed to be at the Brockles', taking their statement.'

'I was on my way, but I wanted to . . . pay a visit to Canon first.' If Sexton tells her the truth – that he thinks Lucy might have hired Canon to bump someone off, his whole plan to protect her from prosecution will unravel. Melissa Brockle is dead, it's too late for her. Sexton has had every intention of telling McConigle that Canon was linked to Melissa's death, he just intends to find out exactly what his links to Lucy were first.

In any event, McConigle doesn't seem to be waiting for an answer. They both know if she hadn't taken the credit for informing Dan about the suicide video being sent to the kids' phones, she'd never have been put in charge of the investigation.

'If I find out you're withholding information pertinent to this investigation, I'm going to make sure it costs you your job. Now is there anything else I need to know?'

Sexton blinks, and then shakes his head.

46

Sexton sits on a couch with Marie Brockle, the mother of Melissa, who is scrolling furiously on her iPad now the conversation has dried up. Her sixteen-year-old niece, Beth, who has silver piercings in her face, is on the couch, watching the late news intently. Beth sighs a lot, Sexton realizes. He knows since the introduction on first arriving a quarter of an hour ago that she moved in with the Brockles a few months ago after her mum, Martin Brockle's sister, died of cancer. Her body language suggests she would rather be anywhere else. They are waiting for Melissa's dad to get home from work, even at this hour. He's a portfolio manager in a bank, Marie explains. 'They're under a lot of pressure.'

Sexton looks over his shoulder at the sound of a key turning in the lock. Martin Brockle is a tall man with dark circles around his eyes. He glances into the room, registers Sexton's presence but doesn't say anything before taking his suit jacket off and hanging it on the coat stand in the hall. Sexton waits for a 'Hi, love, I'm home,' or a 'How was your day?' or a 'Dinner's in the oven,' but nothing.

When Martin enters the room, he shoots his wife a look that suggests he thinks she's a waste of space, which is at least more than Beth gets. She may as well be invisible.

'The detective is here to talk to us about the bullying,' Marie says, barely looking up.

Beth stands to leave the room, but Sexton asks her if she wouldn't mind sticking around.

Martin unbuttons his shirtsleeves and folds them back. 'I need a drink,' he tells Sexton. 'I've seen enough cop shows to know you're on duty.'

Marie clicks her tongue disapprovingly.

Martin loosens his tie and heads out of the room. When he returns, he's got a stiff whiskey in a tumbler. 'You want to know how I find out about my wife's day?' he asks Sexton, giving Marie a disparaging look. 'I look up Facebook.'

Beth squirms.

'The night my daughter died . . .' he says.

'Our daughter,' Marie corrects.

'The night my daughter died, I came home and asked my wife where she was, and she said, "I'll check her Twitter feed". You know why they call it Twitter? Because it's for twits.'

Marie shoots him a pleading 'Don't start' look. Martin knocks back his drink.

'You made a complaint that Melissa was being bullied,' Sexton prompts.

'Yeah, and I told the school, and the HSE, and anyone who'd listen when she was alive. Nobody cared. Now she's gone, and' – he motions to Beth – 'she's still here.'

Beth stands and leaves the room, silently. Sexton lets her go this time. The atmosphere in here is too toxic for a kid.

'Do you know who was bullying Melissa?' he asks.

'A gang of bitches in the school,' Martin says. 'They were jealous of her.'

'But did you ever hear any names?'

'Plenty.'

'What about the ringleader?'

'Lucy Starling.'

Sexton swallows. Martin stands to refill his glass.

'Are you sure?'

'Positive,' Marie adds.

'It started after Amy Reddan took her own life. Lucy got the others to gang up on Melissa, because she – Lucy – had been so friendly with Amy. That Reddan girl's death had nothing to do with Melissa. They scapegoated her. I wanted to take her out of the school, but her mother—'

Marie's eyes fill up. 'I thought it would settle down. I thought it would cause more problems than it would solve.'

The front door slams in the background.

'I'm not going after her,' Martin says.

'It's a Wednesday night,' Marie says. 'She'll have gone to the Back Gate. It's half price tonight.'

Martin is clearly not interested in Beth. 'Melissa met that Lucy one on the night she died, and now she's dead. I know this because I looked my wife up on Facebook and saw her cyberstalking our daughter about some exchange between Lucy and Melissa organizing to meet. As far as I'm concerned, if Melissa was bullied by Lucy right before she died, that's tantamount to murdering my little girl.'

'Can you show me the Facebook page?' Sexton asks Marie.

'We deleted Melissa's account,' Marie says. 'The comments people were leaving were too upsetting.'

Sexton doesn't recall seeing anything on Lucy's Facebook page about meeting up with Melissa. Perhaps the messages between them were sent privately.

'Why don't you talk to Lucy's father? He knows about it,' Martin says quickly. 'That Nigel Starling. You should talk to him. He rang a couple of days ago.'

'What did he say?' Sexton asks.

209

'He didn't get a chance. I gave him a piece of my mind.'

'Well, how do you know he knew the girls were together?'

'I know,' Martin says. 'I didn't give him the time of day. Lucy Starling might as well have strung up Melissa's noose herself.'

47

The atmosphere in the Back Gate nightclub is charged. A quarter of an hour after Sexton arrives and begins to quiz the kids at the cloakroom counter, word has got around who he is and why he is there. He hoped to find Beth, but there's no sign of her, so after persuading the bouncers that they don't have the option to send him packing, he sets about touching base with every teen handing in their coat, although most have begun bypassing the queue and heading straight for the dance floor with their coats still on.

The dwindling few left in the queue stare back blankly when he explains what he's trying to find out. Some grunt; others rise to a shrug. They all shake their heads. He knows he is being stonewalled.

'Pervert,' a girl says, appearing at the counter.

'Excuse me?' he asks. She smears lip balm on with a fingernail chewed down to the stub. She could be nineteen with all the make-up, but the disco is for over-sixteens, and she still has train tracks on her teeth.

A jock behind her in a rugby shirt backs her up. 'Yeah, bud, if you want to question us, you like should definitely have paperwork.'

'And if my aunt had balls, she'd be my uncle—' Sexton begins.

'Inappropriate!' The girl cuts him off. 'You're dealing with minors here, mister, which means we've got a right to a parent or some kind of guidance.'

The elastics in her mouth restrict her jaw, so there is a satellite delay as Sexton interprets what she's saying.

'Didn't your parents ever tell you children should be seen and not heard?' he asks, taking her coat and passing over a ticket, noting the number . . . He's been checking out all the pockets of the kids' coats in the hope of finding an illegal substance, preferably prescription, that might indicate contact with Lucy. But the pockets are all suspiciously empty. There isn't even loose change.

He goes back to the counter, where a girl with a love bite on her neck and a pierced nostril, septum, lip and chin is waiting in the queue. She hasn't taken her military jacket off. Underneath she's wearing a Victorian boned corset and a ruffled tutu with a petticoat, and long Dr Marten boots.

It's Beth.

So far, he's divided the teens into distinct tribes: girls, like the last one with braces, who are grown-up versions of the *Toddler & Tiara* tots. Their clothes are the brightest pinks and limes on the spectrum and they look as if they belong in a chorus line.

They're the polar opposite of the rock kids in skinny jeans and T-shirts who headbang with the heavy metal set if the music's right.

The skater kids come somewhere in between. Their clothes are grunge, they have long hair and open shirts and sneakers and want to look like pot heads.

There are the nerdy kids, über-self-conscious because of their virginity and dressed in clothes still bought by their folks. They're the next generation of lawyers, politicians and app-inventing millionaires.

But Beth has changed since he saw her at the Brockles'.

Her look is biker chick meets Steampunk – a cross between Edward Scissorhands and Vivienne Westwood. Her short black hair is long on one side and shaved on the other, and small silver rings run all along the outside of one ear.

'My aunt and uncle have no right to be so hard on Lucy,' she says.

Sexton cups a hand to his ear to indicate he can hardly hear her. The music, if you can call it that, is belting, the lights flashing strobes of blinding colour.

'Did you know her?' Sexton shouts.

'You could say that.' She glances over her shoulder. 'Me and Lucy, we were . . . are . . . in love.'

In the passenger seat of the squad car in the car park outside Beth stares at her hands as Sexton flicks the light on and guns the engine so the battery won't run down. He puts the heat on full blast.

'It's so unfair,' she says, voice breaking. 'All Lucy ever wanted was to help people. That's why she's ended up worse than dead. Her favourite book was, like, *Wuthering Heights*. She was deep as the ocean. She just got the intensity of things, you know . . . ?'

Sexton is surprised she's talking about Lucy, and not Amy Reddan. Also, he's aware Lucy had condoms in her bag. Whatever her orientation, she was underage.

'Was she seeing a guy too? She had contraceptives in her personal belongings.'

'That was just to freak out her Dad,' Beth responds. 'She knew he was going through her stuff and she wanted him to think she had a boyfriend, so Nigel might back off.'

'How long were you two' – Sexton coughs – 'an item?' He shifts uncomfortably in his seat. He's no problem with homosexuality, just Lucy's age.

'A couple of months.'

'Did Lucy confide in you?'

'We told each other everything.' Beth turns and stares intently. 'We were soulmates. Still are. Even if she dies and stuff, I'll never let her go.' She pushes up the sleeve of her jacket. Sexton realizes she's got the word 'love' carved in the same part of her arm as Lucy.

'Are you in Benedict's?'

She shakes her head. 'I go to the local comp.'

'So how did you meet Lucy?'

'My social worker brought me to see Lucy's mum, because I was having panic attacks. Lucy rang me afterwards. She'd scanned her mother's notes and wasn't happy with her treatment plan.'

'Rang you?' Sexton probed.

'She said she could help me. She said she'd seen what her mother had prescribed for me and it wouldn't work. I'm fifteen and three quarters. If I'd gone to see a doctor at sixteen, I'd have been prescribed Serozepam. Lucy said it had helped get her through the bad times. She was sick.'

She glances at Sexton and clarifies, '"Sick" as in a *good* way.'

'But why would Lucy take it on herself?' Sexton asks. 'And how would she know, anyway? She's only fourteen.'

'She used to live in a town where kids were topping themselves for no reason. Kids she knew. Her dad had treated some of them with herbs . . .' Beth scoffed, and zipped open a pocket and took out a cigarette tin, 'But when Lucy complained of feeling down, her mum put her on Serozepam straight away. Lucy said it was like a wonder drug. She was only twelve years old at that time. The only reason kids were being refused it was because the pharmaceutical companies are, like, terrified of lawsuits. Do you mind if I smoke?'

'I'd be delighted.' Sexton closes the window.

Beth fills a cigarette paper with coils of tobacco, licks the glued edge and offers it to Sexton. He shakes his head and takes his electric cigarette out, then changes his mind and sticks it in the ashtray. Beth pulls the lighter from the dash and sucks her roll-up against it until the tip sparks. Little embers of the sparking paper float away and burn out.

'Lucy was like a lifeline for a lot of kids around her. They'd started coming to her directly, bypassing GPs, drug dealers, whatever their previous buzz was.'

'Did you have to pay her?' Sexton asks.

'I didn't have to, but I did,' she answers fiercely.

A loud bang makes Sexton's shoulders jump. A teen acting the maggot has slapped a hand on the bonnet and turned his back to them. He is running his crossed arms up and down his own back to indicate they should make out. Sexton honks the horn and he clears off.

'What about other prescription drugs?' he asks.

'What do you mean?'

'Rohypnol, Viagra – drugs that can get a good price on the black market. Maybe Lucy wanted to start a business, and make some real money.'

'That's bullshit, just Lucy's enemies spreading rumours.'

'She had enemies?'

'A lot of people felt she was doing them out of business.'

'What kind of business?'

'Take your pick: weed, mind-altering substances, anything that gives a buzz.'

'Do you mean Eric Canon, in the Damm shop across the road?'

Beth shrugs. 'Among others.'

'How was Lucy competition to them if she was dealing prescription drugs?'

'You really are *old*. The kids don't care about the name of the drug giving them the high or whether it's prescribed or not. It's all about the buzz. Lucy was doing underworld dealers out of customers. End of.'

'When did you last talk to Lucy?'

'On the day of the crash,' Beth says, pulling open the ashtray and flicking some ash inside. 'We spoke every day, several times. Lucy was happy because this troll who'd been taunting some of the kids had agreed to meet her. Demand had gone way up since the troll came on the scene. Lucy couldn't keep up. That's the person you need to blame for Lucy's crash.'

'Troll?'

Beth's face became taut. 'When I said you were old, I meant more, like, *vintage*, man. A troll is someone who harasses someone – bullies them, basically. They're keyboard warriors who make people's lives hell. We were convinced it would turn out to be Lucy's dad, because he'd been acting really weird, but in the end it was Melissa. I couldn't believe it of my own cousin. She was a pain, but I never thought her capable of that. She'd been taunting the kids who'd expressed suicidal thoughts on the chatroom, was even having a go on the Jacob's Angels Facebook page.'

'What's that?'

'Jacob's Angels? It was set up by the mother of Jacob Larson, an American kid who was bullied so badly in middle school his teeth were knocked out. It's somewhere kids with dark thoughts can go to get help. Lucy made all the kids she was treating agree to get help on it, to talk about their troubles, but Melissa was egging them on, telling them to do it, to take their own lives. It was horrible, vile abuse. She'd tell kids they were worthless, useless, and deserved to die.'

Beth looks out of the window and Sexton can see the glint of tears has filled her eyes.

'Lucy had guessed it was someone she knew because the troll was aware of things about the people being taunted that could only have been learned by mixing in certain circles. Lucy wasn't scared, though, even of someone that evil. When she found out it was Melissa she organized to bring her to the wood to meet someone there who could show her what it felt like to be at the receiving end.'

'How was she so certain it was Melissa?' Sexton asks.

'Melissa admitted it in a pizza parlour one time when she got pissed. That's how Lucy knew.'

Beth reaches for her phone and runs her finger over the screen. 'This will give you a sense of how evil my own cousin was.' She hands him the mobile.

Sexton squints to read the miniature Facebook page. Beth leans across him and pulls open her finger and thumb on the screen. The comment reads: 'You should do an Amy. Everyone knows you rode Darren Maguire in the Back Gate car park. You two deserve each other.'

'Your aunt said that page had been taken down,' Sexton said.

'It was. I grabbed a screen shot of it.'

'But why would Melissa kill herself, if she was the troll?' he asks.

'Guilt?' Beth suggests. 'She must have known everybody had found out. She was probably scared of more trouble. She was already completely isolated over bullying Amy. She must have been terrified of how bad things would get when things got out.'

'Why would Lucy have left Melissa alone in the wood like that?'

'Maybe she wanted Melissa to spend some time with the

other kids' ghosts, see how it felt to be made to feel like she had no friends, that nobody cared about her and her life was worthless. Maybe it was Lucy's protector's idea. I just don't know.'

'But if the someone Lucy had organized to teach Melissa a lesson was Eric Canon, how did she get him onside if she was competing with his business?'

'It wasn't the Damm guy. What makes you think that? Lucy had paid this really dangerous guy to help her bully the bully. Eric is small time in comparison to this guy.'

'And who was he?'

'I don't know his real name. She said he'd killed someone and that everyone was scared of him.'

'Did you ever meet him?' Sexton draws a breath as he remembers that Rory told him about the old IRA guy Lucy had mentioned at the party. 'Did he have a scorpion tattoo?'

'I never met him, but Lucy did call him Red Scorpion, yeah.'

Sexton bangs the heels of his hands off the steering wheel as the penny drops. One of the country's notorious killers had set up the Red Scorpion Debt Collection Agency when he'd got out of prison after a twenty-year stretch. His slogan was 'Don't Get Mad, Get Even'. Bert McFarland aka Red Scorpion traded on his reputation as a hard man, hiring himself out as a heavy for businesses who wanted to collect bad debts. Sexton is willing to bet his life that that's who Lucy Starling had turned to, to stop the troll. He should have realized who it was straight away.

'Did Lucy ask Bert . . . the scorpion guy . . . to murder Melissa?'

'Lucy kill? What are you talking about?' Beth's hand moved to the door handle as she shoots him a look like she's just discovered he's Jack the Ripper. 'I just told you he was just to scare Melissa off. Lucy was trying to save people. Don't you listen?'

Sexton leans across and grabs her arm.

'Rape!' she screams.

He releases, puts his palms in the air, and says, 'I spoke to Lucy,' just as Beth pushes the door open.

She pulls it closed again. 'Lucy can speak?'

'No . . . well . . . sort of. Listen, she told me about going to the scorpion guy herself, but the way she said it made it sound like she'd hired him to kill.'

'What exactly did she say?'

'She said, "I hired a hitman."'

'So?'

'So? *So!* Maybe he killed Melissa.'

Beth stares at Sexton like he's the stupidest guy in the world. 'My old man hired a plumber once to cut the grass. When the plumber called, he had a lawnmower and not a set of monkey wrenches. Just because Lucy hired a hitman to settle old scores and get even does not mean she wanted him to kill anyone.'

She gets out of the car and takes off.

Sexton gets out too and calls across the roof of the car: 'Beth, wait, please.'

But Beth has disappeared into the pitch-black night.

Thursday

48

Sexton rubs sleep from his eyes in the driving seat of the car as he watches the mourners leaving Anna Eccles's funeral. He's been here since 9 a.m., with McConigle in the passenger seat, to spot them arriving. She wants a list of names of the people they recognize and a set of photographs of the ones they don't, to be ID'd later. Her latte is stone cold, perched in the cup holder, but she's still taking the odd sip. There's no policing science to people-watching; it is what it is. McConigle wants to see who associates with who, and if anyone is isolated by the mourners. She wants to watch the adults intermingling as much as the teens, she explains to Sexton. They bully in a different way to kids, but they do it just the same. At least teenagers are upfront about it, obnoxious as it is. Adults snub behind people's backs. Sexton had tried to argue that Oakley would be better suited to this job, but she wasn't having his excuses and had been waiting outside his gaff at 8 a.m. this morning. He gets the feeling she doesn't plan on letting him out of her sight.

Now the service has ended they have a better view. The mourners had their backs to them as they arrived, heading straight into the church. Now everybody's hanging around the church car park until the hearse leaves.

'What's Rory Mason doing here?' Sexton asks, spotting

the kid in his oversized black suit jacket in disbelief. 'Jo's here too. Bloody hell!'

McConigle giggles and writes the names down in her pad, where she'd earlier written the words, 'Suspect list' across the top. 'Any sign of the chief?'

Sexton scans the crowd. 'Blow me, there he is. Chief Superintendent Dan Mason.'

McConigle mutters, 'Any time,' and writes Dan's name down with a flourish.

Sexton checks to see if she's serious before his eyes dart to another couple he knows. They're barely able to move forward because of all the handshaking and hugs. 'Melissa's folks: Marie and Martin Brockle,' he says.

'How did it go with them last night?'

'Fine. They'd nothing to add,' he says.

'Nothing?' McConigle starts. 'I thought they were the most vocal. Tell me they named names?'

'What did Canon say about the deer?' Sexton asks quickly.

'He exercised his constitutional right to silence,' McConigle said. 'But we can re-arrest him and hold him for a week, thanks to the drugs you found, and we will.'

'Who's quizzing him?' Sexton asks.

'Oakley.'

'Anyone would crack under that kind of pressure,' Sexton says flatly.

McConigle opens her mouth to pursue it, but Sexton has moved on. 'Who's that?' he asks, pointing a finger over the steering wheel at a face in the crowd. 'To the left of Rory, the man with red hair in a ponytail, leather jacket, trainers.'

McConigle spots the guy he means in a group of three men isolated from the rest of the crowd.

'Dunno,' she says. 'But he's talking to that scrote Frankie Brown from Fatima Mansions.'

The block of flats McConigle is referring to had produced some serious drug dealers over the years, but Brown was a talented artist who sold reproduction artwork, before he was caught and convicted of fraud and forgery.

'Yeah, that's Frankie all right,' Sexton says, stunned. 'What the hell . . . McConigle, look.' He points. 'That red-haired guy is the arsonist Johnny McCann. I knew I knew him.'

'Bloody hell, it's like a criminals' convention!' McConigle says.

Sexton keeps his trap shut. He twists around and reaches between the seats for the long-lens camera on the back seat, lifts it up, points through the window, closing one eye before he snaps. The shutter makes a *clack-clack-clack* sound. He snaps to the left and the right, on high alert, as he peers through the magnifier for any sign of Bert McFarland. He checks the image on the camera's mini-screen, then returns it to the back seat. He doesn't want any trouble here. 'Got him,' he says. 'I'll confirm that ID later.'

'Who's that?' McConigle asks about a woman working the crowd.

'Bronwyn Harris, the headmistress, and students from Benedict's College,' Sexton answers.

He watches Bronwyn Harris walk across the church car park and approach a well-dressed man who has just come out of the church. She puts her hand on his shoulder, shakes his hand. Other people in the crowd approach him.

'Must be another of the dead girls' dads.' McConigle remarks, reading Sexton's mind.

Sexton clicks his fingers. 'I know him. He's . . . he's Amy Reddan's dad. I saw him in the school the day of the lecture. He looks different, though. Thinner.'

Sexton takes his phone off the dash and dials Rory's number. He puts it on speakerphone so McConigle can listen. They watch Rory glance at his phone, say something to Jo and step aside to answer.

'Rory, do you see that guy the principal is talking to in the car park to your left?' Sexton asks.

Rory looks around in confusion to locate Sexton and then gives him a brief wave. Then he tries to find out who Sexton means.

'Rob?' Rory says.

'Yeah,' Sexton reacts. 'Rob Reddan, good. And see the dodgy blokes to your right?' Sexton says, referring to Frankie Brown and Johnny McCann. 'The red-haired one in the leather jacket and the men he's with? Have you any idea how Anna might have known them?'

Rory shrugs. 'I don't have a clue. They're in the choir. Lucy's dad's in it too. He's in some weird church. The music is good, though. If you're into hymns and stuff.'

'How come your folks are here?' Sexton asks.

'That was Mum's idea,' Rory says, not hiding his disparagement. 'She wanted to show her support. I wanted to come with my mate, the one who went out with Amy.'

Sexton's eyebrows go up and he shoots McConigle a look. 'Right. Which one is that?'

'You mean Darren?' Rory asks, putting his arm around a youth's neck. 'That would be this blond-haired faggot.' He rubs his knuckles in Darren's scalp, and Darren tries to jostle free. 'I keep telling him to get it cut,' he tells Sexton, struggling to keep the phone pressed to his ear. 'He looks like a queer, doesn't he?'

Darren puts his hair behind his ears and asks Rory who he's talking to.

'Tell him to come over to the car for a sec,' Sexton says.

'Are you nuts? My mother will kill me if she knows I'm talking to you.'

'Don't tell her then, just send Darren.'

Sexton hangs up and watches Rory point out the car to his friend, who puts his hands in his pockets as he lopes across the street.

Sexton gets out of the car to talk to him.

'I'm sorry about Amy,' Sexton says.

'Yeah, I know,' Darren says. 'Adults think it's a good idea to go up to you at a funeral, shake your hand and tell you they're sorry for your trouble. What else would they be, unless they're psycho? Why are you guys here, anyway? Don't tell me you think Anna was murdered?'

McConigle pounces. 'Murdered? Woah, why would you say that?'

Darren shifts his weight uncomfortably.

Sexton smiles. 'It's just part of the Talk About Feelings programme. I'm the juvenile liaison officer; this is the family liaison officer. We're here to support the kids, and their parents.'

Darren nods.

'Did Amy's mum die when she was young?' Sexton asks. 'I read Amy's funeral notice before. I didn't see her mentioned.'

McConigle glances at Sexton in surprise.

'No, she's still alive,' Darren says. 'Amy was real close to her mum.'

'Is she here?'

'No, she doesn't go anywhere the dad is. They don't get on. That's why she wouldn't have been mentioned in the funeral notice. She didn't even go to Amy's funeral. She lives in England.'

'Do you want to update me?' McConigle cuts in.

'Amy's own mum didn't go to her funeral?' Sexton asks in disbelief.

Darren shakes his head. 'She absolutely hates her ex-husband, Rob.'

Sexton's gaze moves to Rob Reddan.

'Could you get me her number?'

'Look, you should really talk to Rob about it,' Darren says. 'He's over there. I can get him if you want.'

'That's OK,' Sexton says. He still has Rob's card in his pocket.

'I don't have Amy's mum's number. Amy didn't like talking about it. It kind of broke her heart when her mum went.'

Sexton nods. 'OK. What does Rob do for a living?'

'He makes TV ads, or he used to. I don't know if anybody advertises anything any more, though. I've got to go back, OK?'

Sexton climbs back into the car and watches him go.

'What's going on?' McConigle asks.

'What's the only thing that would have kept you away from your own daughter's funeral, if the two of you were real close?'

'What are you thinking?' she asks.

'That she's scared,' Sexton says.

'Or a cold cow,' McConigle says.

They both stare at Rob Reddan.

'Write him down,' Sexton says.

'What about Nigel Starling?' McConigle asks, spotting Lucy's dad emerge from the church. 'And his weird church?' Nigel is heading over to Frankie and the other criminals, and together they walk to a Volvo and climb in.

'Leave him out of it,' Sexton says. 'He's all right.'

49

McConigle wanted Sexton to tail Nigel, but that proved impossible with the funeral cortège. They head back to the station for a midday conference on developments. McConigle updates thirty-odd officers on the operation, which she has code-named 'Dracula'. She pauses every couple of minutes to take another bite from a dripping tomato sandwich, angling her body away to avoid being hit by red blobs. Behind her, posed school photos of Amy Reddan, Melissa Brockle and Anna Eccles have been stuck to the whiteboard. There's also one of Anna taken at her post-mortem. The contrast is so great, it could be a fourth victim. Sexton knows Lucy's picture should be there too, but is relieved it's not.

Sexton tunes out as McConigle talks, and studies the pictures. His gaze moves from Amy's shy, tilted face to Melissa's. Anna's PM picture is the only one with the haunting symmetrical blood circles on her neck, but Sexton is willing to bet that if the other girls had had autopsies the same marks would have been found.

'Bugger!' McConigle curses as a spat of seeds manages to land on her white shirt. Sexton tunes back in as she details the main lines of enquiry she wants actioned.

'Right, if there's a "How To" video out there, we need to find it. Sexton heard Anna's siblings talking about it, so

229

that's where we're going to start looking. Those kids need to be interviewed – sensitively, they've just lost their sister – but they can't fob us off this time either. Did either of them see the video on Anna's phone? If so, what did they see? If not, did Anna tell them about it? Did she discuss it with school-friends? Did anyone else get it?

'Then there's the wood where all three died. I want it fine-combed with a dragnet and using the sniffer dogs. Who knows what might crop up.

'Also, we need to contact the parents of all of the other children affected, and the doctors who proclaimed them dead and the undertakers who buried them will have to be contacted and asked if they remember any strange markings on the neck. Despite what you might think, it's not the norm to carry out PMs in suicide cases.'

Sexton shifts uncomfortably in his chair as McConigle brings up Lucy Starling.

'I need someone to concentrate on her father, Nigel, to find out if he's got any previous. Nobody hangs around the kind of crooks he does without good reason.' She names the criminals whose company Nigel was in at Anna's funeral and details their crimes.

'I'll do it,' Sexton offers.

'Got him!' a voice pipes up. Sexton turns and sees a uniform sitting at a computer and displaying a little too much initiative for his liking.

McConigle grabs a napkin, wipes her blouse and heads over. The others crowd around the screen for a view.

'Bloody hell!' McConigle remarks, leaning on the desk. She reaches for the mouse and scrolls down the page.

'What is it?' Sexton asks.

'He's only just found a photo of Nigel Starling in a Welsh newspaper with a bunch of schoolkids in Bridgend,'

McConigle says. 'You know, that place in Wales where all the kids topped themselves.'

'I know the place,' Sexton says, as if he's hearing it for the first time.

McConigle reads from the screen. 'The caption says: "Registered homeopath Nigel Starling, who specializes in depression, gives a talk to pupils at the local comprehensive."'

'A lot of people don't like taking drugs for depression,' Sexton says calmly.

McConigle is bobbing on the balls of her feet, clicking her fingers, trying to summon up a memory. 'Something weird came up in Anna's bloods,' she explains excitedly. 'The prof rang me during the conference yesterday. He said it was hypericum. Ever heard of it? It's more commonly known as St John's Wort. It's used in the treatment of depression.'

'It's common as house salt,' Sexton says.

'I wonder if any of the suicide victims came to see Nigel Starling,' McConigle says, as if she hasn't heard.

'Oh, now he's Harold Shipman, is that it?' Sexton asks, referring to the serial-killer GP who murdered hundreds of his own patients.

'Thanks for reminding me,' McConigle says. 'Better bring his wife in too, see what Dr Death has to say for herself. Sexton, can you do it? If they come voluntarily, we won't need arrest warrants and we won't have to worry about the clock ticking.'

50

'How's Lucy?' Sexton asks when Nancy opens the front door. To his surprise, Nancy steps forward, throws her arms around him and hugs him tightly.

'What is it?' Sexton moves back, holding her by the shoulders at arm's length so he can see her face.

Nigel joins them in the hall and puts an arm around her. 'I'm afraid Lucy's condition has deteriorated a lot,' he says.

'What do you mean? Is she . . .?' Sexton can't bring himself to ask how sick Lucy is. His emotions have taken him by surprise.

'She doesn't communicate any more,' Nancy explains with a sniff. 'Come in, won't you?'

Nancy takes Sexton's arm in hers. 'I'm sorry,' she says. 'It's just the sight of a kind face. You understand, you always have, and you have shown us great kindness. You think we don't know, but we know. Tim McMenamy wrote to us. He's dropping his case. He told us what you did. Thank you for that. But you have news for us, that's why you're here. What is it?'

'We need you to come into the station for questioning,' Sexton says. 'It's just routine, nothing to worry about.'

'We're just about to sit down to lunch,' Nancy says. 'Can it wait half an hour? We can't both go, obviously, because of

Lucy. But we could stagger it once we've eaten. Can we eat first?'

'Of course.'

'You'll join us?' Nancy says. 'We can talk properly that way. Not like in a stuffy, sterile station.'

Sexton nods reluctantly. 'All right.'

As they walk towards the kitchen, he stops and turns to glance towards Lucy's room. 'Want to say hello?' Nigel asks him.

'I'd like that.'

Nancy lets go of his arm and steps up to the bedroom door ahead of him, pushing it open a chink. She peers inside and turns back to Sexton.

'She's asleep,' she whispers with a smile. 'We'll eat first.'

'I'll just have a quick peek,' Sexton says. He enters the room and walks up to Lucy's bedside, appalled by how different she looks to last time. She is so frail now. He checks over his shoulder and lightly moves the hair from her neck so he can see it properly. No stun-gun marks, he notes with relief.

In the kitchen, Nigel is pushing the handles down on a bottle of wine, uncorking it.

'Not for me,' Sexton says.

'Don't be silly, you're our guest. And we owe you so much. We've had a rough few days with Lucy, and I need a drink. Please join me.'

'All right, just one,' Sexton says.

Nigel examines the bottle. 'It's a nice one too,' he says, sounding desperate to change the subject as he holds it up by the neck to examine the label. 'I picked it up in Venezuela in 1985, would you believe, and have been saving it for a special occasion. But, actually, a shit day is equally deserving. Isn't it, darling?'

Nancy sighs. 'Probably more so, if you ask me. And it's not one shit day, it's thirteen.'

'What has happened to Lucy?' Sexton asks.

'She has total Locked-in syndrome now,' Nancy says. 'We have touched base with the leading experts in the world, based in Florida, consulting on her treatment plan. We'd volunteered for a new clinical course of a wonder drug that is on trial, you see, but they can't tell without monitoring Lucy's progress how she's reacting to the drugs. She's one of only three people in the world who is eligible for testing, because the patient must have suffered the syndrome within a window of just over two weeks in starting the trial, otherwise there can be no benefit. Without seeing Lucy and scanning her brain, they don't know if there's a problem and whether she needs to have her dosage adjusted. Today's Thursday . . .' She pauses to take a sip of her drink, and it's clear she's holding back tears. 'By tomorrow, Lucy will have been locked in for two weeks.'

'Can't the tests be done from here?' Sexton asks.

'The equipment we're talking about is so sophisticated it isn't even available in the specialist brain hospitals. This research is being funded by private donations. It's taken ten years to get it to this point.'

The atmosphere grows morose as Nigel walks Sexton over to the table. 'Talk about something – anything – else. My head hurts with worry and dread.'

Sexton takes a breath and tries to get his mind off it. 'What were you doing in Venezuela?'

Nancy pokes her husband's elbow with her own. 'Carve,' she says, eyeing the roast.

'Studying the medicinal practices of the Yanomami tribe,' Nigel tells Sexton as he slices the meat. 'They've got a huge botanical knowledge.'

'Cannibals!' Nancy says.

Sexton is relieved the mood has lightened.

She grabs the set of whiskey glasses Nigel has poured the wine into, tut-tuts and carries them over to the sink, where she sloshes the wine into proper glasses.

'Sampled some hallucinogens too while I was there,' Nigel says, lowering his voice and nudging Sexton. 'Don't mention the war!'

Nancy hands out the wine glasses. 'Here you go,' she says, passing them around.

Nigel raises his glass and gives her a doleful look. 'To Lucy.'

'To our beautiful daughter pulling through, and to these nightmare teenage years finally coming to an end,' Nancy says. 'Only five years to go.'

Sexton clinks his glass against theirs. He sits at the table as Nancy lights candles and Nigel dishes the food on to the plates.

'Can I do anything?' Sexton offers.

'You can eat and drink and tell us what you need to know so badly,' Nancy says, sitting down too.

Nigel places Sexton's plate in front of him. Ham, spuds, carrots and broccoli and a spoonful of mustard are arranged on it – like a still life.

'Did you use a ruler then?' Sexton jokes, waving his fork at their plates. Each plate is like a carbon copy of the next – the food, the portions, exactly the same on all three.

'Mild autism,' Nancy jokes, tucking in. 'It has its advantages. Lucy's medication is administered like clock-work as a result. Now go on, tell us what's up?'

Sexton shoves a forkful of food into the side of his mouth. 'I noticed some of the members of your choir are not exactly . . . how shall I put this? . . . men of good repute.' He smiles.

'How did you come into their company?'

'God forgives sinners,' Nigel says earnestly. 'So does Conquest.'

'Conquest?' Sexton asks.

'Our church,' Nigel explains. 'We wouldn't have got through the bad times without it. It's still small, but we're spreading the word. We originally belonged to the Free Presbyterian Church, but we broke away because it was too unforgiving, especially when it came to Lucy's rebellious year. Our pastor's advice was to read her the Bible!'

Nancy smiles at her husband, and motions at him with her shoulder. 'He goes around the prisons now,' she says lovingly. 'Trying to find people who might be open to new ideas – that love is the answer, not humiliation, not guilt, not penance. I think sometimes' – she checks to see Nigel won't disapprove of what she's about to say – 'even you have to admit, my love, that some of the people who join us believe it might increase their chances of parole.'

'Without question,' Nigel says. 'But you also have to admit that some of them can really sing!'

Nancy grins. 'Plenty of practice at karaoke machines in dodgy places.'

Sexton wipes the corners of his mouth on a napkin and finishes what's left of the wine in his glass. 'You have to take Lucy to Florida,' he insists urgently.

'It's impossible,' Nigel says.

'Lucy has never had a passport, believe it or not,' Nancy explains. 'She's never needed one.'

'She was going to apply this summer. She wanted to go to some music festival or other in Spain with a bunch of friends. She filled in the form and got her photos ready, but the paperwork takes days to process. Her photos have to be verified, and the form stamped by a garda. Even if you were willing to do that for us and went and sat in Molesworth Street tomorrow, there are no guarantees they'd process it for us on the day. It's entirely dependent on how busy they are, and they're closed for the weekend. By Monday we have no hope of trying to get the drug levels right in her system, and even after there'll be red tape setting her chances back even further.'

'Book the flights tonight,' Sexton says. 'Contact Lucy's consultant in the States. I've got a contact in the passport office who'll put the paperwork through for me. You can bring Lucy's paperwork to the station and I'll stamp it for you.'

'Are you serious?' Nigel asks, sounding like he's afraid to hope.

'We'll do it,' Nancy says decisively. She starts to cry.

Nigel tops up the glasses and holds his up. 'To you then, Gavin. And everything you've done for Lucy.'

After coffee and warm apple tart that slides down his gullet much more easily than the dinner, Sexton goes to see Lucy. He hides his alarm for the sake of Nigel and Nancy. She's awake now but, as he could see earlier, Nancy and Nigel are right: she looks so much worse than when he was last here. He senses she knows it's him, but her eyes barely flicker and the spark has gone.

'How are you, love?' he asks her gently.

But when her eyelids droop down they do not reopen.

51

Sexton drops Nigel Starling off at the station, where McConigle intends to interview him herself, and after organizing to have Lucy's passport form stamped he heads straight for the Red Scorpion Debt Collection Agency, based in a Portakabin in an industrial park off the M50.

Parking up, he walks past a couple of white vans outside with scorpions painted on them and the caption: 'Settling Scores – Don't Get Mad, Get Even'.

Sexton buzzes the door and flashes a grin for the camera on the intercom before pushing the door at the sound of the lock releasing.

The blonde behind the makeshift counter looks bored as she hands over a clipboard with a sheet containing a questionnaire asking how much was owed, by whom, and what his credit-card number was.

'Bert doesn't see anyone without an appointment,' she says when Sexton asks if the boss is in.

He holds up his ID card. She reaches for the phone and mumbles something into the handset, telling Sexton to 'Take a seat.'

He glances at the couch, which is covered with a picnic-rug-style throw that smells of wet dog. The seat is so low down he'd have needed a cherry picker to hoist himself out of it again. Instead, he walks past her towards a door set in the linoleum-covered wall behind her.

'You can't go in there,' she says, but Sexton ignores her and pushes through.

Bert is leaning back in a dentist-style chair set in the middle of a room. He pulls towels furiously from around his neck. A woman dressed in a nurse's outfit as if she's just come from a hen party is holding a barber's shaving knife in one hand – the old-fashioned type.

'What?' Bert bellows at Sexton.

He is sixty-something with over-dyed black hair that has a plum hue, substantial sideburns and a scorpion on his right forearm.

'You missed a bit,' Sexton tells the nurse, pointing to the spot between Bert's eyebrows.

'Out!' Bert roars at her.

'Well, well, well,' Sexton says, taking in the wood-panelled interior that looks as if it has been furnished from skips by Del Boy. A naked mannequin stands beside a lap-dancing pole. A collection of tarnished brass ornaments takes up most of the desk space.

'Such grooming, such finesse,' Sexton says. 'Are you saving all this shit for a visit to the *Antiques Roadshow*?'

'Get on with it,' Bert says.

Sexton kinks a net curtain to look out of the window. 'Your scorpion looks more like a crab. A crab is a crustacean. It comes from larvae. A scorpion is an arachnid. I know because I had a pet tarantula when I was a kid. Used to read up on it.'

'You didn't come here to give me a National Geographic lesson,' Bert says. 'What do you want?'

'What did Lucy Starling pay you ten grand to do?'

'Who?'

'The fourteen-year-old schoolgirl, Bert. There can't be many of them on your books.'

'Honeytrap?' Bert asks.

Sexton's eyes widen.

'Unless you intend paying the money back, I'm going to do you for extorting money from a minor,' Sexton says. 'Who did Lucy pay you to put the squeeze on?'

'Wouldn't I be breaking a professional code of client privilege or something?' Bert asks with a sneer.

'As Lucy is hanging on to her life by a thread, she's got other things to worry about,' Sexton answers.

'I know nothing about that.'

Sexton tilts his head. 'Here's the way I see it. An internet troll was taunting the kids online, encouraging them to kill themselves. Lucy thought the troll was a girl in her class called Melissa, and blamed her for sending the suicide clip. So she paid you to scare Melissa off. But maybe Melissa wasn't the troll. Nobody is who they say they are online. What if you were the troll? Maybe Lucy was paying the very person who was stalking those kids. Melissa didn't come out of the wood alive. Maybe Lucy was paying you to scare you. Was Lucy your little Lolita?'

'That's funny. You got the first bit right – she wanted me to put the mockers on someone, like you said. The rest is more of your shitology.'

'So who did that person you had to put the frighteners on turn out to be – if it wasn't you, I mean?'

Bert walks over to his desk, pulls a drawer open, a DVD out and sticks it in a player under a TV on a swivel arm at a height in a corner.

'Let's just say, Lucy thought it was someone, but it turned out to be someone else.'

Before Sexton can probe, an out-of-focus sepia image fills

the screen. Sexton squints, trying to make out what he's looking at. A pair of hands fills the screen. 'It's best to use a soft rope,' a voice booms through a distorter.

Sexton steps back to get a better view of the screen. There is no face in the frame, though, because, as far as he can tell, the camera is on the ground and the man is standing over it.

'This is how you tie a hangman's knot,' the voice continues, weaving one end of the rope over the other slowly. 'It breaks the neck more easily than the gallows knot . . .'

The hands fill the screen – they look male, Sexton notes.

'Sick, isn't it?' Bert says. 'Would you blame Lucy then for wanting to get me involved?'

Sexton scans the background, notes the cabin-like interior.

The voice over on the tape continues, 'A rope at least six feet long is best . . .'

'Why didn't Lucy just come to the authorities?' Sexton asks.

'Maybe she didn't want to have to wait a week for her call to be answered, and a couple of years for a case to come to court. Maybe she thought it was more serious than that, and not another second could be wasted. You could always try asking her, copper. This has nothing to do with me. I'm the guy the kids came to for help. You got it all the wrong way around.'

Sexton turns back to the screen and listens: '. . . a smaller loop at this end . . .'

'Did you find out who made it?' he asks Bert.

'Now you want me to do your job. I won't. I'll do my own. Like I said, Lucy organized to bring the person she thought responsible to the wood.'

'Melissa?' Sexton asks.

Bert doesn't object. 'Only, when the bullets started flying, I wasn't about to stick around. That's the beginning and end of my involvement, and no, I won't be signing a statement to that effect.'

'Why didn't you warn the girls to stay away?'

'There wasn't time. Me and Lucy had thought it was Melissa we'd be talking to. We weren't expecting some other nut to show. So we were kind of taken by surprise, too busy ducking the shooter's fire to have a conference,' Bert says.

'How would this other person have known Lucy and Melissa were going to the woods?'

'I've no idea. That wood isn't the easiest place to get to either.' Bert switches to a different DVD. When he hits play, the voice on the TV changes to one of a young girl. 'Amy Reddan was my best friend . . .'

Sexton sees Lucy's face fill the screen. She's unrecognizable compared to the girl in the bed. Make-up makes her look ten years older. 'All Amy ever wanted was to be accepted for who she was – kind, gentle, talented,' Lucy continues.

The camera pans back and McFarland's weathered face appears on the screen. He is grinning maniacally and whacking a baseball bat into the cup of a hand.

'I know who you are,' he says, peering into the screen. 'And I'm coming to get you.'

Sexton gets him by the scruff of the neck. 'If you want a chance of immunity from prosecution, you can tell me who was firing, or . . .' He becomes distracted by the sound of Lucy talking again: 'You might as well have murdered her,' she hisses, brushing a tear from her eye. 'I won't let you murder anyone else. Next time you hurt someone, you answer to Bert.' She makes her signature 'L' shape with her forefinger and thumb and stretches her arm out. 'Hope you understand what it's like to be made to feel small and scared . . .'

The footage ends.

'So what was Eric Canon's role in it all?' Sexton asks, giving McFarland's collar a rough shake.

'That scrote on Rutling?' Bert asks. 'I've no idea.'

52

'It wasn't your fault,' McConigle says. She needs to wind the interview up, to get back to the station, as Sexton has texted her that Nigel Starling is waiting for her there, but it would be too insensitive to leave immediately, in the circumstances. Katie Eccles buried her sister this morning. 'You do know that, don't you?'

She reaches forward and clutches Katie's hand, breaking her own 'No physical contact with members of the public' rule. The interview has turned into more of a counselling session anyway. Thirteen-year-old Katie hasn't said anything yet; her mum is there too and keeps talking through the silence.

McConigle thinks Katie is holding back, but also that she's still too deeply traumatized by the death of her sister to talk. Katie needs a bereavement counsellor, medication, and to be watched like a hawk, McConigle reckons. The kid's fingernails are chewed down to the quick, and her hair – pulled back in a ponytail – looks like it hasn't been washed in days. Probably not since Monday, when she found out about her sister, McConigle expects.

'Katie, are you listening to me, my love?' McConigle pushes.

But Katie continues to stare out the kitchen window, as she has since McConigle arrived to try to find out what she

244

knows about the suicide 'How to' video clip that is supposed to have been sent to Anna's phone.

'Katie shared a bedroom with Anna,' her mother, Maggie, explains quietly. 'When they were little, they used to fight over who'd get the top bunk; when they got bigger, it was over who was underneath. They were always at each other over clothes, or pals, or phone credit. But when their nan died, a couple of months back, I found them holding hands in bed at night. Anna would let her arm drop down over the side, and Katie would hold it.'

'Mum,' Katie says, cringing.

McConigle is so relieved she's finally said something, even if it's only a word, she can't help but exhale loudly. Sizing up the situation, she decides her only chance of getting Katie to talk is to get her on her own. Perhaps she doesn't want to admit knowing anything because she's worried it will come back at her when the next stages of grief follow the loss: anger, recrimination, blame. Perhaps she's just unable to relax around her mother. When McConigle was JLO, she came to the conclusion that self-consciousness drives every teenage impulse.

'Maggie, would you mind if I spoke to Katie alone?' she asks. Technically, the child's entitled to a guardian present at the very least, but McConigle wants to make it as informal as possible, and she's out of time.

Maggie glances at her daughter, who doesn't object. 'I don't want her put under any more pressure. If she doesn't answer you the first time, please let it go.'

McConigle nods. She waits until Maggie's gone and then heads back to the kitchen table where Katie's sitting and kneels down in front of her, taking her hands again.

'When did Anna get sent the video?' she presses, still without any confirmation that it even exists.

'A few days before she did it,' Katie says so quietly McConigle has to strain to hear.

'Did she show it to you?'

'No. She didn't even tell me about it. I just heard her talking to her friend on the phone the night she went missing.'

Which they are still desperate to recover, McConigle realizes.

'And what did you hear her say?'

'She was kind of joking about it, but Anna always laughed when she was nervous.'

'Do you know which of her friends she was talking to?'

'Darren, Amy's boyfriend, I think.'

'Did Anna say who'd sent it to her?'

'Anna said she didn't recognize the number it had been sent from. She told him what it was, and asked him if he knew it.'

'Did you hear his answer?'

'No.'

McConigle nods. 'Can you give me Anna's phone number?'

Katie reels it off. McConigle draws a breath. The phone provider will be able to give her the records and they might get a lead on who sent that vile clip.

'I could get you the number of who sent the video, if you want,' Katie says, reading McConigle's mind. 'It's probably still on Anna's phone upstairs.'

McConigle checks she's hearing right. 'Anna's phone is here?'

'Yes. It's upstairs.' Katie breaks down. 'She gave it to me the night she died, which I should have realized meant something major was going on in her head. Anna never went anywhere without her phone.'

53

Sexton goes straight to Amy Reddan's ex-boyfriend Darren's front door as soon as McConigle rings him to tell him what Katie's told her.

Darren's father is shocked to find a garda standing there when he opens it. Brendan Maguire is tall, clean-shaven and dressed in a soccer dad's tracksuit and trainers. He explains that he's training for the marathon, and is just about to head out.

'Should I be worried?' he asks Sexton intently.

'As long as your son tells the truth, there's nothing to be worried about,' Sexton reassures him, explaining the conversation they've learned Anna had with Darren shortly before she died.

Brendan steps out of the house and walks Sexton around to the side, where he releases the garage door. As it glides up, Darren can be seen inside playing drums.

'What is it, Dad? I thought you were gone for a run.' He looks past him and sees Sexton. An expression of resignation spreads across the teenager's face.

'Oh, give me a break,' Darren says, tucking his hair behind his ears.

'Don't talk to a policeman like that,' Brendan says, appalled. 'He's trying to get to the bottom of this. Tell him whatever it is you know.'

'Look, I don't know anything, OK?'

'Darren, why did Anna Eccles ring you the night she died?' Sexton demands.

'Answer him,' his father warns.

'Someone had sent the suicide clip to her phone. I'd put a post up online saying I was keeping track of the mobile numbers it was being sent from, that I had identified all of them, and people could touch base with me to find out if it was the troll's number.'

'You knew who the troll was?'

'Sort of.'

'And?'

'I thought it was Melissa. Everyone thought that.'

'I need that list,' Sexton says, 'and the chatroom site where the troll was stalking the kids.'

'OK,' Darren answers. 'It's all on my laptop.'

He stands up to go.

'Wait. Was Amy sent the video to her phone before she died?' Sexton asks.

Darren puts his drumsticks down. 'If she was, she never mentioned it, and I think she would have. Everyone who got it since has talked about it.'

'Did you get it?'

'Yeah.'

'When?'

'About two months ago.'

'Around the time Amy died?' Sexton clarifies.

'Yeah, that's right. That's what made it even worse. Melissa didn't even wait until her body was cold.'

'What made you originally think Melissa had sent it?'

'I tracked back the numbers. The person who sent it to me was sending it because they thought it was terrible, not because they wanted me to top myself. So I got the number they got it from, and it was the same story. Kids were just sharing it to warn each other there was a psycho out there. The time on her phone was earlier than any of the others. And, like I said, any time it was sent on from that point was because kids were talking about it, they were disgusted. People wanted to see it. I went back as far as I could and, when I got to Lucy, I discovered she'd got it from Melissa. She was the first kid to send it, so we presumed she'd made it.'

'So why didn't you tell anyone?'

'I was going to, but Melissa said someone had sent it to her. Nobody believed her. Then, when she died, there didn't seem any point.'

'Who did she blame? Who sent it to Melissa?' Sexton asks intently.

'She was being a bitch,' Darren blurts. 'It's what Melissa did. It was kind of her default setting. She said she sent it to Lucy to show her that she was a victim too.'

'In that case, Melissa must have accused someone of sending it to her,' Sexton says, as Darren's father looks on in disbelief. 'Who was that person?'

Darren sighs. 'Rob Reddan – Amy's dad. But she had it in for him. She'd already sent these photographs of him to Amy.'

'Photographs?' Sexton asks.

'You know . . . dodgy ones . . .'

'Explain,' Brendan states.

Darren sighs. 'Look, if you must know, Melissa's mum was seeing Amy's dad, Rob, on the QT.'

'Really?' Brendan asks.

'What?' Sexton asks slowly.

'Melissa found these photos on her mum's phone of Rob . . . you know?' Sexton's eyebrows go up. He shoots an apologetic look at Brendan, whose curiosity saves him the bother of probing.

'Do you mean Rob Reddan was naked?' Brendan asks.

'Yeah, naked, and the rest,' Darren says. 'Melissa discovered Amy's dad was a pervert, so she sent them to Amy to let her know: "By the way, your dad's a freak." The pictures totally grossed Amy out. She asked her dad about them, and he apologized, said he was seeing Melissa's mum on the side, and not to tell Melissa, as it was all top secret.'

'Did Amy send them to you, or anyone else?' Sexton asks.

'Nope, they weren't the kind of family snap you shared on Facebook.'

'So, no copies.' Sexton is thinking aloud. 'And then Amy died. And then Melissa sent the video clip to Lucy and blamed Rob?' Sexton clarifies.

'Yeah, but Lucy didn't believe her either.'

Sexton pats his jacket pocket for the card Rob Reddan gave him in the gym hall on Tuesday, and takes it out. 'Can you get your laptop now? Is this the number Melissa said she got it from? Can you check?'

'I don't need to, that's it all right. Fuck. It really *was* Rob.'

54

Melissa's mother, Marie, looks shocked when she opens the door. Sexton realizes how bad he looks – panting, wild-eyed with adrenaline, sweat patches soaking his armpits – but from the look on her face he knows it's not his appearance she's reacting to. She knows he knows.

He watches Marie closely as he puts the extramarital affair to her, trying to nail down the last details before he goes to her boyfriend's house. She doesn't react at all, not so much as a flicker. He feels betrayed himself. Her performance is Oscar-winning. So, he puts it to her that they both know what's going on:

'Are you sure there isn't something more you want to tell me, Marie? Something you want to get off your conscience? Something gnawing away at your insides because of what has happened to your daughter? Let's remind ourselves of that, shall we? The daughter you brought into the world, your only child, the one who went to a wood on her own and died alone. Melissa.'

The look on her frightened face changes to horror and as quickly again to something hard. Sexton recognizes this face from countless interviews, when the interviewee starts feeling sorry for themselves and the survival instinct kicks in. Marie is calculating what's best for her at this point. She's not thinking about her daughter lying cold in the grave. It's too late for her. She's thinking about herself and how she can extract herself from the whole pile of shit she's now in.

'He used to say all women want this – sure, that's why *Fifty Shades of Grey* sold millions,' she says, tears springing from her eyes.

'Who used to say that?' Sexton presses.

'Rob, before he'd tie me up.'

'Did he ever talk to you about Melissa?'

She looks up in surprise. 'What do you mean?'

'Your daughter and his daughter didn't get on. It must have been strange that the two of you, on the other hand, got on so well.'

'No, he never talked about Melissa,' she snaps.

'Do you think his interest in you had anything to do with Melissa?' Sexton can see the question is torturing her, but he also senses how close he is to cracking the case.

Her face turns red with anger. 'You mean was he using me to get to my daughter? Did he ever say her name when he was fucking me?'

'Did he? Melissa had lewd photos of him on her phone.'

'No. No. No. She got them from my phone. They were for me. Rob wanted me for my sake. Don't you listen?'

'That's right, I forgot, he wanted to hurt you for your sake.'

She starts to sob silently.

'He sent Melissa a video showing her how to kill herself.'

Marie shakes her head in disbelief. Her face contorts. 'What are you talking about?'

'That's what Melissa told people.'

'She was wrong. Rob wouldn't have done that.'

'Where did you meet to have . . . relations?'

'Why? What's that got to do with anything?'

'If it was a hotel, I can check with the staff if they ever saw Melissa go there with him.'

'You've got it all wrong. Melissa was not seeing Rob. I told you. Anyway, we never went to a hotel. We went to this log cabin he has.'

'A log cabin?' The hackles on Sexton's neck are on end. He's picturing the images on the suicide video Bert has. 'Where is it?'

'I don't know.'

'What was the address?'

'I've no idea. He'd blindfold me on the way there and back, again say this is what women want.'

'Here's what I can't understand,' Sexton says. 'Why would you want to go somewhere voluntarily with a man who has blindfolded you and intends to hurt you?'

'Because, at least he was willing to touch me. Not like Martin. At least if I was sore because of Rob, it meant I wasn't invisible. We met in a queue at a parent–teacher meeting. I knew he was on his own. Melissa had mentioned Amy's mum doing a flit. I knew Rob was flirting with me. I liked it. I was so sick of feeling I repulsed Martin.'

'Is it over?'

'Yes, a couple of months now. He broke it off after Amy died, said he couldn't go on.'

'Because you have a husband?'

'Because Amy caught us, together, in the cabin. Came in on us one night. I don't know how she found us, or how she got there. I pictured where we were going in my head, got to a point where I was pretty sure I knew where it must be. I even drove the roads I thought he'd taken afterwards by myself, but I couldn't find the hut, so I wasn't sure.'

'And where did you end up?'

She stares at Sexton as if she's just seen a ghost. 'The

woods. Where the girls went. Amy and Melissa. The kids are calling it Amy's Wood, and Everlasting, but it's Boley, near Enniskerry. Rob had said nobody else knew about it, but Amy walked in. I will take the way she looked at us to the grave with me. Rob was doing one of his . . . things.'

'What things?'

'I can't say it.' She breaks down. 'He couldn't get hard unless I was in pain. Get it now?'

55

'What was Rob like to me?' Amy's mother, Susan, repeats down the phone as Sexton watches Rob Reddan's house from his car, which is parked outside. Sexton is doing some last information-gathering. McConigle is on her way now with a team. She's told Sexton to wait until they get there, but he doesn't have that much self-control.

'Cold as a stone. Rob was abused as a kid; he's incapable of intimacy. He associates it with what happened to him when he was little.'

'How long were you married?'

She laughs bitterly. 'We were never married, but we lived together for ten years. I woke up every morning of every day for most of them and went to bed at night plotting my escape. But I couldn't leave my little girl. Then one day it occurred to me that if I stayed, he'd probably kill me, and my daughter would lose her mother anyway. Ironic, isn't it? That she's the one who's gone.' She starts to cry.

Sexton watches the curtains twitch in an upstairs bedroom, sees Rob Reddan clock his car outside. He climbs out of the car and starts to walk towards the house. 'Why did you say you thought he might kill you, or the other way around, if you stayed? Did he have a history of violence?'

'No, he never hit me. But . . . it's hard to explain . . . there was just a look in his eye when he lost it. Like he hated me.

Like he could have hurt me. It sounds mad now. But he had the worst temper I've ever seen.'

Sexton puts a hand on the garden gate and presses down the handle. 'It can't have been that bad, if you left Amy with him.'

'Rob never touched, or hurt, Amy, in any way. If anything, it was the opposite – he idolized her. When she was born he was afraid to pick her up. He pretty much stayed that way around her all her life. He thought she was the most perfect thing, called her his angel. He told me he didn't want any more children, because it would take away from the amount of time he devoted to her. The worst thing about it was he was barely able to show her any affection at all. He didn't want to hug or cuddle her, because he associated that kind of contact with what had happened to him.'

Sexton is standing at the front door. He puts his hand up to the bell.

'Did you suspect him of having any involvement in what happened to Amy?' he asks.

'No.' Susan is shocked. 'I hate him, but he wouldn't have done that.'

'You didn't come back for the funeral?'

'You still don't get it. He's a whack job, a maniac. I was scared he blamed me for what happened and would have killed me.'

'Why didn't you go to the Gardaí?'

Susan gives a bitter laugh. 'I'm talking to the wall. They couldn't have protected me. Not from Rob.'

The front door opens.

56

Rob Reddan doesn't look the least bit surprised to see Sexton standing on his doorstep. He must have spotted the squad car earlier, but it's rare to meet someone who doesn't want to know, or isn't prepared to fake wanting to know, what a policeman is doing on their doorstep. He stands back for Sexton to step in without saying a word, and then leads him in to a reception room off the hall, which is like a shrine to Amy. There are pictures of her everywhere, and a coffee table has a stack of photo albums that Sexton presumes are full of her too. Old homework copies written in a child's spidery crawl sport the name Amy Reddan. The fireplace, and even the mantelpiece, bear a granite marble heart that belongs on a grave.

'I thought you were going to ring,' he says, and Sexton can hear the slight jeer in his voice. It was a tone that would have been better suited to a question like: 'What took you so long to figure it out?'

'Rob Reddan, I'm arresting you on suspicion of murder. You have the right to remain silent . . .'

'You're arresting me?'

'Yes, but first I have to get this caution out of the way . . . Anything you say can and will be used against you in a court of law. You have the right to a solicitor. If you cannot afford one, one will be provided for you.' Sexton pauses. Rob doesn't respond. 'I should tell you that, in my experience, innocent people never want a brief,' Sexton continues. 'Don't you have anything you want to say?'

'I'm still waiting on the first question.'

'Do you own a Taser, Rob?'

Rob jerks back his head and slams it into Sexton's. There is a loud crack and blood spurts from somewhere. Sexton reels and reaches for his nose, establishing that's what's bleeding and broken as Rob takes off. He follows through a veil of pain and dizziness, sprinting out on to the road after him.

Sexton's bulk makes it impossible for him to run far, and when he stops, panting for air and leaning over on his knees trying to draw a breath, he glances back over his shoulder at the open door, and then back at Rob, in the far distance, getting smaller.

Blinking away the colour spots dancing in front of his eyes, Sexton turns and walks back to the house, pulling his phone from his pocket and dialling McConigle's number. 'Where are you?' he says as the call connects. 'He's just bolted. He's wearing a white shirt, jeans and a pair of runners.'

He listens as McConigle begins to ask a question, then shouts: 'There he is!' The siren screeches to life, and the call goes dead.

Inside, he bolts the door and calmly walks to the back one to do the same. Then he goes into each room; everything's so neat he suspects that Rob suffers from OCD. He finds a room upstairs with an editing suite, but he goes first into the only bedroom that could have been Amy's, as there's a poster of Amy Winehouse on the wall.

Sexton is presuming that if Rob is refusing to let his daughter go, if he has avenged himself on the people who persecuted her in life, it's here he'll have brought any trophies.

He stands in the middle of the room and takes a pair of baby-blue plastic gloves out of his pocket, snapping them on. He starts pulling open the drawers of the dressing table, Amy's bedside locker, and emptying the contents.

He spots a DVD with the name Melissa written on it sitting on a DVD player in the corner. He heads over to it and pushes it in, turning on the TV. The DVD won't go in, there's one jammed in there already, and when he presses eject, it slides out. It has the name Anna on it.

His *Perfect Day* ringtone trills to life and Sexton answers, sandwiching the phone between his shoulder and his ear, and pushes the DVD back in and presses play.

'We've got him,' McConigle says.

Sexton can hear Rob's shouts of abuse down the line as he stares at the screen. He hits the pause button on the player, and his face changes to one of immense pity.

Anna Eccles's terrified face is frozen on the screen.

He answers McConigle's latest question: 'Yeah, it's definitely him.'

57

In custody, Rob Reddan shows no remorse, but in the face of the overwhelming evidence against him has begun to admit his crimes. The crucial question is how many of the twenty kids' deaths he's responsible for. Sexton – who has a plaster across the top of his nose and two black eyes – is glad McConigle didn't argue that he should be the one to try to find out. For now, at least, she's put aside the fact that he withheld evidence. If it weren't for him, they'd never be at this point. She's watching from behind double-sided glass, taking notes so they can build the case.

'We have the tape you made of yourself showing kids how to take their own lives,' Sexton says. 'We know where you made it. We have the two tapes you made of Anna Eccles and Melissa Brockle, a girl I recall you described as a "poor mite" when we first met, you cynical bastard.' Sexton studies him before going on: 'There's a team in your house right now collecting hair specimens, your fingerprints, fibres, sweat drops – every possible cross transfer of evidence is being tagged. Why?'

'They may as well have killed my baby with their own bare hands.'

'Who?'

'You know who. Melissa Brockle.'

'Why did you kill Anna Eccles?'

'She left a horrible message about Amy's song after she'd died, dishonouring her. She was trying to kill her all over again.'

'What song?'

'One Amy uploaded on YouTube.'

'Jesus. How many others?'

He shrugs. 'I didn't kill any of them. They did that themselves.'

'Anna Eccles had marks on her neck from your Taser.'

'I told you, that bitch taunted her in the grave Melissa put her in.'

Sexton makes a fist which he pumps forward. 'Didn't stop you banging her mother, though, did it? How did Amy feel about that? Was it the ultimate betrayal, you sleeping with her torturer's daughter? Or did you kill your own daughter too?'

Rob glares. 'I didn't know how bad it was until after-wards. I loved Amy. But after she found me in the wood, she couldn't go on.' Sobs rack through his frame.

Sexton puts the DVD marked Melissa into the player, turns it on. Rob sobers up.

The images are in dark greens and greys and blacks because of the glare of the camera's night-light shade. The camera is jigging up and down because Rob is running, panting. A girl ahead is running. She trips and falls.

'It's too easy,' Rob tells her on the tape. 'Run.'

The angle shifts as he climbs the ladder into a watch tower. His breathing quickens. Seconds later a shot rings out.

'You hunted her?'

'I wanted her to know what Amy must have felt like to be at the mercy of a pack of wolves. I wanted them scared, as my daughter was. I wanted them to know what it felt like for her to have the life squeezed out of her. So, yes, I shot at them, then I strung them up. I'm glad I did it. Just don't ever accuse me of harming my daughter again. I loved Amy. I was away on business that night. You can check it out. Look, I know it's all over for me. I'm prepared to cooperate, but if you accuse me of hurting Amy again, that's the end of it, I won't say another word. Yes, I killed Anna and I killed Melissa, because of what they did to my daughter. But not the others. The rest did it all by themselves.'

'What about Lucy?'

'I wasn't interested in Lucy. She was good to my baby. I only got Melissa because she crashed the car.'

Bile rises in Sexton's throat. He swallows it back. 'And the suicide video? Who did you send it to?'

'Melissa, and Anna, because I wanted them to die.'

'What did you do with their phones?'

'I got rid of Melissa's and I warned Anna not to bring hers once I got talking to her in the chatroom.'

Sexton glances at the glass. On the far side McConigle closes her eyes and thanks God. The information stacks up with what Katie told her.

'How did you get the girls to the wood?'

'Lucy got Melissa there for me. She kept me filled in after Amy died on what was going on. She told me they were bringing Melissa to the wood to teach her a lesson, so I went too.'

'What? Are you saying Lucy was your accomplice?'

'No, no! Lucy's a good kid. She stayed in touch with me after Amy died. She just wanted me to know that Melissa was going to get a fright for what she did. She had no idea what I had in mind for the little bitch.'

'What happened when Melissa got there?'

'She almost got away. I fired some plastic bullets, but she

made it back to a car. She had some help. There were men there. No idea who they were. Otherwise, it would have been simple. They sped off once they got Lucy into her car. Fortunately, Lucy crashed the car and I got a second chance.'

'What about Anna? How did you get her to the wood?'

'I got her number and sent her the video I'd made. She texted me back she was too scared. I offered to help her. I told her it was the most peaceful place on earth, a chance to say a special goodbye to the girls, and I'd go with her if she was afraid. She met me willingly. If I hadn't done it for her, she'd have done it anyway.'

Sexton punches the table with his fist.

58

McConigle heads into Interview Room 2, directly across the corridor from Sexton, with Eric Canon, who has been brought back in.

'Do you want the good news or the bad first?' she announces, hoping to appeal to Canon's most basic instinct – himself.

'Go on then, give me the good,' he says, sneering.

'We've found the man what dunnit,' she says. 'You're off the hook.'

He checks to see if she's kidding.

'If' – she lets the word linger – 'you explain to me what you were doing in the wood that night, how you came into contact with Melissa Brockle and why the blood and hair from the deer in your yard match that on her clothing. Otherwise I'm going to have you brought before a court this afternoon and charged on multiple counts relating to drugs and obstructing an investigation.'

Canon is unruffled. 'Is it any wonder coppers get a bad name? I'm going to break my own golden rule and tell you, if you turn that off.' He points to Big Brother.

McConigle considers, then zaps the recorder off.

He smiles. 'If you must know, I'm the one who saved Lucy. Thought I'd got the other girl out of harm's way too, but he must have caught up with her—'

'Give over,' McConigle says. 'I don't have time for this. There's a court sitting in' – she checks her watch – 'half an hour, and a van outside. I'm going to have you put in it.'

She stands.

'Ask her. Ask Lucy if you don't believe me,' Canon protests.

'She can't talk, Eric, as well you know. This is getting boring.'

'Look, it's true. She was dealing drugs. I was trying to put her off. She was dealing prescription, and the shit you can get over the counter is heavy duty: Zimmos, Methadone, Ritalin. Had an unfair advantage. So you've got nothing on me.'

McConigle glances wearily at him. 'What were you doing in the woods? Why did you have a dead deer in your yard?'

He checks the video camera is still off. 'I wouldn't want to get a bad name, have gangsters thinking I've gone soft. If you must know, I saw Lucy heading out that night and I knew she was up to no good. Call it my radar for trouble; it's built in. Me and Gok figured maybe she's meeting some dealer, planning on getting someone else in on our territory. When Gok took her phone apart he found Bert McFarland's number in it. We wanted to know if she and Bert were going into business. She was done up like a tart. So, yeah, we followed her, went to get a heads-up, ended up in the woods. All I was going to do was watch, maybe warn her to stay out of my patch, to go back to her homework. But she goes into the woods in the dark with her mate and me and Gok think maybe they're going to top themselves. There's this dead deer lying near the entrance. We can hear shots being fired in the wood and reckon the shooter knows something we don't, like it might be worth a few quid if we hack it up and sell it to one of those posh restaurants. We try to drag it back to the car, only it's too big, so we have to start hacking it up there and then. Next thing we see the girls come tearing through the wood like they've just seen a ghost. I'm there covered in fucking blood like Freddie Kruger. But whatever the fuck is going on in the wood is worse than that, 'cos they took a lift off us back to their car. We heard the gunshots for ourselves. They said they'd parked up outside the wood.'

McConigle clicks her fingers. 'If you'd left Lucy there and she was killed, and your fibres and footprints were all over the place . . . Was that what you were really worried about when you did your Good Samaritan impression?'

'Doesn't really matter, does it? I'm the one who got her out and back to her car. I heard after, she crashed it and her friend died in the wood. That is what happened, on my kid's life. I didn't kill anyone, I saved them. I got them out.'

McConigle shakes her head super-slowly. 'I believe you,' she says. 'You can't make shit like that up.'

59

'I know what happened to Maura,' Jo says as Sexton enters his flat.

'Jesus,' he says, starting. 'How did you get in?'

'Your landlord.'

Sexton makes a beeline for a bottle of gin and a waiting glass on the kitchen counter. 'Drink?'

She shakes her head. 'I'm driving.'

'Still got the sense of humour.' He gulps back the drink. 'There's something to be said for that after what you've been through.'

He carries his glass and the bottle over and, after pouring another, puts it on the glass-topped coffee table and collapses on an armchair that's only feet from the TV. Jo turns her head in his general direction.

'We solved the other suicide mystery too, did you hear?' he asks, sounding distracted.

'Yes, Dan rang me. Congratulations. I knew you had it in you. End of your J-Lo days.'

'Not in this lifetime,' he gripes, knocking back his drink and topping up again. 'That bitch did a number on me.'

Jo pauses. 'Who do you mean?'

'The psychiatrist they hired for post-traumatic stress and anger management,' he says. 'She's a man-hater . . . like the rest of them.'

'All women are out to get you now, is that it?'

'Not you too . . . it was a joke. God, the PC brigade is taking over the world. My point is that someone seriously fucked up in the head is in no position to fix mine.'

Jo waits. 'Why haven't you asked me who killed Maura yet?'

Sexton points the remote at the TV and hits mute before the sound comes on. 'Sorry, who did it then? Anyone I know?'

'Definitely, based on your reaction tonight,' Jo answers.

He pulls a handle in the arm of the chair and the foot rest springs up.

'Don't you want to say anything?' Jo asks.

'Just getting comfortable. Chill.' Sexton flicks through the channels and settles on *Come Dine with Me*, as any show that features people pretending to be pals, eating their food and then bitching behind their backs and going through their stuff gets his thumbs-up. That's the real world. He pours himself another shot and downs that one too.

Sexton sighs. 'It's been a long day, Jo. It's been a longer week, and the longest year yet. Do you mind if I change? I want to get out of the clothes I spoke to Rob Reddan in tonight. They're contaminated with the air we sat in that got soaked in his fucked-up mind. They belong in the washing machine on the boil setting.'

'Sure,' she says. 'I've only been here four hours, what's another ten minutes?'

'I'll be five, promise. I won't shower until after you've gone.' He pauses. 'What have you been doing for four hours anyway?'

'Trying to get into the killer's head, to work it out,' Jo says.

'And you have? You know who killed Maura?'

'I know.'

Sexton blinks and leaves the room.

Jo scrolls through her contacts while he's gone, selects the number for the taxi company she uses, and calls it. She gives them Sexton's address and says, 'Give me half an hour.' Jo hangs up at the sound of Sexton coming back.

He is wearing a T-shirt and boxers, ready for bed. He's too tired for that shower now.

'OK then, hit me,' he says. 'Who dunnit?'

'You know exactly who did,' Jo says. 'Why are you playing this game?'

Sexton closes his eyes. 'When did you find out?'

'Tonight. I mean, up until tonight I wasn't sure. Up until you came home, I still had a margin of doubt. That's gone now.'

Sexton takes a deep breath. 'Somewhere along the way she'd started hating me. I couldn't believe she was plotting to leave me, without even having the decency to say goodbye. She'd compromised me with her lowlife friends. She'd got this whole other life planned out for herself that she thought I didn't know about, because she forgot that what I did for a living was spot the lie.

'So I told her that her little plan wouldn't work, because I knew what she was up to, and I wouldn't let her go, and she could forget about the big insurance payout she thought was coming in month thirteen.'

'What's month thirteen?' Jo asks. There's a slight quiver in her voice, because she already knows about month thirteen from the bank documents.

'It's the time limit some life-insurance policies set before they will pay out on suicide claims. I didn't think they'd cover suicide, but it turns out I was wrong. They don't pay if you do it within a year, because anyone who needs to kill themselves for money needs money straight away, and the thought of any kind of delay puts them off topping themselves.

'Maura wouldn't admit it, but I told her the bank had rung one day wanting to speak to Patricia Sexton. I told them there was a mistake, no Patricia lived at the house. The banker asked me to confirm who lived there and I told him. When I told Maura that last night, she said she knew nothing about it.'

Sexton points a finger to his temple and shoots an imaginary gun.

Jo stares straight ahead blankly. 'Then you left the flat, and when you came back, you found her.'

'It was only much, much later that I put the pieces together. She must have phoned the guy she owed money to – Philly Franklin – and told him that it was all over, their little plan to defraud the insurance company. That her one shot at being someone else who'd lived and died was gone. She only had one middle name on her passport to set up another account and that was "Patricia".' He looks at Jo. 'I thought you'd think it was me,' Sexton said.

'In all the years we worked together, you never hit anyone until you attacked Philly Franklin,' Jo says. 'And you've met a lot worse than him in your time. So I realized it was personal.'

'Some time after she died, Franklin called to me to collect the money he claimed she owed him,' he goes on. 'I told him in no uncertain terms that the next time he called I'd do him in with my own bare hands. But it was only when I eventually read Maura's suicide note that I realized the role he must have played in her death. As soon as I saw her suicide note, I knew she wouldn't have signed it Patricia. He must have come over, decided she was lying, and gone through with it.

'It took me months to find him. I spotted him once at Maura's graveside, but he took off before I could get to him. I picked him up a while later for extortion in an unrelated case.

'He confessed it all, how he'd dictated it to her, made her write the note. He was still convinced, when he killed her, that he was going to get the insurance money. The original policy had been made out to him – he'd made her do that, he told me. But, it turned out, Maura had had a change of heart a few weeks before she died. She'd written to the bank, asked them to change the beneficiary. Franklin still killed her, believing he was going to get the payout off me. I only found that out after I caught up with him, when I went to the bank and saw the policy and her letter.'

'And the insurance payout? What happened to the money?'

'I told the company the truth, so the policy was void. I didn't want the money anyway. It was tainted.'

'You loved Maura, right to the end, didn't you?'

'Of course I did. And . . . I think, in the end, she loved me too. That's why she changed her mind. The irony of it – no, the fucking tragedy of it—' Sexton breaks off to gather his emotions '— the tragedy is, if she had just told me that day, told me everything, I wouldn't have stormed off, we could have sorted things out – and she'd probably still be alive.' Jo said nothing for a while as Sexton took a deep breath. Then he went on: 'Laying into Franklin, beating him to within an inch of his life, that felt good – much better than any charges would have. If I hadn't used force, I still wouldn't know.'

Jo stands, and lifts her bag up. 'Maybe he confessed because you were using force. I've got to go. My taxi's outside.'

Sexton looks over at her slowly. 'What are you going to do?'

'I told you once that I was to blame for the death of someone I loved without ever having lifted a hand against them,' Jo says. 'You and I are exactly the same, Sexton.'

Friday

60

The traffic is gridlocked around the Green, and Sexton is glad he walked from the station to try to meet Beth, as arranged on the phone. He needs a break from putting together the paperwork on the case, and he suspects she'll be the one who can answer some remaining questions for him. She stands out a mile, near the top, chatting to a bunch of girls in Benedict's uniform. They disperse when he approaches.

'Were you Rory Mason's chatroom source on Lucy?' he asks, offering her a real smoke – John Player's. The e-fags were great, but now there's all this concern about the vapours in the atomizers needing clinical tests to make sure they're not bad for you.

She shrugs a yeah and pets a straggly mongrel dog curled at her feet beside a guitar that's covered in peeling stickers. An empty McDonald's cup is perched on the street for change. It's a place where Maura used to busk. That's how they'd met. A lifetime ago.

'How come you didn't tell me about Rob Reddan and your aunt?' he asks.

Beth looks at him, surprised. 'I like my Aunt Marie. I didn't want her in any kind of trouble.'

'But you were the one who told Darren about their affair, weren't you?'

'Actually, I told my cousin, Melissa, who told her archenemy, Amy, who told her boyfriend, Darren. Which is why for a long time I thought he had something to do with all this.'

'How did you find out in the first place?' Sexton asks, taking a deep drag of the smoke.

'My aunt was getting all dolled up every Tuesday around five and heading out. Martin has tennis on Tuesdays, so she wasn't meeting him, and Melissa had a singing lesson.

'Marie's default setting was miserable, so when she started getting all tinkly and happy every Tuesday, I knew she was up to something. I decided to follow her. It wasn't hard. She doesn't drive, so it wasn't difficult to keep up. I followed her to a bus stop the first Tuesday. The following week, I got on the bus at an earlier stop and watched from upstairs to see where she went. I saw her get off the bus four stops later and walk to a café across the street from Rob Reddan's ad company. If she'd spotted me, I'd an excuse ready for the coincidence of bumping into her. She didn't spot me, though, because she doesn't do heights. The next Tuesday, I'm in the café too, only on the mezzanine level. I see Rob come in and kiss her hand, pay for her coffee, then the two of them head off together and I know I'm on to something.'

'You went to a lot of trouble.'

'My uncle's a dickhead. It was payback time. Marie was nice to me, but I didn't feel like I was shitting on her because I was glad she'd found someone who made her happy. I wanted her to leave that asshole.'

'Were you there the following Tuesday?'

'I went in my friend's car. It was a piece of piss. Marie doesn't know him, or his car.'

'Where did they go?'

'Dunno. We lost them.'

Sexton stubs his cigarette out on the ground. 'You're like a regular Miss Marple.'

'Anyways, I went through Marie's phone one time she left it down before it locked, and I found all these pictures Rob had sent her of himself in . . . you know . . . sexual positions. They were gross. Think he thought he'd turn her on. And one day, when I was pissed with Amy for always getting between me and Lucy, I sent Melissa the pics of Amy's dad. I shouldn't have done it, but I did.

'I couldn't tell Melissa where I'd got them, and that it was her own mother who was so interested in Rob in the buff. But I didn't expect Melissa would send them on to Rob's own daughter, Amy. I feel so bad that they must have tipped her over the edge.'

'You still got the pictures?'

Beth gets her phone out, opens up an album and shows Sexton an image of Rob Reddan.

Sexton winces.

'Yup, gross, told you,' she says.

'Did Amy talk about her problems . . . to Lucy?'

Beth shakes her head. 'Amy never said much at the best of times. That was kind of the problem. She internalized everything and then . . .' Beth tilts her head and jerks an imaginary rope from it. 'Will Rob Reddan go to prison?'

'Yes.'

'Marie?'

'I doubt it, but I have seen people done for withholding information pertinent to an investigation before.'

'So I could face charges too?'

'Not on my watch.'

'What about Nigel and Nancy?'

Sexton blinks. 'What about them? Come to think of it, if you were Rory's source, why did you tell him that Nigel was a pervert?'

'You know . . . for being someone he's not?'

277

'What do you mean?'

She hesitates.

'Don't stop now, not when I've just offered you immunity.'

She takes a drag. 'Lucy found this dodgy passport Nigel had hidden one day, and these receipts for money he used to wire to a nursing home to pay for the upkeep of his dear old ma, since deceased.'

Time started moving in slow motion for Sexton. 'So what name was on it?' he asked, as it begins to sink in.

Beth shrugs.

'Do you know where they came from, originally?' Sexton's tone is urgent.

Beth sticks the fag in her mouth and strikes a pull-out match. 'They were Yanks from some West Virginian hillbilly, banjo-strumming shit-hole. That's where the nursing home was anyways.' She rubs the dog's head.

Sexton jumps to his feet. 'So why didn't you tell me about them before?'

'I was scared Lucy would be the one who suffered. They are taking such good care of her.'

61

Sexton refuses to believe that he could have been duped by the Starlings. He speeds from Grafton Street to see Lucy's consultant, Dr Anthony Dean. Could Nigel and Nancy possibly be involved in what has happened to the other girls? He's here to double-check. The doctor sits opposite him, on the far side of a walnut desk. He has Michael Heseltine eyebrows and when he opens a glasses case on his desk and puts a different pair on, they poke over the frames like an owl's. He takes a Manilla file from his secretary.

'I remember Lucy, of course I do, it's just I've never been good with names. Ah, here we are, Lucy Starling. I've no idea what clinical trial you're talking about, though.'

Sexton tilts his head. 'Isn't Lucy still under your care?'

'No, her mum made it clear to me that she intended to take over the management of Lucy's case.'

'Oh?'

'Before you ask me if it's strange that Lucy should have been released so soon after surgery with such a serious diagnosis,' the doctor continues, 'I want you to know we're bursting at the seams here, in case you hadn't noticed. Her mum was adamant she should be the one to take care of Lucy following the op, and to be honest, the way litigation has gone in the profession, I wasn't about to object.'

'What does that mean? Lucy did have an operation to reduce swelling on her brain, didn't she?'

'Yes, of course, but we record everything now, and the last thing I wanted was her mum requesting the tape and bringing it to an independent expert who would tell her whatever it is she wants to hear because she would of course be the one paying him the bobs.'

'Sorry, I don't follow.'

'Look, in many ways, the brain is the last frontier of medical science. We know so little about such a complex organ. What today might have been the right thing to do might not be tomorrow. What on this side of the Atlantic is common practice is medieval in other parts of the world. For instance, in the States, freezing is now considered the best way of preventing the brain from swelling. A bilateral decompressive craniotomy is carried out, leaving only a strip of bone down the centre of the head. The exposed brain is then treated with ice. Initially, the skull was often transplanted into the stomach until the time came to replant. But hindsight showed that the bone leaks calcium, so now it's considered best to stick it in the deep freeze. In terms of us catching up with these advances, we haven't even got to the point of putting the skull in the stomach yet. Do you see where I'm coming from?'

Sexton has to swallow to stop himself retching. 'You're saying you let Dr Starling take her daughter home rather than be accused of doing something wrong?'

'I'm saying we're neither equipped nor trained here to carry out the best international-practice procedures yet.'

'And you feared, if you'd botched it, she might object to something you'd done and decide to sue?'

'I stand by everything I did, but I think you can read between the lines.'

'Is that why you haven't continued to monitor Lucy?'

The medic moves uncomfortably on his seat. 'Once the patient leaves the hospital, it is entirely up to the parents to decide how she should be treated.'

'So who decided on Lucy's course of treatment?'

'Whatever neuro-specialist they hired after me.'

'But did she have Locked-in syndrome?'

'According to her mother – but it's highly possible she was just recovering from brain surgery. There's no way I could have diagnosed that without, well, watching her progress over a period of time.'

'You're saying you didn't diagnose Locked-in syndrome?' Sexton asks slowly.

'No, her mother did.'

Sexton stands up. He can't believe this. 'But Lucy was supposed to have been on some kind of clinical trial. I know you haven't heard of it, but is there anyone you can think of who might know, someone you could ask about it?'

'There's no point. If I haven't heard of anyone doing any-thing like that here, there isn't one. I promise you, if it was legit, I would know,' he says.

62

Sexton runs through Dublin Airport's departures hall, crashing into people but blundering on. He had gone straight to the Starlings' house from the hospital, and pounded at the door to no avail. A smirking Gok had emerged from Damm and casually told him. 'You missed them. They got in a taxi, all three of them, couple of hours ago. Suitcases and all.'

He has to find them. He stops to study the flight-info display board, sees that a flight to Orlando is about to take off and bolts for the area where the Aer Lingus desk is located. He bends under the rope controlling the queues, stepping over suitcases and shoving trolleys out of the way, panting like a sprinter. His heart is not up to this. He needs to get fit.

'Take it easy,' a man says.

'He's skipping the queue,' a woman complains.

There is no sign of the Starlings among the dwindling stragglers at the desk demanding to be allowed to check in and being told they're too late. Sexton barges his way up, apologizes to a couple who are trying to argue they can still make it – the woman bursting into tears in frustration. He slaps his hands on the counter to get the stewardess's attention. She's clearly adept at ignoring what she presumes is another impatient traveller, and she remains completely focused on the task. She studies her computer screen and speaks over Sexton's shoulder to the couple. 'I can get you on the six o'clock flight this evening. There are still a few seats available.'

'Hey!'

She looks back at Sexton witheringly. He holds up his ID. She doesn't turn away from him but she doesn't stop what she's doing either. She's on automatic.

'Did Nigel and Lucy Starling board this flight?' Sexton demands.

She sniffs and uses a perfectly painted finger to hit an arrow on her keyboard. 'Nope,' she says eventually.

'What?' Sexton asks.

A woman taps him on the shoulder. She's got a crying child in her arms. 'What's your problem? We could have boarded already' – she glares at the stewardess – 'if we didn't have to put up with shite.'

'Gardaí,' he says, turning back to the counter.

'I don't care who you are,' she continues to rant. The child is screaming and she changes arms and keeps yapping in Sexton's ear.

'Have they even booked?' Sexton asks the stewardess.

'I'm going to make a complaint about you,' the aggravated woman tells Sexton. The couple let out a final expletive and give up.

The stewardess is jabbing her arrow key. 'Nope,' repeats.

'Bloody cheek,' the disgruntled mother says, abandoning the effort too.

'Get his number, that's what you're supposed to do,' someone grumbles.

'How can a couple travel with someone incapacitated, someone in a wheelchair?' Sexton demands, glad he's got the stewardess to himself. 'Would they have used a separate gate? How does it work?'

She's confused. 'I've already told you there's nobody like

that on the plane. If there was . . .' Her phone is ringing. 'Sorry, I have to take this.' She picks up the phone.

'Yeah, that's it,' she says into the receiver, glaring at Sexton. 'I know, but what am I supposed to . . .'

He reaches over, grabs the phone, slams it back down. Now he has her attention.

'Check your list again. I want to know if you have any couples travelling with a teenage daughter.'

'Jesus, take your pick,' she says. 'It's a Boeing 747; there are 520 of the 524 passengers already onboard. They've closed the gate.'

Sexton pushes his hair back. 'How many, roughly?'

'I don't know!'

'Right,' he sighs, 'how many couples in their late fifties, early sixties?'

She glances at the screen. 'Off the top of my head, fifty. I don't keep track.'

'But no disabled teenagers?' he asks urgently.

'No,' she states categorically. 'There was a teenage girl we thought was drunk, but her parents explained it was her medication. She was able to walk with their help.'

Sexton blinks. 'What age were the parents?'

'Late fifties, early sixties, like you said.'

'And the plane hasn't taken off yet?'

'Not yet. There's a backlog on the runway.'

'Which gate?'

'109, area B,' she says.

Sexton starts to run. It's one of those bloody gates that takes a quarter of an hour to get to, he realizes, panting again. He spots a motorized wheelchair and jumps on board. It's almost as slow as he is. He sees a golf buggy and hops off, waving the driver down.

'Gardaí,' he says, squeezing in. 'Get me to 109.'

The guy stares at him blankly.

'Now!' Sexton roars.

A couple of minutes later, they pull up at the gate. The stewardess on the desk refuses to let Sexton out on to the airfield; she doesn't care who he is.

He tries to barge through but the gate is locked and he can't get out. Through the window he scans the passengers in the plane and spots Lucy. She is sitting upright, looking dazed but curious, turning her head, pointing out something that has interested her on the runway to her mother.

63

McConigle listens with a frown as Sexton fills her in on the phone. 'Dr Dean said he never diagnosed her as Locked-in,' Sexton concludes.

McConigle nods and puts him on speakerphone. She walks to the top of the room and claps her hands to get everyone's attention. She wipes the whiteboard clean then writes Nigel and Nancy's names on one side of the board and Rob Reddan's on the other, with chunky markers that squeak. Under Rob's name she lists Melissa and Anna, and under Nigel and Nancy Starlings', she writes Lucy.

'It's not over,' she begins, briefing the team on the latest development. 'We need to establish before Sexton gets them back here for interview if these cases are linked. Personally, I don't believe in coincidences.' She draws a double-pointed arrow in the space between the columns.

She lists the gangsters Nigel was consorting with at Anna's funeral and dispatches some officers to go and interview them, to find out if they know Rob Reddan. Then she hurries over to a computer and takes a seat, propping the phone against the computer as she types the words 'inducing Locked-in syndrome'. She stares at the screen and then reads aloud, for Sexton's benefit: 'According to Wikipedia, curare is a paralysing poison used by indigenous South American people. Prey was shot with arrows or blowgun darts dipped in curare, leading to asphyxiation, owing to the inability of the victim's respiratory muscles to contract. Recovery is complete if the animal's respiration is maintained artificially. Acts on the voluntary muscles rather than the nerves and the heart. Introduced into anaesthesia in the early 1940s as a muscle relaxant for surgery. The patients, however, reported feeling the full intensity of the pain, though they were not able to do anything about it, since they were, essentially, paralysed. The time of onset varies from within one minute to between fifteen and twenty-five minutes. And there's an antidote.'

She lifts the phone, switching off speakerphone, holding it to her ear. 'Do you think Nigel and Nancy were involved with Rob Reddan in hunting down those kids?'

'I want to believe all they did was induce their daughter into a coma,' Sexton replies.

'They would have needed all kinds of criminal connections to get the paperwork they have to create new identities,' says McConigle. 'Which may be where the Conquest Church comes in. Think about it: if you set up a church, you can approach all kinds of morally dubious people to come on board.'

Sexton doesn't answer; he starts giving out orders. 'McConigle, get on to the Medical Council. Nancy must have had documentation to set up a practice, right? And something else . . .' Sexton clicks his fingers, summoning the memory back from last night. 'Nigel mentioned he went to Venezuela in 1985, which may be where he learned about curare. Maybe he was using his real name back then.'

'Sure,' she reacts.

'When Rob Reddan was charged with the murder of Melissa Brockle, where did they take him?'

'He was remanded to Mountjoy,' McConigle says.

'Get out there, see if he had any links to the Conquest Church's choir himself, or can fill in the blanks.

'I've got to go. They're letting me on to the tarmac now.'

McConigle stands up. 'Right, I need a team of ten to take apart the Starlings' house in Rutling Street. Spacesuits, people.'

64

Sexton sits in Interview Room 1 opposite Nigel, who has yet to meet his gaze and has so far only sighed in response to questions. Nigel stares at a spot on the ground between his feet, flat on the ground.

'There must be a lot of pressure being a dad today,' Sexton says, watching him closely. 'You've got to be your kid's friend, if you want to keep the lines of communication open. You need to know what they're thinking so you can anticipate for them. Otherwise . . .' Sexton pauses, but nothing.

'Then, you've got to protect your kid from all the evils you know are out there in the world,' he goes on. 'You've experienced them yourself, because you're older, you know what's best for them, but how do you enforce your take on the world on a teenager? And if your child is a daughter – an only daughter – it must be that bit harder, right?'

Nigel is showing remarkable restraint. He hasn't run a finger along the inside rim of his tightly buttoned shirt, he hasn't loosened his tie, he hasn't taken off his anorak, or the V-neck jumper over his shirt.

'Why? Lucy wasn't paralysed as a result of the crash. You and your wife did that to her. What were you afraid of?' Sexton asks. 'Sex? Lucy was an attractive girl. There must have been any number of horny males out there sniffing around her. She was sexually active. Her handbag was right there in her room for you to see that. Don't tell me you didn't look. It's human nature.'

Nigel sighs again, but doesn't say anything.

'What is the Conquest Church stance on teen pregnancy anyway?' Sexton probes. He leans forward. 'Maybe your own feelings for her were changing. She'd become a young woman. Maybe you started seeing her differently, couldn't control your own feelings for her. She was young and nubile and – no offence to Nancy, but she's getting on a bit. You were watching her inappropriately when she came out of the shower. You'd taken her underwear. Were you peeking through the keyhole when she got dressed? Lucy was calling you a pervert on the chatrooms. A bit strong, isn't it, that choice of word? Why would she say that about you, her own flesh and blood? Had you touched her? Was she going to say something? Was that what you were afraid of? Why you forced her into that state of living death?'

Sexton stands, puts his hands in his pockets and walks behind Nigel. 'Then again, maybe you did it out of sheer concern for your finances. Maybe you thought she was out of control. She's stealing drugs from the surgery, money from my account . . . she's brought all these nasties to my door . . . she's making life hell. I'm going to teach her the ultimate lesson. I'm going to slow her down for a bit.

'All those drugs you'd learned about in South America. You just couldn't help yourself, could you?' Sexton bends to speak directly into Nigel's ear. 'Was. That. It?'

Nigel turns his head sharply to give him a sidelong glance. Their faces are inches apart. 'We did it to get her through puberty,' he hisses. 'We did it to get her through the teenage years. So she wouldn't top herself. We did it to save her from herself. To keep her alive.'

65

As Sexton crosses the corridor, McConigle takes him aside to fill him in on their progress.

'All the crims are saying the same thing. They knew him from the church, considered him an oddbod, but that he doted on Lucy. They're all denying knowing Rob Reddan.

'Nancy used the name Norah Starling to register with the Medical Council,' she continues. 'She's qualified in the States, according to the records, but had changed her name by deed poll from Norah Bantam, and she practised as Norah Bantam in Venezuela and Turkey for most of her career, before moving to Bridgend in Wales three years ago. Mean anything to you?'

He shakes his head. 'Should it?'

She pauses. 'There was an American couple named Bantam who were suspects in a big child-abduction case years back in Turkey. I don't know if you remember?'

'It's ringing a distant bell,' he says.

She stalls. 'It's just a thought, it's just one of those mad, "what if?" random thoughts, but it's niggling . . .'

'Go on,' Sexton presses.

'It's just that in 2002, I'm fifteen, right, and my parents are planning to take me and my little brother, Josh, on our first summer holiday abroad, and there's all this excitement about where we could go . . . Greece, Spain, Italy?'

Sexton glances at his watch. 'I don't mean to hurry this trip down memory lane, but the detention clock is ticking.'

'All right, I'm nearly there. It's just Josh is three and he doesn't know what's going on, but I am totally in with a vote with regards to where we can go. And my mum goes, "As long as it's not Turkey, I don't mind." And I'm, like, "What's wrong with Turkey?" And she says, "Oh, this little girl was taken from a beach in Turkey. She was the same age as your brother. One minute the kid was collecting shells with her parents, and the next, she's gone." So I spend the whole holiday holding Josh's hand, afraid to let him out of my sight, and ever since then I kind of still have a shit attack at the prospect of going anywhere that involves a plane and sunshine. So, as a result, I've kind of retained a lot of the details about that kid who was abducted in Turkey, such as the name Bantam, for instance.'

There's a split second of silence. 'What are you saying?' Sexton asks.

'That's the little blonde girl, a few years before Madeleine McCann?' the chief asks. 'She looked like the little girl in *ET*?'

'Elizabeth Lipton?' Sexton says. 'No wonder Lucy had no passport.'

'Set up a church, convert the damned, it's the perfect front for mixing with the kind of people ordinary decent folk run a mile from,' McConigle says.

'And you based all this on a hunch?' Sexton asks.

McConigle shows him a sheet of paper she's been holding. 'Well, I ran a search on Elizabeth Lipton first.'

Sexton reads it aloud: 'An American couple living in Bodrum . . . A dozen failed IVF attempts . . . It was all the more frustrating for her because she was a medical doctor . . . Only became suspects because they left the area immediately after the child's disappearance without ever saying they were going . . . Never subsequently located . . . The emergence of other suspects led the inquiry in another direction.'

He looks at McConigle, 'Lucy's being treated in the Mater?'

She nods.

'So where did you end up going on that first holiday?' he asks.

'Bundoran,' she grins.

66

Lucy's spacious high-dependency room in the hospital is as stuffy as the cramped ward Sexton had to cross to reach it. He's already shrugged his jacket off while filling her in, and he unbuttons his shirtsleeves and rolls them up to the elbows.

'I still can't believe it,' Lucy says, shaking her head slowly. 'I mean, I always knew they were weird, but I thought everyone's parents were weird. I know I should feel like I've lost something, but all I feel is anger. Ever since we moved to Ireland, and my Dad . . . I mean Nigel . . . stopped practising so he could concentrate on stalking me, I just felt so suffocated by them. All these years without my real mum, and dad.'

Sexton can see she's struggling to hold back the tears. He leans forward in the chair, towards her bed. A nurse has told him Lucy is recovering well, but she's still so frail, propped against a stack of pillows and nibbling a slice of toast, barely able to manage even the tiny bite she has just taken, that he knows it's going to take time. Her voice is croaky.

'What did my mum . . . I mean, Nancy, say?'

'Much the same as Nigel . . . that they wanted to get you through the teenage years – alive, but without the . . . difficulties of puberty,' Sexton tells her.

'How could they do this to me? They've taken my whole

life away from me. What they did to me with drugs, I will never forgive them for. That's not love, it's warped. It's evil. They could have killed me. It probably would have suited them better.'

'Maybe that would have raised too many questions for them?' Sexton speculates.

'I never felt connected to them, you know? They always kept me at a distance. Like they were watching me all the time instead of just giving me unconditional love the way parents are supposed to. When I was little, I was convinced I was adopted, that they were keeping it from me, because there was no family, like, anywhere, and no stories of family either. That's why I got on so well with Beth, and Amy. They understood exactly what it felt like to be on your own.'

Sexton nods. 'How much do you remember about what happened the night of the crash?'

Lucy swallows with difficulty and puts the toast back on the plate on the tray.

'I got to the hut in the forest, and this freaky guy appeared in a black ski mask, holding a rifle. I started shouting for Red Scorpion to help me, but he'd gone. I thought he might have been killed already. This madman was shooting at us. Then Melissa started shouting back, and we found each other. The gunman chased us, but Eric appeared with Gok in his car and we jumped in the back. At first, I wasn't sure what they were doing there. I thought maybe they were in on it. You should have seen them, they were covered in blood and guts. We were terrified. Eric and me had had our run-ins, but kill me? There wasn't time to think it through, we didn't have an option. We knew we were going to die if we didn't get out of that wood. So we got in, but it was a mess in that car – blood and body-parts, it looked like. So I thought he was definitely going to kill us. Instead they got us to the entrance to the wood, where Mum's . . . I mean, Nancy's, car was parked. We thought we were safe but I couldn't get the car going properly. It started, it took off, but then it cut out. We were so scared. We could see him coming behind us. That's it. That's all I remember.'

'How did you persuade Melissa to go with you to the wood in the first place?' Sexton asks. 'You two didn't get on, did you?'

Lucy reaches for a tissue and wipes her eyes. 'Poor Melissa . . . I thought she was behind that video, leaving all those horrible messages on the Internet. When she sent me the video showing me how to kill myself, I thought it was a step too far. Amy was already dead because of her, but when I confronted her about it, she claimed that she hadn't sent it to intimidate me; the only reason she'd sent it was to show me that she was being tortured too.

'I didn't believe her. So I told Melissa I'd hired this Red Scorpion guy, a real-life gangster, to teach the person who'd made that video a lesson, which was true. I thought she'd admit straight away that she was lying because she'd be so scared of Red catching up with her, but she didn't. So I tried another tack. I asked her to come with me to meet Red Scorpion in the wood where Amy died, thinking that would guilt-trip her into a confession, that she'd never be able to go through with that, would be too scared, but she agreed. She said she'd had enough too.

'When we got there and all the shooting started, at first I thought maybe she'd arranged her own little Red Scorpion to scare me even more, but it turned out Melissa was telling the truth. She really didn't send the video. She wasn't the troll.'

Sexton stands and puts his hands in his pockets. 'You told Rob where you were going?'

'Yes, I touch . . . touched base with him most days. I

thought it would help him. I told him everything that was going on, about bringing Red Scorpion to the wood with Melissa. I had no idea that I was signing Melissa's death warrant.' She breaks down. 'If it wasn't for me, Melissa would still be alive.'

'There are counsellors who'll be able to help you to deal with all of this.'

'I just need to talk to a friend. I wish Amy was here. I miss her so much.'

'I can't bring her back. But Beth is waiting outside. She came as soon as she heard the news . . . And I can arrange for you to meet your real mum and dad.'

'They're here? In Ireland?'

'We've traced them. Your mum lives here. Your dad's in the UK. He's flying in tonight. There's something else. We're trying to understand if Nancy and Nigel had any links to Rob Reddan.'

Lucy shakes her head. 'They were always drawn to dodgy people, but I never remember Rob phoning or calling over.'

'How come you didn't ask any of the people in the Conquest Church's choir to scare the troll for you?'

'I was scared they'd report back to Dad – Nigel.' She shifts in the bed. 'Please, can we leave it at that? I'm shattered. I'd like to see Beth, and then get some sleep.'

'Sure, I'll send her right in.'

A red-eyed Beth was pacing the other side of the door. He smiled at her and nodded, and she raised her face.

But before he could leave the room, Lucy spoke again. 'Detec— Gavin?'

'Yes, Lucy?'

'Thank you. For everything. I knew when I saw your face that I could trust you.'

Now it is Sexton's turn to gulp back the tears.

Saturday

67

McConigle sits in a little café in the Mater Hospital with her arm around Nicki Lipton, who is clutching a shredded tissue. She's a handsome woman, but dressed in clothes way beyond her years – a baggy coat, frumpy trousers. And her shoes are practically old folk's home, McConigle observes.

'Do you have other kids?' the detective asks kindly.

There are four empty coffee cups on the table, and McConigle transfers them to a waiter's tray as he comes to wipe it down.

'Three,' McConigle says with a sniff. 'The youngest's one and a half. Lizzie was my first. It broke my heart. I kept having babies to keep busy. Me and Jack . . . Lizzie's father . . . broke up two years later. We weren't married when it happened, and there was just too much grief afterwards for us to cope with each other's as well. I haven't seen him in ten years. I mean, we always contact each other on her birthday, and the anniversary of her disappearance, just to touch base with a quick call or email, but it was too painful . . . we had to let each other go . . . I still can't believe this. I keep thinking, Don't get your hopes up, just in case. There were so many false leads and knockbacks over the years that I just stopped hoping.'

'Lucy's DNA matched,' McConigle says. 'I mean, Lizzie's.'

A man walks briskly through the entrance and glances

over, heads for them. He's got a shock of white hair and a handsome, tanned face.

'Jack,' Nicki says, standing and opening her arms awkwardly.

McConigle can see the tension in her face as they hold each other.

'How are the kids?' he asks politely.

'Good, thanks. Yours?'

'Great, yeah. Keeping me busy.'

'Time flies,' Annie agrees.

He turns to McConigle. 'This is one hundred percent, right? I mean, I don't want to . . .'

'It's her,' McConigle promises.

Tears roll down his face.

'We can head up to see her now, if you like,' McConigle says.

There's no more conversation in the elevator up, just a tense silence. When they reach the correct floor, McConigle walks them towards the TV room, off the ward, where Sexton is waiting with Lizzie, who's in a dressing gown and slippers.

She breaks off her conversation with him and glances up, sees McConigle, and looks at the couple she's with.

Her faltering steps break into a sickly run. The three hug each other like the world is about to end. Or begin.

McConigle wipes a tear from her eye. There's a reason she does this thankless bloody pain-in-the-arse job.

'You know the way you fancy the arse off me?' Sexton asks.

'Yeah.'

'What are you doing tonight?'

'I'm going to Sergeant John Foxe's retirement do . . . with my new boyfriend.'

68

Dan pulls the keys from the ignition and gets out of the car, walking around to the passenger seat to help Jo out. He hands her a Tyvek jumpsuit as he surveys a squat, disused warehouse in the docklands. Sexton had contacted him to tell him that a woman's body had just been found inside by a bunch of kids drinking cans of cider. Jo wanted to tag along.

It's a Saturday, but Jo can't resist. For the first time, it feels safe to leave Rory home alone. She's found out he was setting up a Facebook page for kids under pressure – researching the whole suicide subject. He's persuaded counsellors to give their time – for free. He's going to organize youth-club events and regular 'meet up' events to bring the kids together to talk about their feelings while hiking, or camping, or whatever. That's why he has been doing so much research. It's going to take up a lot of his time, but Jo doesn't care about exam results any more. She just wants him happy. And who knows, maybe this will be his calling and he won't need points to go to college.

Dan links arms and leads Jo to the scene. Her walking stick taps between their steps.

'Bins out?' Jo asks, picking up the sickly-sweet stench.

'Yeah, rats got at them too, by the looks of it,' he answers.

'Or foxes,' Jo says.

'Trust me, this is no 'burb,' he says. 'You sure you wouldn't rather wait in the car?'

'I'm sure,' Jo says.

'The boys OK?' he checks.

Jo glances at her phone, and nods. 'Rory's got Harry with him.'

'Foot,' he says.

She bends her leg and holds it at the ankle behind her, leaning against him. Dan covers her shoe with an elasticated cover. He slaps the other leg. Jo obliges.

'How did she die?' she asks.

'Sexton didn't say. He just said there was a lot of blood.'

'Did he bag anything at the murder scene?'

'A monkey wrench.'

'Any missing-persons reports spring to mind?'

'Sexton said she was fresh. He said she's just inside the door. Cordon.'

Jo ducks and Dan raises the 'Garda No Entry' navy-and-white tape over her head.

'Wish I could wait in the car,' Dan says. 'Doesn't matter how used I am to the smell, it gets me every time.'

He pushes open a rattling metal door and guides her in.

'No officer outside?' she asks.

'What? Oh, right. He's probably gone for a leak.'

'He should be reprimanded for that.'

Sticky cobwebs brush her hair. Another smell mingles with the fungal must and mould: petrol.

'What was this place?'

'A tyre factory, I'd say. For HGVs, judging by the size of a stack over there.'

'Any signs of that blood so far?'

'None.'

Water is dripping somewhere. Jo starts at the sound of

metal clanking. A bird's wings flap. She pictures a pigeon.

'Stay here,' Dan says. 'It's one of those old lifts. There's no way it could still be working.'

'Wait,' Jo says.

'Don't move,' Dan warns. His voice is low and urgent. 'There's a mechanic's pit six deep, three wide, eight long to your right, and a hydraulic platform straight in front of you. This place is an obstacle course of pain. Stay here.'

Jo reaches out to grab him, but he's gone. She holds her hands out in the pitch dark. Something glimmers in the distance – a flashlight?

'It doesn't add up,' she whispers, as her old instincts kick in. 'You bring a victim somewhere like this, it's to die. That means premeditation and nothing left to chance. A killer here would bring their own weapon, not grab the nearest thing to hand. And Dan hasn't seen any blood . . .'

Something lurches towards her. Hessian sackcloth. It's over her head. Jo thrashes.

'Dan!'

Arms grip her from behind, hands locking on her stomach. A fleshy man lifts her off her feet.

'Got ya!' he shouts, pulling the sack off her head.

The place floods with blurry light. Jo's pupils cannot constrict and she closes her eyes, whacking Sexton on the chest.

'You've put on weight, you fat bastard,' she says.

'You need to,' he says. 'Turning into a bag of bones.'

Two other detectives from the station jump out from behind a stack of barrels, jeering and clapping amid peals of laughter. Jo recognizes DS Aishling McConigle's magpie laugh.

Dan comes back; she can hear his uneven steps – quicker than usual.

'Is this supposed to be funny?' he asks, panting.

'Thought if I got Jo's blood flowing, she might remember why she loves what she does and come back to us full-time,' Sexton says. 'And give Foxy one last taste of the job before he leaves.' He points to the pit, where Sergeant John Foxe is lying in his underpants, bound and gagged.

'He was initiated when he started this job, and he's getting the same before he leaves. We didn't think you'd want to miss it, Chief.'

Foxy looks up at Dan with a 'Get me out of this' expression and tries to speak through the duct tape over his mouth.

Dan heads over to help him.

'No girl with a caved-in head?' Dan clarifies, unpeeling the duct tape.

McConigle is doubled over, laughing.

'Give me my clothes. I'm freezing,' Foxy says, taking a gulp of air.

Dan is not amused. 'Since you've decided to take the afternoon off, you'd better pray there hasn't been a real murder.'

'Actually . . .' McConigle says, reading a text that's just beeped in to her phone.

'Tell me you're joking?' Dan demands.

'No, I mean, he's solved one. The Segway murder? Lucky Kernick has just walked into the station to confess.'

Sexton claps and rubs his hands together. 'I might even stretch to dinner tonight, if you're lucky,' he tells McConigle.

'I hate to interrupt,' Jo says. 'Under normal circumstances, Foxy in the buff would have been the only time in the last year I'd have been grateful that I couldn't see. But . . .'

'Love?' Dan asks.

'Oh, I can see him all right,' Jo says, pointing. Dan lifts her up in the air and gives her a twirl, amid a round of whoops and cheers.

Jo steadies herself against her husband's arms. 'It's good to be back.'

Author's Note

The case that brought teen suicides to the fore in Ireland was that of Phoebe Prince in Massachusetts, because it showed the pressures kids are under. But nobody could have predicted what happened after her death in 2010, or the surge of incidents involving youths who'd decided to follow the same path.

Earlier this year, I interviewed the coroner for south Kerry, Terence Casey, for the *Sunday World*, after five of the six cases he had for hearing in April returned suicide verdicts.

'The worst part is there were two sixteen-year-olds,' Terence Casey explained. 'I could find absolutely nothing from the information gathered by the Gardaí which would lead me to understand why young people of this age could take their own life.'

'Number one, I can't understand how a fourteen- or sixteen-year-old child would have troubles that would force them into a situation that would take them into taking their own life.

'What would a fourteen- or a sixteen-year-old have in their own brain that would trouble them that much to take their own life? It doesn't solve any problems.'

Terence Casey said all the stories coming before Killarney coroner's court were harrowing.

'If you can envisage my coroner's court. I'm sitting down, I'm facing the gallery. And I'm facing, on the last day, six families, mothers, fathers, brothers, sisters, aunts, uncles sitting there looking for an answer. You can see them crying, the anguish, the fear, the self-inflicted blame on their faces.

'It's practically impossible to convey what the families go through. If the people who committed suicide could only see the anguish and the grief and the pain and the suffering left behind them, they'd think twice about doing it.'

We're all familiar with the cases that have made national headlines. I won't name them or go into detail here, because this is a work of fiction and it wouldn't feel right or fair to package them with what's supposed to be a potboiler. I will, however, use some of the things their parents said in the aftermath: 'My heart turned to stone when I found him' . . . 'We forget what it is like to be fourteen, fifteen or sixteen. We forget how they feel about things' . . . 'We could fill the ocean with our tears.'

Tragically, in Wexford Coroner's Court that same month, suicide accounted for ten of the fifteen deaths.

All these issues I wanted to try and explore in this book. Ultimately, I had to conclude that, when hope is lost, evil thrives.

Helplines

1lifefreephone: 1800 247 100
Aware: 1890 303 302
Console: 1800 201 890

Help in a Crisis: Text Headsup 50424
Pieta House: 01 6010000 or email mary@pieta.ie
Samaritans, 24-hour service: 1850 60 60 90
Teen Line Ireland: 1800 833 634

Acknowledgements

My name is on the book but so many people were involved in getting it to the point of publication, it's a bit embarrassing that theirs aren't there too. Without my husband, Brian, there'd be no time or space for this passion that is writing books, I'm very lucky he has it too.

The other Brian in my life is my editor, Brian Langan, who brought so many insights, solutions and alternative scenarios to the book that he worked wonders. Actually, that's putting mildly what he did. Editor Cat Cobain and publisher Eoin McHugh believed in this story from the start, and I'm indebted to them too. My skilled, vibrant agent Jane Gregory is wise, kind and funny, and I'm very grateful for all her sound advice. I'm also very lucky to have made good friends with many people I've met in the book world – and a special thanks to Helen Gleed O'Connor, who is also an amazing publicist.

My parents, Sheila and Eamonn, are always there to help and never ask, 'Is it finished yet?' They help convince me chaos is normal. 'Hi' and thanks also to my pals on the *Sunday World*, especially editor Colm McGinty, and to my great friends Siobhan Carmody Collins, Carmel Wallace, Vanessa O'Loughlin and Maria Duffy, thanks for putting up with me pulling out of everything. Again!

Without Liz Byrne and her magic way with children and big smile, I'd never have got to the finish.

Finally, thanks to the inspirational, brilliant women who helped get me on this road: Selina Walker, and Cathy Kelly, and the ones who believed in the books once they were published – Orla Bleahen Melvin, and Kate Triggs. A heartfelt thanks again.

ABOUT THE AUTHOR

Niamh O'Connor is one of Ireland's best known crime authors. She is the true crime editor for the *Sunday World*, Ireland's biggest selling Sunday newspaper. Her three novels, *If I Never See You Again, Taken* and *Too Close For Comfort* have introduced a refreshing heroine in feisty CS Jo Birmingham and two have been shortlisted for Irish Book Awards.